THE RED PAVILION

"And thou—what needest with thy tribes' black tents,
Who hast the red pavilion of my heart?"

FRANCIS THOMPSON

The
RED PAVILION

By

JOHN GUNTHER

HARPER & BROTHERS PUBLISHERS
NEW YORK AND LONDON
MCMXXVI

THE RED PAVILION

Contents

Chapter One

i

ON FRIDAY, the 10th of May, 1924, at about seven o'clock
in the evening, Richard Northway stood before a mirror,
tussling with studs and things, dressing for dinner. Outside the window he could see a scribble of roof-tops
against the sky: along his own street he saw the trees
shining in bud, bowing precisely toward the glossy pavement like etiolated green umbrellas. He sighed. He
wrenched the two ends of his collar to contact and
lifted his chin to the mirror, cursing the evil genius which
had devised starched collars, dinner parties, and other
such ornamentalia to masculine civilization. Richard
was bored. He was bored enough to think idly: he
surveyed in perspective a vagrant company of idle
thoughts parading through his brain. He wondered why
spring had been so late this year and why no one wrote
clearly on the quantum theory and why no one had
ever invented nail-scissors satisfactory for the left
hand.

He thought:

" The real crux of the problem must remain small
issue advertising."

He thought:

" $K_2SO_4 + Ba(OH)_2 \geqslant 2KOH + BaSO_4$. Precisely. But
that doesn't give me 1.33."

He thought:

" It is perfectly true that love is not a reciprocal
process."

He thought :

" I must find out if El Greco was a contemporary of Ferdinand's."

Richard moved from the mirror, looked to the street again, and tied his tie with wide flaring butterfly wings, wondering why evening clothes always made him look so thin.

By the time he slipped into his dinner coat his thoughts had progressed as far as little Marjorie. But it was extremely silly of him, she probably being in love with young Paul.

Richard dusted a little powder on a red spot left from shaving and scrutinized himself. He was hardly a remarkable looking young man. He had thinnish dark hair, not bright except when the sun glinted on it directly. Then people were apt to think it was exciting hair, so casually did the light reveal soft brown and even a few insinuating stray threads of gold. His face was moulded in planes rather than curves, so that when it took the light each particular feature was striking. It was a general mould, well made, with cheek-bones high and the forehead roomy. It was a difficult face to describe because it was so integral ; it was easy to pick out the nose and mouth and analyse nose and mouth, yet they didn't exist except as part of the whole, they had importance only in equipoise and balance. His eyes were grey, set wide apart under a dark ridge of brows. When Richard turned suddenly high lights were apt to gleam across his cheek-bones, plastically flowing into the planes of his cheeks. He had a habit of burning with an idea, and then indeed his face appeared to take on an energy of its own : the planes shifted and became alive : he was irradiated. His mouth, too, was very mobile, and, when he talked, it articulated his words palpably, with precision and clarity. He was not at all good-looking, as that phrase is ordinarily used. At this time he was about twenty-six.

" I like his face because it's so eager and sometimes so severe," little Marjorie said once.

Richard meditated which of two top-coats he should wear, chose one of fawn, and drifted toward the garage. He paused a second before the laboratory door, but did not enter. After all, he must not be late, and he had three people to pick up on the way, all bound for Mary Detmers' dinner party. He was not sure he liked dinner parties. He was not sure that he liked women, for that matter, except occasionally to tantalize his own asceticism. It was much more fun to sit at home and work or think. That was why, he supposed, so many people thought him queer. Perhaps if he kept on thinking so much, some day he might go mad, like his father. Meanwhile there was the dinner, and it would be bearable because all the guests were his good friends, and all of them amusing in a vague sort of way. Besides, little Marjorie would be there. He hadn't seen her for several weeks.

First Leon. Then Doris. Third Austin.

Yes, he was to pick them all up on his way south, all three of them. Richard tuned the engine of his car, put on driving gloves, and was careful of the cuffs of his dinner jacket. He liked to hear the motor purr, and to feel the smooth, latent energy under his foot in the accelerator pedal. He hummed in tune to the engine. He hummed comfortably.

Richard lived just off Sheridan Road, far enough out of the noise of the city to make that noise sometimes attractive. He had a small apartment crammed with books, the use of the garage, and a room in the garage for his laboratory. Sometimes the laboratory smelled, in which cases there was trouble. His neighbourhood was one of those typically Chicago neighbourhoods with the lake close by, the murmuring thunder of the elevated trains muted in the distance, wind and smoke at all hours of day and night, and a few trees nodding primly along the pavement. Richard's apartment building was like most apartment buildings. It had six stories and it was faced with cream-coloured limestone. Inside his apartment were mostly books. He had a great many books. Books and a bed.

He shifted gears and swung the car into the alley behind his apartment. Bryn Mawr Avenue, Catalpa Avenue, Argyle Avenue. They drifted behind him quickly. Near the Edgewater Beach he turned into the boulevard, just missed hitting an omnibus—one of the new ones, coloured caramel—and then shot south. The evening was warm and mellow, with a faint mist in the trees and a fluid grace to the long shadowed streets. To the left, the lake placidly shifted blue waves round and about. Far ahead were the green shadows of the park.

" Hell ! " suddenly muttered Richard.

He had forgotten that book for Marjorie.

But he decided not to return for it, since he was a little late, and another time would do almost as well. Dear little Marjorie !

He sat low in the seat and turned swiftly to the right down Irving Park boulevard to call for Leon in the mean little flat near the elevated tracks. He pulled to the curb and sounded his horn. He slipped out of the car and decided he might as well go up and hurry Leon along. Leon was a slow and listless person.

" I wonder," Richard murmured to himself as he climbed the steps, " just what that young fool is up to now."

ii

Leon, Leon Goodman, had just finished a poem. It was, he thought, a good poem. Perhaps it was even a great poem. Leon had strange ideas on such matters. He was very young, he was a Jew, and he was hyper-sensitive. Also, he was a romantic with an awkward body, which in hypersensitive people is likely to be unfortunate.

Leon's poem was untitled. When he read it, his voice thrilled. He was thrilled:

> " I would thou wert a grape,
>   Soft and fragile, with tender skin,
>   That I might take thee
>   In between
>   My thumb and finger,
>   Crush thee slowly
>   And watch with dark voluptuousness
>   Thy body swell and burst . . .
>   And spurt
>   Green
>   Blood,
>   O'erdripping my still fingers."

Leon was sitting before the window of his dirty little flat. There was dust on every article of furniture. He was very poor. That was because he preferred to live on a meagre allowance rather than to work. He had been a student for two years at the University and had then been expelled ; now when he talked about the University his tone was very dark indeed. He rumbled.

" Cafeteria culture," he would say.

" Rumble " hardly expresses it. Leon's voice, like most of him, was curious. It had a profound timbre—at times—but mostly it squeaked. It was a deplorably uncertain kind of voice, just as Leon was a deplorably uncertain kind of person. You could never tell what either would do. He had no humour whatever, which was a curious matter. He was tall, thin, and stooped, his blond hair dangled before his horn-rimmed spectacles, and his elbows and knees were always getting out of line.

That afternoon, that evening, Leon was drumming with a pencil on his desk. He was accustomed to drum with a pencil on his desk whenever he wrote a poem. This was often. The tattoo of his pencil increased sometimes to a barrage. This was when he wrote a great poem. After completing the poem about the grape, he read it over, very slowly, very carefully, until each word dripped off his tongue, as he tasted, savoured, each word. " Green blood "—that was a triumph. It was epochal. Leon leaned back and ceased his tattoo : he was satisfied.

But the satisfaction did not persist. A few moments later he was lost in contemplation again ; and his contemplation approached his favourite topic : Death.

Leon thought a great deal about death. The focus of his mind was perhaps aslant because he was interested in obscure, in horrifying modes of death. There were times when he read Motley and Frazer because of the tortures therein described ; and once, when he discovered a sheaf of old prints in the Field Museum, illustrating such tortures, his happiness was unbounded. Ah ! The extraordinary nicety of the thumbscrew, the terrific poignance of crucifixion, the superb ecstasy of death on the rack ! Imagine being torn apart by horses ! Bones slowly pulled out of their gristly, blood-dropping sockets ! Leon shivered in exaltation. He was fond, too, of obscure tortures : the oubliette, the jungfernkess, the plumbatæ, the Tormento de Toca (pouring water into a gauze bag which was then forced into the stomach), the strappado, even peine forte et dure. Torquemada ! The Duc d'Alba ! The Marquis de Sade !

And diseases could be very pretty too. There was a good deal to be said for diseases. Scrofula and endocarditis ! Carcinoma and beri-beri ! The divine perfection of peritonitis—the uneasy comfort, the racing pulse, the quick awful pain, the puncture, the ooze of intestines into the bloated abdomen, the exudation of yellow lymph, coma, convulsions, death. And plague ! And Kalà-Azar ! And hydrophobia ! And, after all of them, death, desiccation, putrefaction, slow green decay, and then the burrowing hooded worms. Leon was thrilled. He was happy. He was a poet again.

Yet the worst thing that had ever happened to him was a case of measles. That and staphylococcus pyogenes. And hay fever. He had never even suffered.

Suffering! Leon remembered an incident two years before; and his sudden memory of that incident caused him to rise and walk excitedly in his little room. He had been eating his sparse lunch in the University commons, where the dyspeptic bust of John D. Rockefeller gazes enviously on a thousand students clattering knives and forks. After lunch, a discussion. How often those discussions! Leon missed them now, though he wouldn't admit it. His eyes were hungry when they were in his mind. Brave youthful discussions of life, art, constipation, the value of sacrifice, fox terriers, the law of diminishing returns, Mossourgsky, strabismus, the function of criticism, spirochæta pallida, what not. How many noble words; and how wasted.

That day it came out that Leon was a poet. Near him, across the table, was an older man, new to that discussion group. A dark, youngish old man, bowed and unshaven, with heavy hair, he had deep brooding eyes, extraordinary eyes. Leon still remembered them. This older man turned to him that day, very quietly, and asked:

" You want to be a poet? "

" Yes," said Leon, embarrassed, feeling a little punctured.

The older man turned to him and with a tremendous quiet intensity, his eyes burning, uttered:

" Have you ever suffered? "

Leon was blank.

" *Have you ever suffered?* " repeated the stranger. And then, when Leon still was blank, he laughed, laughed shortly and unpleasantly, an "I-told-you-so" sort of laugh.

Leon never forgot that. Had he ever suffered? Well,

It was all over. Of her own free will. She had met emotion for the first time in her life and she had let it conquer her. But Doris smiled. It was a wistful sort of smile. Her eyes were still half closed and she could hear her heart beat.

She tasted her lips, drawing a finger over them. She put her hand to her mouth and kissed her fingers, then her fist. In the soft light she saw her bare shoulder, gleaming. She leaned over and caressed it with her chin. Then she crooked her arm and noticed the soft shallow before the elbow. She put her lips to the smooth flesh and bent the arm so that it hugged her face. Stirring her legs under the blankets, she passed her lips up and down her arms. Yes. But it was different, somehow.

Cautiously she felt her sleek hard thighs and her breasts, giving roundly under her fingers, then cautiously stretched herself to comfort and relaxed.

The whole thing had really been very curious. The way she had felt herself melt. The boom-boom-boom of her heart and the choked feeling she had. Her breathlessness and the silence.

"I *asked* him," she whispered to herself in amazing recollection.

But it might have been anyone. It was herself and her mood. It was the soft silence of Spring, the placid water lapping up to the beach, so silently you could just hear the ripples, the blur of colour in the trees along the shore. It was the moment. *Any*body might have fitted it. Still, something was gone.

"At last," she said again.

She thought suddenly of her father and wondered if he had known this would come when without a word he let her go.

All these years . . . cool and aloof. And now . . . Oh, but what difference did it make? It was all experience. He didn't count. Ah, he didn't know that! But

Doris did and was glad. Wait till he tried to see her again! But all these years . . . cool and aloof. . . .

"It wasn't him," she said to herself in ungrammatical scorn. "It wasn't him. It was *me*."

She yawned slightly. She felt the silken coverlet whisper against her toes, whisper that it was time to get up and dress for Mary's party.

She was glad Richard would be at the party. Dear, nice Richard, and how shocked he would be. She must tell him. Right away.

Anyway, an epoch was over. It was an end to that *damned* curiosity. Well, she was nineteen. A bad age, nineteen. If you got over nineteen safely, then it was apt to be all right thereafter. Nineteen was a sort of climax. It was when you first got de-adolesced.

"After all," she thought, in gradual reversion, "it wasn't so tre-*men*-dous. If that's all . . ."

A few minutes later, when the low purring claxon of the car sounded outside, she was ready, but she didn't want especially to go, except, perhaps, to talk to Richard. She was excitedly anxious to talk to someone, in a way to boast of her lost innocence. She smiled to herself. If she were a man, now, she would go down the street sauntering or whistling, smoking a large cigar.

Richard appeared at the door, having left Leon outside : and her smile as she held his hand was dazzling. And he thought indeed she was one of the loveliest girls he had ever known, rather like a blond Joan Tilford, better looking perhaps than Joan, not quite so beautiful— really beautiful—as, say, Shirley Bowdoin. But still . . .

Doris was very slim. When she wore close-fitting tailored suits she appeared poured into them, a living breathing mould of fawn colour or taupe or biscuit grey. Her arms were outlined like gloves and her body swung from tight supple hips. Her hair was golden, of soft hammered gold, with just a touch of red in it ; somehow

it looked like gold-foil in the sunlight, smooth, burnished
gold-foil. It was cut closely to a triangle over the neck,
waved softly and transversely to a thin golden blur on
the white neck. She had a small white disdainful face
under arched brows, and very red lips.

Richard greeted her.

" Leon is downstairs."

" Oh," said Doris, " bother Leon."

She slipped into a wrap and he led her down the steep
dark stairs. Her greeting to Leon was mocking, as she
prepared to sit with Richard in the front seat. But
before she entered the car she looked about her, at the
brilliance of spring and the soft warmth of the city,
looked pensively and appraisingly and with a certain
condescension ; and she was glad.

Something was gone. Yes.

" Look ! " exclaimed Doris. " What a lovely evening ! "

iv

Their next stop was on the way south. Austin Devery
had telephoned, asking to be picked up down-town at a
bath establishment. Richard drove across the bridge,
down the shaft of tall buildings into the Loop. Driving
here was a madness ; the long stops for the twittering
signal lights, the crowded lanes of cars, the mist and
smoke hanging low over the city. He drove beneath the
groaning elevated structures, twisted between the zigzagging steel girders. The crunching roar of the trains
deafened him, but he loved it. Chicago ! He reached
the bath, drove up to the curb, and slid out.

" Just a moment," he said to Doris and Leon. " Just
a moment and I'll get him."

Austin Devery had just finished having a shave, a hair-
cut, a manicure, a Turkish bath, a steam bath, a swim in
the cool water of the tank, an alcohol rub, a towel rub, and

a long rest in the vaporous air of one of the steam rooms. When Richard appeared he was finishing off with a pedicure.

Austin was a most particular young man and his chiropody, his pedicure was one of his most fantastic and cherished luxuries. He was fond of luxuries. When he discovered chiropody as an outlet for dissipation he compressed his thin lips and laughed. He laughed precisely. Austin was not a demonstrative creature and such laughter meant that he was entranced with sardonic emotion.

Both of Austin's feet were exposed. His ankles were hairy and a thin fluff of hair grew between metatarsus and phalange before each big toe. The toes were outspread, splayed in hot pans of water. Austin leaned back sucking a cigarette, watching the toes. The attendant, who was something of an artist, deftly clipped away nail, smoothed away cuticle, cut off cartilage, and expunged dirt. The water was a pale blue colour with soap. The attendant continued to clip, smooth, expunge. Austin watched.

" Another," said Austin perfunctorily.

Another came. It was in a large glass. In the glass was an amber liquid, chill and clear. Austin raised it to his lips. First he sipped, then he tasted, then he drank. He kept on drinking. This was because it was his custom while being pedicured to drink a few dry Martini cocktails. It added, somehow, to the luxury.

In silence then the work progressed. The artist in white gloves fished Austin's foot, now as red as a lobster from the heat, out of the water and held it couched in his lap, tenderly clipping and polishing. Austin wiped from his close-clipped blond moustache a tiny bead of the liquor and watched. The artist enveloped the foot in soft cloths, coddling it. Debris—clipped bits of nail, a speck of hard black dirt, a smudge of soft yellow dirt, bits of cuticle, remnants of polish, spirals of cartilage—littered the towels on the floor. The artist worked. Austin drank.

When it was done Austin admired his pink rosy feet, so nicely embowered in the white towels, and drank the remnants of his cocktail. It was time now to dress. When would Richard come? Austin hoped he and Richard could get together for a quiet little chat. And he must show Richard through the bath establishment.

Richard came when Austin was just ready leisurely to leave the bath.

" My God ! " said Richard in horror. " You podophile ! "

" The care of the feet," commented Austin, with a disarming smile, " is endorsed by the best writers."

Richard grunted.

v

Richard sat low in his car and drove. He swung back into Michigan Boulevard, and the lights strung like fireopals on a straight necklace glimmered before grey buildings overlooking the lake. The Blackstone was a huge lantern swung at one end. In the daytime the windows looked like the articulations of waffle-irons, but now they shone, flickering with a thousand lights. Richard drove his car in the steady columns and waited for the red and green signals to wink their directions to the traffic. He pulled up at the intersection of Twelfth Street and looked at the Field Museum, like a ghost in grey marble warning the lake.

" Richard," Doris began, just lightly touching his arm, " I have something to tell you."

" Yes ? "

He was occupied watching the traffic and only slightly turned to her. Strange sort of girl, Doris. Innocent little thing. He must have a long talk with her some day.

He prepared to swing to the left at 33rd Street, through the flat negro quarters, but again he felt her hand on his arm.

"Richard," she began again.

"Just a moment," he pleaded.

The driving was ticklish. Indeed, at the moment, a truck sidled out of an alley and Richard jammed his wheel sharply in the other direction. On the back seat he heard Leon and Austin talking. Leon was not saying a great deal. He did not approve of Austin. This was probably because he envied Austin. Richard got his car back in the swell of the traffic, narrowly missed a safety island, and heard a policeman yell at him as he swung to a comparative ease in the open surface of Drexel Boulevard. But even here the cars stretched out in solid procession, nuzzling one another.

"If you do anything like that again," pronounced Austin, "I shall get out and take a taxi."

"Always bad this time of night," commented Richard.

Leon looked at the heavy squidging wheels of another great truck bursting into the boulevard and considered how it would feel to be run over. A wheel like that, now —how flatly would it squash your foot? As flat as a blotter or only as flat as a pancake? What would it do to your head? Leon's eyes quickened as he wondered. A head, he calculated, would probably be compressed to a thin smear several yards in diameter, a faint glaze of ooze on the pavement as big as an umbrella. Leon leaned out of the car to watch the truck. What torture!

"Well, if you don't want to hear, I won't tell you," said Doris, suddenly and tartly.

Richard had indeed forgotten.

"Oh, sorry," he apologized. "Just a moment, please. Wait till we get clear of the park."

Doris bit her lip. She was somewhat annoyed.

Richard was, in fact, almost entirely oblivious of Doris

and had hardly heard her first tentative remark. In the foreground of his mind was the nervous preoccupation of driving a heavy car south on the screaming boulevards during the rush hour. That took most of his mind, that and the bedlam of violent noise. But he was also hovering vaguely over the thought of avoiding that potash precipitation.

"If I can only get it up to 1.33 !" he muttered.

Doris was still biting her lip. Nothing, she decided, is quite so annoying as an interrupted confession. To outrage innocence is a bad business, but to outrage a lack of innocence is a good deal worse. It took the edge off, somehow, with Richard like this. She had imagined Richard surprised, and then tolerantly smiling, and then very stern. But now he was paying no attention to her whatever. She looked at his clear brown face in profile over the steering gear. The car was almost out of Washington Park now and the green fluidity of spring was washing down the avenue of the Midway. Well, she would try once again.

"Richard," she said ; "this afternoon . . ."

"Look out !" suddenly cried Leon.

Richard dodged just in time. A taxi and a mad one.

Doris closed her lips in disgust.

They wheeled down the Midway, past the squat towers of the University, into Jackson Park, and then jogged a little way north into 57th Street. Strange city, Chicago, where it takes a good car and a good driver on direct roads almost two hours to get from the middle of the north side to the middle of the south. To the west, the smoke from the factories was lazily circling in the air. . . .

"Yes ?" prompted Richard, turning to Doris.

"Oh, nothing."

They were nearing Mary's house now. Only a few blocks more.

"What's going to happen to-night ?" asked Leon.

"Oh, just announce the engagement," Doris called over her shoulder. "That's all."

Richard turned, puzzled, as he slowed up by the curb. "What engagement?"

"Why, Paul Millis and little Marjorie—didn't you know?"

Richard was stunned for a moment: and then discovered himself with open mouth softly laughing. He opened the door and slipped out, giving Doris his hand. What a ridiculous thing? Well, it was lucky he hadn't been altogether a fool. Lucky he found out in time. Anyway, it served him right. Silly jackass, to meddle with babies! He laughed again.

"I'm very glad," said Richard to himself, as they walked up to the door, "that I forgot that book."

Chapter Two

MARY DETMERS ENTERTAINS

i

MARY was busy apportioning her charm. This was something she did very well.

"Richard," she said quietly, and Richard felt himself peculiarly and intimately welcomed, with cordiality in the single word and friendliness and also quiet humour ; and "Doris," she said quietly, and "Austin," and "Leon," she said ; and each of them felt the same thing.

Mary had a quick wide smile and a charming attitude of negligence.

"Oh dear," she would say, "whatever shall I do ? " And all the time she knew precisely what she would do.

Just the same, Mary was a lonely young woman and sometimes she did feel helpless. At this time she was about thirty-two, perhaps thirty-three. Often she was unhappy and she took particular delight in this small circle of friends for whom she cherished her humour and her gentleness. In an unpretentious way, to these friends and to many other people at the University, she was a notable hostess, and even a famous one. A great many amusing people passed within the doors of her charming house on 56th Street. They liked Mary, and often too they admired her. "Brave Mary," they would say.

Her husband had been a famous professor of anatomy at the University, and he had died, quite suddenly, quite tragically, about six years before. The associations which he had made for her at the University persisted after his death. She was as well known a figure on the

campus as many a dean. Her cousin Marjorie lived with
her and was a student there. Mary liked to have " young
people," as she called them with quotation marks, around
her. She had gathered Leon to the group when he
first began college, and Doris a little later, while Richard
had been her friend almost as long as she could remember.

" Richard, I have a surprise for you," she said when he
slipped off his coat and entered the wide drawing-room
before the others. " Oh, Richard," she almost chuckled,
" I have a surprise for you ! "

He had had one surprise that evening and he thought
one was enough.

" You mean Marjorie and Paul ? "

" Oh, no. Something much more exciting than that."

" What is it, then ? "

Mary took him aside as Austin and Leon and Doris
sauntered in, and then whispered :

" Shirley is back."

" What ? "

It was a simple ejaculation, a simple " What ? " but
it contained passion.

" Yes," Mary appeared to be meditating aloud,
" Shirley is back."

" You should have told me ! "

" But she only just came."

In an instant all his preoccupations of the day were
gone, washed clearly from his mind—experiments,
business, ideas—and every vestige of a thought of little
Marjorie, every trace in his heart of little Marjorie.
She vanished from his mind, obliterated, and it is doubtful
if he ever thought of her twice in his life again.

" And there's nothing very much," continued Mrs.
Detmers, " that you can do about it—in case you should
want to do anything." She looked at the ridge of his
brows and continued : " Now, Richard, don't be angry
or stupid."

" Yes," he said shortly.

" And remember . . ."

" Oh, God ! " said Richard passionately.

" Sh-shhh. Please don't look like that or talk that way.
You'll make me feel guilty. I asked her to come."

" Is she here now ? "

" Yes."

" Where ? "

" Upstairs dressing. She'll be down any moment."

" Does she know I'm here ? "

" Of course."

" What did she say ? "

" Why, she smiled. She smiled rather softly, and
then didn't say anything at all."

Paul and Marjorie then came down. They made a
minor sensation. Marjorie was wearing his fraternity
pin tucked close against her breast. Marjorie bobbed
her little tousled corn-coloured head and Paul was very
straight and shy and thrilled. Austin was pleasantly
ironic and Leon aloof and yet vaguely excited. Doris
kissed Marjorie and then everyone kissed everyone.
Richard congratulated Marjorie and Paul sincerely
enough, but he was not thinking intimately of them, his
mind was still staggering with Mary's news. Further
congratulations and kisses came and it was all very
happy and young and gay. Soon would come the official
announcement and then there would be a wait, these
fresh youthful children would wait ; and then marriage,
and more laughing and crying and flowers at the wedding,
with Paul still very upright and shy and Marjorie bubbling
in her bubbling way. Then the honeymoon. These
children. Strange word, honeymoon.

Shirley came down in the middle of the excitement
flowing around the children : and if the children made a
sensation so did she. But the meeting was a simple one.
Everyone was quiet for a second, a breathless sort of quiet

after the gush about Paul and Marjorie, and everyone
wondered just a little, the while Richard cursed them for
wondering. " Hullo there, Ricky," was all she said.
Just like her to use that old pet nickname. " Hello,
Shirley," said he.

That was all : and then Mary led them into the wide
low-ceilinged dining-room, aflame with orange flowers,
with orange flowers heaped burning on the great soft
brown table. Except for the silent frosty tinkle of glass-
ware and the orange flowers, the table was bare, grained
and glossy, and from the raftered ceiling orange clusters
of ribbons were hanging while an orange lamp shone on
the serving table. They sat down.* They were all a little
breathless. They began to eat.

" Syzygy is a term used in zoology, architecture, and
algebra," Austin turned to Mary at once, " but it also
means, biologically, the intimately united and apparently
fused condition of certain low organisms during conjugation."

" Charming," murmured Mary, detached, " syzygy ..."

While the sole marguery was being served there came a
calamity, because Leon sneezed. The flowers then had
to be removed because he kept on sneezing. That hay
fever. " Poor Leon," muttered everyone.

---

* In this formation

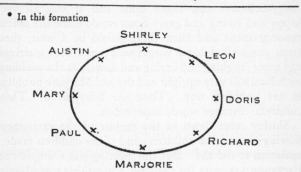

Outside they could see Japanese lanterns floating on invisible wires over the lawn. But they did not watch them carefully. They were too interested talking. The conversation was extremely miscellaneous. It would have puzzled a microphone.

" As soon as Paul had his real stroke of genius," Mary was saying, from the head of the table, " as soon as he was intelligent enough to suggest that he wanted to marry Marjorie to reform her, then she accepted him."

" Oh, *Mary!* " Marjorie protested.

" I think," Austin was saying in his precise, deliberate way, " that Pliny's remarks about the conduct of bodies floating downstream are utterly uncalled for."

" Bother this asparagus," said Doris, for she had lost a piece of asparagus during its adventurous journey from the plate to her lips. " *Bother!* "

Richard and Leon were talking about diseases in an undertone, but Doris, recovering the asparagus, heard Richard say :

" Just the same," in a very confidential tone, " it is always wise to wear a cholera belt east of Suez."

Leon was very pleased with himself, after the awful moment of sneezing. In the glass opposite he could see his face, and his face seemed to win something, to gain lustre, even to appear handsome. Besides, he thought he could see a new Line in his face, and this was something of a triumph : he watched for Lines very carefully, almost as carefully as years before he stood before a mirror and watched his Adam's Apple grow. They denoted Growth. Still, that sneezing had been disastrous.

While Shirley talked art to Austin, Doris muttered across the table about complexes.

" I really do think Simone Martini was the greater colourist," Shirley was saying.

But Austin's reply was lost when Doris suddenly turned to Richard with :

"Tell me, has a dream about an apple any Freudian significance ? "

"Apples, no," said Richard judiciously. "But watch out for snakes. Church steeples and snakes."

Then Shirley was heard to say to Austin again :

"Of course, Corot painted about a thousand pictures in his lifetime—and four thousand of 'em are in the Louvre."

Meanwhile Mary's voice threaded out in literary conversation with Paul :

"I like young Huxley because he enjoys so much laughing at himself laughing at himself laughing at himself."

Richard watched Shirley. He had had no time to see her alone. How extraordinary this meeting ! When had she returned ? She was still very beautiful. He looked at the lustre in her clear cheeks and the heavy bell of dark hair cupping the cheeks. She was wearing green, a powdery glossy pastel green. A rope of coral nuggets hung from her throat.

Leon leaned back in his chair. Food. Food was a curious business and eating also. He would write a sketch about food and eating. What might he call it ? Well, perhaps *The Primal Necessity*. Yes, that was a good title. Leon's cold eye gleamed. He would picture great steaming piles of rich food and porcine men grubbing and eating. Eating. Chewing. Masticating. Swallowing. Regurgitating. Digesting. And so on. . . .

Richard watched Shirley. She talked little ; a few words to Austin, that was all.

Mary was still bantering Paul and Marjorie, but paused at mention of a name from Leon and said :

"I wonder if he writes so little because he drinks so much, or drinks so much because he writes so little ? "

Leon began to think of his poem. " Like a grape, " he said aloud, " spurting green blood . . ."

" What was that, Leon ? "

He had no idea Doris had overheard him. He stammered, blushing, and managed an artificial sneeze.

" Poor Leon," said Mary tactfully.

Everyone stood a little bit self-consciously a few moments later for a toast to Paul and Marjorie. Richard felt somewhat ridiculous and Leon, who did not approve of toasts, scowled. Marjorie was blushing and Paul made a speech. It was a very bad speech, but everyone laughed and cheered.

" God have mercy on them," acidly breathed Austin.

The dinner was done then and they moved to take coffee in the little lounge room with blue panels and flowering chintz curtains. And still Shirley was very silent. As they left the table, Richard reflected how very curious it was to sit opposite a beautiful young woman at a more-or-less formal dinner party, and remember that she had a small birth-mark at the end of her third rib. It was curious and also somewhat startling. He laughed abruptly. But he did not want to laugh.

ii

Later, before Richard could talk to Shirley, Doris cornered him, and this time she had made up her mind.

" You were frightfully rude in the car," she began. " Richard, I wanted to tell you something."

" Oh, yes. Sorry." It was difficult to concentrate. " What was it, Doris ? "

He only half-considered. But he liked Doris. He liked to look at her, at the close shining cap of her hair.

" You see . . ." she began.

" Yes ? "

" Well, Richard, I did it."

Did what? He hadn't the faintest idea what she was talking about. Had she been arrested for speeding?

" You did what? " queried Richard innocently.

Doris paused, and a faint smile upturned her lips. She uttered, still smiling, one monosyllable. She said :

" It."

Then Richard, stupid no longer, understood ; and he was a little surprised.

" Oh," he said. " *Oh!* "

Doris was beaming to him like a little child sucking a lollipop, like a little child who wins a prize in Sunday-school.

" Yes," she said.

Richard paused with lips pursed a long time.

" Theoretically," he stated at last, " I am a firm believer in the virtue of chastity. I believe that chastity can be a very beautiful thing. I'm not sure, Doris, that I approve."

" Theoretically," she put in. Nice, grave Richard. . .

" Yes. But I suppose you know what you want better than I. Who was he? "

" That," she said, " is a secret."

He laughed a little.

" But he didn't count," she continued. " It was me— *me*."

" Well, that's good, if it's true," said Richard. " But just the same I think I'm sorry." He proceeded slowly, feeling for words. " After all, something is gone. Isn't that always tragic, to have something gone? Forever, irreparably gone? I've often thought that's the most tragic thing in life. I've often thought the only thing in life to produce a genuine pang is Finality—Finality of any kind. Not just in this sort of connection. And you have achieved, Doris, your first finality. An important finality, too. Besides, it puts you at a loss, psychologically.

c

You have nothing to lose now. What interest is there in life if you have nothing to lose ? "

She pouted.

" What did you expect me to do or say ? " he continued, as he saw she was a little nettled. " Why did you tell me, and what did you expect me to do ? Congratulate you ? "

" Brutal Richard," breathed Doris.

" If you boast," he shrugged, " what else is there for me to say ? "

" I don't think," she said, " that I'm exactly *boasting*. . . . "

This fresh, radiant *baby*, thought Richard.

" Yes," Doris shrugged quickly, " something is gone. But anyway I'm glad. And I'm glad, I think, that you're a little shocked. And I did want to tell you, Richard, I wanted you to be sorry. I wanted to talk to someone who might . . . understand."

" Oh," said he quickly, " I understand."

There was an active pause. He decided there was nothing more he could say, and Doris moodily made as if to go on. He smiled and bowed a little, as if in ironical congratulation ; and Doris, as she left him, pouted a little again. " I'll lecture you next time," he laughed.

Somehow she felt he wasn't properly impressed.

iii

Some of them were playing bridge and some talking as the lanterns flowed in colour outside, dancing on the high wires ; Leon was sneezing in a corner, with his hair dangling over his eyes ; and Austin, roaming before the books as he always did, condescended to them a little. But Mary, as she rose from the bridge table, was thinking of her dead husband.

She thought how much he would have liked this group,

with his quick abundant humour and expressive hands ; how he would have hovered over it paternally, eagerly irradiating its several surfaces, like a light directed on facets of a slowly turning stone. Yes, he would have become this party well. Dr. Detmers had been a very abundant man. Mary's eyes clouded, but then focussed to the present when she felt Austin move beside her and heard him say :

" I was wondering what you were thinking about so gravely."

" Oh . . . nothing," said Mary.

And Dr. Detmers would have liked Austin too. Austin knew a great deal, more even than Richard knew. Well, Austin was almost ten years older than Richard. Anyway, her husband would have liked to talk to them both, to wag his thin beard toward them and throw back his head for laughter. Mary fluttered her hands with her familiar helpless gesture and poised over the table to resume her bridge hand. Strange thing, the way people interworked. " Dear, dear, two no trumps," said Mary. Throw any half-dozen people together and watch them react. This group, for instance. What would happen ?

" Marjorie," said Mary casually, after she raised the bid again, " I think that yellow more becoming than the green after all."

While all the time hovered in the wash of her mind that searching beard, his long hands, the urgent abundance. . . .

" Oh, let spades have it," Shirley was saying : and Mary began to play.

Meanwhile Doris had approached Austin anchored in solitude.

" You look," pronounced Austin, smiling frostily as he surveyed her with slow grudging approval, surveyed the thin scarlet bulge of her lips, " you look like a dream by God."

Doris stopped with an idea.

"Listen, Austin," she said. "I want to tell you something."

iv

Outside the flowing blur of the lanterns, swaying between the trees. The game had been finished. Paul and Marjorie were dancing to the phonograph, and also Mary and Leon, because there were no orange flowers in that room and Leon didn't sneeze. Austin and Doris were whispering against the tall brown case of books; and Richard and Shirley, alone together for the first time that evening, alone together, went out into the garden, under the lights and the trees, and took a walk.

"Well?" asked Richard shortly, almost brusquely. "And have you come back into my life?"

She looked at him. Such a severe flushed face! She had not seen him for two years.

"My dear," she said, "I rather think, from your tone, that perhaps I never left it."

Pause.

"That, in a way, is true," admitted Richard, startled. They walked beneath the trees, toward the iron gate. "But it is not altogether true. I think you know that as well as I."

"I haven't answered your question," said Shirley moodily. "I have come back—yes. But I don't think I have come back in that sense. After all, Chicago is a fairish-sized town."

"I'm not sure that a fairish-sized town is big enough."

"Well, my dear, we shall have to try to make it big enough. I knew I should come back some day. I knew I should see you. You must have known that too. And here we are. I don't see why we should fuss about it."

"True," said Richard.

"Well, then . . ."

"I don't like it," said Richard. "But I suppose we must face it. Look here, we're bound to see one another. It would be silly of you to avoid me. But we ought to know . . . where we stand."

"Of course," she said, "and there's no sense in being strained about it. We're older and we've changed. We're different now. Still, Ricky, we can talk to one another. After two years."

"It shows," said Richard, and his tone had been becoming softer, "what propinquity . . ." he accented the word ironically ". . . in youth can do."

"I don't think that was it," she said.

"But you must answer my first question," he reverted suddenly. "Goodness knows, Shirley, we must get that straight. It would be simply intolerable otherwise."

"I think perhaps you can answer it better than I," she said seriously.

"What do you want to do?"

"I don't know—I've hardly thought. After all, I've only just got back."

"Paris?"

"Paris."

They were both silent for a moment. They were out of the gate, immediately outside it. They stood there. It was as if neither were willing to step away. If they stepped away together, away from the house, it would be symbolical. It would emphasize their unity, they would be together again. Richard waited and Shirley waited, and they were both very silent, watching the glow of the lanterns and the soft sweep of the new leaves. Then Richard breathed deeply and took Shirley's arm.

"Come," he said. "Let's walk!"

After a little he stopped and turned to her, the planes of his face were fluid, his face was burning and puzzled. Shirley looked up at him and smiled faintly.

There was another question, he thought. Then he asked, very soberly :

" Shirley—*why* did you come back ? "

The faint light of a street lamp silvered her face, awakened her face among the night shadows.

" I don't know," very seriously she said.

v

Austin, straight against the books, smiled faintly, sardonically, and as Doris watched him, puzzled and not at all satisfied, he reached for a yellow-backed volume, fiddled through the pages, and, in almost flawless French, began to read :

" . . . Ce jeune abbé, tout frais émoulu de son séminaire, était un peu nicaise. Il confessait pour la première fois. Avant de l'envoyer au saint tribunal, son curé l'avait chapitré :

" . . . Mon ami, proportionnez la pénitence au nombre de fois que la faute aura été commise. Arrangez cela par nombres pairs : deux fois, tant de dizaines de chapelet ; quatre fois, le double ; six fois, le triple.

" . . . Ainsi, ferai-je, monsieur le curé, dit l'abbé, plein d'innocence ? Et il s'enferma dans le saint placard.

" Une jeune fille s'agenouille, bat sa coulpe. ' Mon père, je m'accuse d'avoir commis le péché de la chair.'

" . . . Et combien de fois, mon enfant ?

" . . . Trois fois, mon père.

" . . . Trois fois ? Vous me prenez sans vert, ma fille. Je n'ai pas de pénitence réglée pour trois. Mais faites cela encore une fois et revenez. J'ai le tarif pour quatre."

Austin finished reading and put the book down. He smiled faintly, a smile that was hardly a smile.

Doris understood.

The beast !

vi

"Oh, it's intolerable," Richard was saying passionately, as they walked down the brusque parade ground of railroad tracks and turned toward the lights of Marquette Road. They had been walking a long time. "It's intolerable. Of course, I'm perfectly willing to admit I missed you. I missed you like hell. You must have missed me. It's impossible for any two people to be as close as we were and not feel a vacancy later. But the vacancy was bound to come. You admitted that."

"Yes," said Shirley. "I admitted that."

"And," continued Richard persistently, "when you did go, why, then I tried to cut you out of my heart—do you hear me?—to cut you out of my heart—out of my life, out of my life completely. And in a way I succeeded. I didn't succeed all the way. I admit that. But I succeeded enough. It hurt like the devil to do it. I had to readjust the whole of my life. In the end I was able to work. I have worked. I have worked out a new equation, in a way, to set myself against things."

"Without me."

"Yes. Without you. And I succeeded. I did reestablish myself. I rearranged my whole existence because we parted, and, when I get it rearranged—why, then, as cool and aloof as ever, you come back. Confound it, you come *back !* It's not exactly fair."

A spasm of pain crossed her features.

"But I can't help it, Richard. You've got to admit that. It just happens. I came and I went, and now I'm here again. That's all."

"And I can go, too, I suppose," he said moodily.

"Ah, Richard, but you won't."

"I could take Phil's* Eastward Quest," he continued defiantly.

* Philip Hubbard.   More of him anon.—J. G.

" It seems to me that you're exaggerating it all," she said, and she shook her head suddenly, so that her hair spilt in the wind as if to shake off that trace of pain from her face. " After all, it isn't quite so bad as all this. I haven't the faintest intention of interrupting you again. I came back to see my family, and to work, and also, in a way, to see you if you wanted to see me, because I like you, Richard, you know I like you. I'll always like you. And that's all, really. We can be friends."

They were nearing a coffee stall, a hot-dog stand, near the corner of Stony Island Avenue.

" I want," suddenly announced Shirley, " some coffee, some American coffee. I suppose that's a reflection on Mary's dinner, but I don't care. I do want some coffee. American coffee ! I haven't tasted it for years. Oh ! Coffee ! "

Somehow that broke the strain. They stopped before the little all-night stall and sat on stools before the counter, served by a moustached dignitary with dirty fingers and a great Latin moustache. And they drank coffee. Shirley laughed, her calm slight laughter, because she could see herself in the tall mirror behind the counter, and she saw her arms and shoulders round and full, gleaming even in that hard light ; and she saw Richard's dinner-jacket shaped over his hard shoulders ; and the other people, tardy taxicab drivers, a few students, riff-raff of a Chicago midnight, eating ham and eggs and staring at them with pleasure. It was not the least of her faults that she knew too well she was very beautiful.

Then they talked eagerly, almost in the old way. After all, once they had been very close friends indeed, and they had been apart over two years. They found a thousand things to talk about. Not only, for instance, of what Richard had been doing, but of what he had been think-ing ; and, what was more important than that, of what he had been feeling, too. And Shirley also. Shirley talked but also she listened : she was no sentimentalist, but she knew the value of sentiment. They were recapturing years.

"I did like," Richard said, " the *Mariposa*—lots of photos of it reproduced here."

"Oh ! That *was* fun. Richard, I worked six months off and on with that thing . . . I hate it now . . . but it was fun while it lasted. And did you like *Diana in High Heels ?* "

And he asked her questions and she answered them, about England, about the shawls she bought in Egypt, and the tea she drank at Armenonville, the grass like green plush in Devon, and the clear blue of the Mediterranean off the Corniche and Estèrel Hills. But Shirley was interested, too, in the new Madison Street bridge.

"And there's something I *must* show you some day . . . a gargoyle on the Tour St. Jacques—people can talk about the Sainte Chapelle and Sainte Germaine all they like, but the Tour St. Jacques *is* the finest Gothic monument in Paris—a gargoyle that looks exactly like you—exactly, and . . ."

He told her that he was still pottering with bad smells in odd moments and that he made too much money.

"What's the apartment like now ? "

"Ah, about the same—wait till you see . . ."

"What ? " asked Shirley.

"Well, lots of things," said Richard negatively.

They finished their coffee, and then drank a cup more each, for nowhere in the world is coffee to be obtained so good as the coffee in any cheap American all-night restaurant ; and then they slapped four nickels down on the counter and walked away toward the lake. They sat down on an old log and watched the lake ; both in their evening clothes, feeling the hard sand through their pointed slippers, watching the street lamps wash the beach with faint yellow shadows and the waves rustle gently up the slope of the shore.

"Just the same," announced Richard, as they walked back later, "something has got to be done about us. Now."

"I suppose so."

"We can't go on like this."

"We can try. Richard, I'm not going to interfere with you. I hope you're not going to interfere with me. Can't we let it go at that?"

"No," he said, "and you know it. What are we going to *do*?"

"Wait."

"It's no go, Shirley," he went on quickly. "As I say, you can't come back into my life—like this—just after I've learned how to live life without you."

"I suppose it isn't fair," she ruminated. "Still . . ."

"And it's impossible that you should stay here and not see me."

And although Shirley was a very wise person and should have known better she said once more:

"Can't we be friends?"

"No," he said.

"Why not?"

"Because you're too beautiful for one thing."

"Oh!" said Shirley.

"Because—hell!" broke off Richard.

"I see," she repeated gravely. "I see! And perhaps you're right."

Richard suddenly burned with passion.

"Damn you!" he cried. "*Damn* you!"

After that there was a long pause and they walked in silence down the velvet streets, toward Mary's house; and Shirley's face was very calm, but a pale flush shone dangerously in her cheeks.

"I suppose," she finally pronounced slowly, "that means you're still in love with me?"

They could see the lights of Mary's house, the lights flickering through the garden and the trees.

"I don't know," she continued, "whether I'm glad or sorry. But anyway, if that's a fact . . . well, we've just got to fight it out again. And I'll keep away, Ricky, if you want me to."

There was a final silence before the iron gate after that. "Humph!" said Richard.

vii

Out in the garden, little Marjorie with her tumbled blond hair, and Paul, young Paul, very straight and solemn, stood and watched each other make faces.

viii

Doris wondered: what can he be up to?

Leon was approaching her, and there was a gleam in his cold eyes.

Doris was not happy. Should she tell Leon? Perhaps not. She knew he was in love with her, and she was cautious in such matters.

He, too, was not happy. In fact, he was deeply distressed. That hay fever. What nonsense that he should be bothered every year, between the 10th of May and the 15th of June, by the smell of flowers. He had heard that one could be inoculated for hay fever; that a doctor injected subcutaneously a small garden of flowers into the victim; the doctor planted into one's arm the pollen of rose seed, dandelion, marigold, golden rod, ragweed, hay, and perhaps even a little grass to make sure. Leon liked that idea. What an amusement, to be planted with a garden of flowers. Imagine it, one's arm

sprouting between scrawny elbow and shoulder with ragweed, dandelion, golden rod, and perhaps even a neat
little cluster of roses. That was an idea for a poem. A
good poem, maybe.

But when he approached Doris, something else was in
his mind. He reverted to his idea of the afternoon. He
would tell her that he wanted to suffer.

"Doris," he began confidentially, "I want you to
hurt me."

"What?"

"I want to suffer. Really, I want to feel pain.
Doris, please hurt me."

"What do you mean—pinch your arm—tweak
your nose?"

"No. No. You are beink* stupid. You are beink
deliberately stupid. I mean much more than that, Doris.
I want to *suffer*. It is necessary that I suffer."

"Why do you want to suffer?"

"Aloysha suffered," he replied mysteriously. "Mysh-
kin suffered. Bazaroff suffered. Even Sanine suffered."

That was another thing about Leon. He was saturated
in Russian books. He lived Russian books. He thought,
quite rightly, that only three great novels have been
written in the history of the world, and that all three
were by Dostoievsky.

"Don't tell me," replied Doris, "that you want to be
a Sanine."

"Oh, no," said Leon seriously. "I could not be a
Sanine. But even Sanine suffered; and as for me, I want
to suffer like the others. Don't you see"—and his eyes
quickened—"before there can be art, or real expression
of any kind, there must be feelink, sympathy, pity; one
must know and understand; and to know and understand,

* At the end of some words Leon never quite managed the full "g"
sound, and said something more nearly like a "k." He was born, I think
I forgot to mention, in Russia.—J. G.

to have feelink and sympathy and pity, one must first suffer."

Doris was interested. She saw Leon was right, largely considering his point. She stood against the tall background of bookcases, watching Leon. He was interesting to watch. When he brushed his hair from his face his eyes shone. He had a mobile sensitive mouth; and it was a pity he was so stooped. "Like Beauty and the Beast," thought Doris.

"Just what kind of suffering do you want?" she asked.

"I don't know."

"Well, that's a difficulty, Leon. Perhaps if you fell in love you might suffer." This was bait. "Yes, perhaps you might fall in love. Do you want to fall in love with me?"

"You are playink with me. Do not be so brutal, Doris. You know that I am already in love with you."

"Which would make you suffer more—if I fell in love with you or didn't fall in love with you? Now, then, there is a fair question."

"I should suffer more if you loved me," he proceeded shrewdly, "because then I should know I was unworthy; and I should be deeply hurt. If you didn't love me it would not matter so much, because it would be natural, I should expect it of you. There is little suffering in banalities. But," and Leon paused, "but if you loved me, and *then* I failed to achieve you, then perhaps it would be real sufferink."

"Ah, yes, Leon." Well, now he had answered neatly and put it up to her, was it worth while? Then she said deliberately: "You may consider, Leon, that for the next twenty-four hours I shall be in love with you."

He considered seriously.

"No," he said, "that will not do. The emotion must come before the statement. You cannot say you *will* ' fall in love ' with anybody. It must come, of itself."

" But didn't you look at me and find me beautiful and choose me from others and say to yourself, ' I will fall in love with her ? ' "

" No," said Leon. " It was spontaneous. Like a poem. Like the poem I wrote this afternoon. Listen."

He recited it to her.

" Poor Leon," said Doris.

" It is a good poem," he said, as he looked at her hands and thought of them grasping his heart. She had un-usual hands, very white and small, with short, firm pointed fingers ; the fingers, with their sharp, glistening nails, were like talons.

" I love you . . ." he began cautiously.

At the moment she rather despised him. She despised him because of her superior knowledge. Her lips curled. Leon was probably still innocent. She knew more than he did.

" Listen, Leon," she began abruptly, rapping out the words. " Remember that at this moment I am in love with you. We love each other, you and I "—she lowered her voice and came to him—" and we're alone. Think of that, Leon ! We're alone—and we love each other." Her hands were on his shoulders now and her face was very near, upturned to his. " I love you—do you hear, Leon ? And you are all mine. And you love me—and I am all yours—almost ! " She was intense : perhaps for the first time that day Doris was experiencing emotion. "And think, Leon—my lips—yours—almost ! Close your eyes and dream ! Close your eyes and think, Leon ! All yours —*almost !* "

She paused, breathless, her eyes glittering.

Leon was poised, bent toward her. He was in a passion of excitement. He choked. His heart burned. Doris was before him, breathing hard. He was intensely

puzzled and a little scared. Finally he reached forward
to take her in his arms; and then she withdrew very
suddenly and laughed.

She said very quietly, "Now listen, Leon," and her
lips curled again ever so slightly, and she told him—about
that afternoon.

Later.

They heard Richard call, "Who's going my way?"
and they realized that the party was over. Outside, the
lanterns still cast a flickering glow. Mary was gathering
her guests together and seeing them off. Doris thought
of her day and the night and then looked once more at
Leon.

But she was disappointed. He smiled. Even if it was
not a happy smile, he smiled.

"You have not made me suffer," he said simply. "I
am sorry, but you have not made me suffer. Good night,
Doris."

"It was the *first time*, Leon!" she said urgently.

"It does not matter. You have not hurt me." His
mouth was twisted in pain, but he kept his eyes clear.
"You have not made me suffer. Good night, Doris."

She was annoyed.

ix

The crowd gathered before the door.

"Kerchew!" sang out Leon.

"Try horse dandruff," suggested Austin.

Shirley got in a final word with Mary about Der
Goldnerschnitt, while Richard turned to Leon and made
some comment on the adrenal gland.

"Kerchew!" sneezed Leon again.

Mary gathered to herself the last remnants of her party;
for the last time that evening she apportioned her charm.
She bowed good night with her wide flashing smile light-
ing her face:

"Richard," she said quietly, and Richard felt himself peculiarly and intimately farewelled, with cordiality in the tone, and also friendliness and urbanity, and also quiet humour. And Mary proceeded to Doris and Austin and Paul and Leon.

They were soon gone. But Shirley stayed.

Chapter Three

RICHARD AND SHIRLEY

i

AND now this record must turn back many years, because much about Richard and Shirley remains to be explained.

They had known one another a long time. Richard was never able to recall anything so tangible as their first meeting. They were casual friends in childhood, brought up in the same city. Shirley had been a definite fact in his life as long as he could remember : and even in the early years he thought she must be a definite fact in his life forever. They began to be friends intelligently when they both found themselves in Chicago. That was as far back as 1915 or 1916. Even then, in a childish way, Richard loved her.

Richard's father was a picturesque madman, an old man with a taut red forehead and a spray of white straggling hair : he died in 1915, mumbling inanities, and Richard helped to bury him. His mother had died a good many years before. An orphan, he turned to the business of life. The war years were crowded. He had college to finish and a living to earn, and it wasn't easy, doing both ; he was worn and thin and sleepless and seldom had any chance to see Shirley intimately or personally. During the summer vacations he worked. During the school terms he assisted in the chemistry laboratory and kept on working. He was a little too young for the war and when the war-fever raged he was bitter and remote, talking about " missing out."

Once a week or so he came to the Bowdoins for dinner, and they were the happiest evenings, he thought later, of his life : his eyes dimmed and his face relaxed a little when he thought of them. It hardly even mattered if Shirley were there. It was just that he was in a home, he who had never had a home since early childhood. He thought of Mrs. Bowdoin, an ample capable woman feeding him like a mother, and Mr. Bowdoin, who sat like a mouse in a corner and told him old Southern jokes as he watched his children play; of Shirley's brother, Jack, a vague restless boy, and of Shirley herself, usually at the piano. Richard would listen to the chant of the booming strings and feel himself carried all the way back through the years, listened and felt his heart expand and his eyes cloud, as the wandering chords sank into his brain, an anodyne to the brusque outer facts of his life.

Years later there were things, little things, he couldn't hear without emotion. Debussy's Golliwog Cake-Walk from the Children's Corner, Edward German's musical arrangement of the Just-So Stories, an obscure song by Cornelius called *Monotone*, Lehmann's Persian Garden, the music to Verlaine's poem, *Les Sanglots Longs*, by Reynaldo Hahn, the Beethoven Minuet in G Major, a gay chant by Borodine, even the *Chanson d'Indu* and the *Hymne du Soleil* of Rimsky-Korsakoff.

He wasn't sure when he discovered himself to be actually in love with Shirley. He never did precisely know. With Richard and Shirley it was a process of growth, an inevitable sort of growth, he used to say, but of that she wasn't so sure. They only talked about that sort of thing, however, very much later. It took a long time to convince Shirley; she had an independent kind of mind.

She liked Richard; she liked to see him and to talk to him; she was a wise and cool and lithe little person, and with faint amusement and vast motherly solicitude (though she was younger than he)* she cooled his adoles-

* She was born in 1899 in Louisville.—J. G.

cent stings and hurts. I mention that Shirley was wise. There is little doubt but that she was genuinely wise. Perhaps it was because she felt things so deeply under her cool grace; she did feel deeply, Richard knew, and her sensitiveness, perhaps, led her to an intuitive cognisance of much that other people could only laboriously find through slow thought.

During those two years they went round the corner to the movies, those familiar corner moving-picture houses so plentifully scattered all over Chicago, with such a thick cluster of them on the north side; they took picnics together north in Glencoe and Edgebrook, far south to the Indiana Dunes, and to Palos Park, where the green of the trees made the city a memory; they went to the theatre occasionally and even to opera, two notable productions for them being the first performance of Boris Godonoff given in Chicago (this was in the fall of 1917) and the thrilling drum-beats of Kismet on the great stage of the Auditorium early the next year. They were often together and they were friends.

She was playing one night, playing the Beethoven minuet, simple and even sentimental music, but profoundly charming in its way, the one which begins:

and she turned suddenly to see him with tears in his eyes beside her. She had never seen him cry before, and she was amazed.

" Richahd ! " she exclaimed.

(She often said " Richahd " like that, without the " r "; perhaps it was a survival of a Southern accent.)

He said nothing.

" Well, I do think," she continued, " that you're something of a fool."

Shirley was cruel perhaps in that, but she knew very well it wasn't the brooding melancholy of the music which affected him, though that might have · been contributory ; no, she knew her Richard, she knew he was pitying himself for something, letting that self-pity sway him. He was very young in those days and she knew that also.

She was sitting at the piano and Richard, with tears still in his eyes, walked behind her and sank his lips in the cool smooth mass of her black hair. She bowed her head, largely because she didn't know just what else to do. He stood then for a long time, crying into her hair and kissing it.

" Don't," she said finally.

He wanted to kiss her lips, but he was afraid. He was afraid to move. Shirley probably knew this and she didn't help him ; she decided, a little uneasy, to play a waiting game. And so he stood over her, kissing her hair, pressing her thick hair with his lips, feeling it brush ever so slightly against his lips and smoothly caress his chin ; and all the time she sat at the piano with her head bowed, and he cried into her hair, and she waited. She wondered what would happen if she played a bar of the music, and then with head still bowed she ventured forward her hands and slipped into the plangent melody : but Richard still kissed her motionlessly, still wept a little into her hair.

Later he sat beside her and reached awkwardly to kiss her mouth.

" Don't," she said sharply.

He withdrew, clouded and flushed. Then he sat apart with his face dark, and when she turned to look at him she laughed.

" What I don't understand," she said, " is why you look so *puzzled*."

" I'm not puzzled," he denied.

"Look," she said, "at your face." She got up quickly. "Richahd, don't be such a fool. You know I care for you. But I care for myself first. I'm a very selfish person, Richahd. And I care for myself first, always." She paused and looked again at his face and then felt a twinge of pity.

"There!" she said suddenly, and reached lightly to kiss him.

Richard groped for her and she was gone; he couldn't reach her to kiss her again, and he looked to see her beautiful oval face become very solemn. She hesitated. Should she say it? Well, why not? It was good for small boys to be hurt . . . once in a while. She would hurt him only because she liked him so. He moved toward her again and she waited:

"Richahd," she said quietly, "it takes two to make a kiss."

He looked up sharply, agonzied.

That was his first great discovery in life and love; and to his credit he realized it himself as she said it, realized it as soon as she did, but he couldn't put it into words, there were no words in his heart, only yearning in his heart: but Shirley did say it because she was wise and she knew: and she knew also that probably he would never forget it, that in his heart those few quiet words of hers would whisper through many years.

ii

Richard found Shirley "incredible"—that was his word for her—and indeed she was often a puzzling character. She was a very complex character. She was born, as I think I have noted, in Louisville. When Richard began college, she was sixteen, a year or so younger than he. When she decided that it took two to make a kiss she was seventeen and he nearing nineteen.

She alone among these people was not educated, as the word is, at the University of Chicago. Instead, after her childhood in Louisville, she was sent by her parents to a boarding school and then to a fashionable " finishing " school in the east. When she returned to Chicago, whither her parents had migrated from Louisville, she was " finished." That is, she knew a smattering of politics, art, geography, modern history, English literature, music, French and Greek. It was pretty awful ; but Shirley had a mind and did her best : her French for one thing was remarkable. So was the way she played the piano. When she left her eastern school, it was with a shrug and a sigh of relief. Now she was ready for the real business of life, which obviously was sculpture.

Shirley had many associations with Richard. She remembered his father from early Louisville days. Children were frightened of Old Man Northway and his vacant lustrous eyes. They saw him, and like Shirley ran helter-skelter down the street. For all of that, the Northways and the Bowdoins were neighbours, friendly in a way. Mrs. Bowdoin was sorry for Mrs. Northway, and when Mrs. Northway died (Richard was eleven at that time) the Bowdoin family attended the funeral en masse, watching the old madman mumble near the coffin. The old man wanted to sit on the coffin, which made something of a scene. Little Mr. Bowdoin, his cheeks puffing, was the one who pushed him off. Then Shirley went away to school and Richard came north with his father. Later, in Chicago, they met again and resumed their friendship, and spent eager days together when she returned west from her school vacations.

Then Richard's father died, about the time Shirley finished school, and when she returned to Chicago to live with her people and study, he was adopted, in a manner of speaking, as one of her family.

Even then, a good many years ago, she was an astonishingly beautiful girl. She had a great many young men hovering about her. Richard couldn't remember the time when she didn't have at least one faithful attendant, madly and hopelessly in love with her. To these she was kind. To the others, whose state approached neither the mad nor the hopeless, she was indifferent. She floated through a swamp of men as aloofly as a child. This is not to say that she was an aëry gossamer child ; far from it, her feet were solidly on the earth and she watched them, but the rest of her was as remote and frigid as the peaks of Shala. Aloofness was no pose with her : it was actively a part of the thick bell of black hair tufted over her ears, of her cool grey appraising eyes, even of the warm colour which made her cheeks lustrous when her aloofness became an active emotion. It did, sometimes.

As to the young men, they simply didn't exist. They made no impingement on her nature. They might have been of another world.

At times, with a perfectly calculated gesture, almost an epicene gesture, Shirley could surrender her aloofness, but always deep in her mind was distance, always deep in her heart a remoteness, a solitude, an inner detached realization that she belonged to herself, that no one belonged to her. And all the time she worked. She worked hard. Richard often saw her, with her fingers still ringed slightly with clay, her hands too tired even for the piano. There were the days of hard, unproductive study—anatomy, perspective, lettering, water-colour, charcoal sketching, free-hand—all of it a tough apprenticeship. She sped through it. Then the first days of modelling. The first feeling of wet clay gave her an overpowering emotion. Her first little completed work, a small figure of a child bending over and touching its toes with long fingers, was exhibited at the Institute Exhibition in the spring of 1919—a triumph for so young

a student. It was a proud day for Shirley. She crept
into the exhibition rooms once or twice, with her lips
slightly apart, and could hardly believe that it was hers,
that *her* supple fingers had given such life to clay. It was
called *The Spring Flight*.* Later she came to laugh at
The Spring Flight, but she didn't laugh then : she was
excited. It was bought for a hundred dollars after the
Exhibition, the first money that Shirley had ever made.
She was transformed.

The Bowdoins lived in Edgewater, on one of the little
side streets which thread a short precarious way between
Sheridan Road and the lake, little streets like Buena
Terrace and Airdrie Place and Edgecomb Place, each
only a block or two long, faced frowningly their short
span with high apartment buildings, so that one looked
down through them from the boulevard to the lake,
as through a narrow crevice, a chasm between deep
buildings to blue water. The Bowdoins were comfortably rich, and Shirley had a car of her own, a little two-
seater, and Jack, two years her junior, had his first dinner
jacket at fourteen, and Mrs. Bowdoin shopped on
Michigan Avenue and bought strawberries in December,
and small, puffy Mr. Bowdoin, busy managing his glass
factory during the day, could smoke Vaneto Abajos in
the evening after dinner and smoke as many of them as
he wanted, which was a good deal. It was a very peaceful
family.

Shirley was fond of them largely because they let her
have her own way. She had her own way a good deal.
Night after night she would sit and play with clay in her
little studio-room at the back of the apartment, while
Mrs. Bowdoin watched and wondered sometimes how
her flesh had produced this strange quiet child, while
Mr. Bowdoin puffed fragrant curling blue smoke and

* It was bought by Mrs. Harley Fitzjohn, 1366 Lake Shore Drive, and
may be seen to-day. Telephone Lakeside 3621.

watched the fractions in the financial columns quiver at the end of the stock quotations, while Jack would disappear, pleading with Shirley for the loan of the car, on mysterious nocturnal excursions.

What a despot she was in those days!

"Go home, Bill," she would say, or "Go home, Andrew," or "Martin," or "Steve" as the case might be; and sometimes "Go home, Richard," to Richard. And they would go, watching her with her serious mouth a straight red line across the pallor of her face and her hair tumbling to her cheeks just a little, watching her vague eyes and her habit of pulling her fingers pensively, gravely over her chin. "Go on home," she would say. "I want to work." And she did work. They were puzzled. But they went.

Richard often remembered a letter she once wrote him, when she was still very young, still, in fact, away at school. He treasured that letter. It was a shock to him when unaccountably, carelessly, he lost it:

"Which is the more fun," she wrote in her precise small hand, " to finish a book or do something or make a discovery, and then get all enthusiastic and rush to the perfect listener and burble everything away—or to long for the perfect listener in vain, and go to bed feeling superior to your room-mate? Well, everything is very good just now. I don't know why, unless it's because the first thing I see every morning is a tree with little new shiny leaves on it. I can't express the feeling by any word but ' brave,' and I can't express it by that. Anyway, I'm free and I haven't any money, so I won't forget that I want certain things, and I *will* get them. And I don't belong to anybody, and nobody belongs to me. And there are always new things to discover and so always new battles to fight. And when I want to die, I will! Even the fact that I'm almost eighteen years old isn't depressing now. Is there anything in the world so secure as an utter insecurity? I should think a soldier would move in an ecstasy."

The grave little *child!*

This was all before Richard became important.

iii

He did become important. There were incidents.

Sometimes Shirley was curious that she had never fallen in love. It was strange, somehow, and unnatural. It was almost embarrassing, as if she hadn't washed her neck and someone discovered it.

One day Richard asked her why she had never loved anyone, as they drove in her little car and watched spring hover over the city.

"Please," she said, evading the question slightly, "don't put ideas into my head."

"But that's exactly what I'm trying to do, to put an idea into your head."

"Such ideas," she went on, still evading him, "are not the property of the very young."

"When you do," said Richard, "the stars will fall right out of the sky."

Shirley didn't say anything as they drove a block. He thought the remark had slipped into her and lost itself. He watched the new green edge the trees. Then she asked:

"Into whose lap, I wonder?"

And it was into his lap eventually.

Shirley and her mother were walking toward Wilson Avenue one afternoon, window shopping and watching the crowds, and suddenly, quite unexpectedly, they met Richard. After he had gone, her mother asked:

"When you see Richard do you always stop dead like that?"

This bothered Shirley a little; and for a time she rather avoided him.

And once they were lunching at the Tip-Top far above the noise of the city. Richard drummed on the table with a pencil and tried to draw Shirley's face as he saw it. Her face in this posture meant a great deal to him. It was the way he carried her face in his heart—directly looking at him with her eyes level and grave, her nose turning up gently at the tip, her straight little mouth with the short upper lip, her hair, her heavy bell of black hair just cupping her face, dancing a little over the ears, with a severe part, a most grave and severe part, in the middle.

He thought he could visualize that oval of her face perfectly. It was with him like that in thoughts and dreams. But as he tried to draw it, for he knew no technical training in draughtsmanship, he failed miserably. It was extraordinary to him that he could feel this visualization of her face so keenly, feel it, but that his poor fingers refused to execute the design. He tried again and made a horrible botch, and Shirley hooted with laughter.

Richard explained the paradox and was irritated.

"You mean this way," she said, and she took his pencil and drew his idea of her face perfectly.

"Exactly," he said. "Now why can't I do that?"

"You should be able to," she said seriously. "You can do things with your hands and your fingers are steady, and your eyesight is good."

"Don't laugh at me," he said. "It's the most outlandish thing. I have that outline of your face in my soul. I live with it. I know its every line and gesture. I see it, but just the same my fingers refuse to draw it."

"Ah," she said, and she was suddenly alight with an idea. "Ah, that's just it, Ricky. You see it, but you don't see it clearly enough. If it were perfectly clear in your own mind, clear as crystal, so that your mind knew every line and accent and gesture, *knew* it as well as felt it, *knew* it—why, then you could reproduce it all right."

" I wonder," he said seriously.

" That's the whole thing," continued Shirley eagerly. " Of course, see it clearly first and then you're all right. I imagine that's the way with all art. All writing too, maybe. You can't just fiddle around and improvise. You must *know*, first. You must see *clearly*."

That little dialogue was profoundly important to him. He suddenly realized (it seemed extraordinary that he had never realized it before) the essential importance of clear sight in everything. To see clearly said it all. If you saw clearly, then perhaps you might be able to straighten out the muddle of things. If you saw clearly, then perhaps those experiments would right themselves, perhaps that story long in your mind would precipitate to clarity, perhaps even your love for Shirley might be distilled and rendered lucid. He came to the conclusion that to see clearly was something vitally important, and thereafter he sought consciously to see things clearly. It became a quest for many years. He was not too successful at first. For a long time he was not successful at all.

He told Shirley what he felt and she smiled and understood.

At this time Shirley often wondered if she'd like Richard more if he were less obviously in love with her. She did like him, immensely : he filled a large want in her life, the want of companionship, and they were friends. They talked. How they talked : they talked tremendously of everything in the world. She recognized now that he was important : and with her fingers poised over her lips but her eyes resolute, she wondered . . .

And he looked back later to this year and the year

which followed, and he was very glad it all happened so long ago.

iv

Richard was indeed very terrible. It was the unhappiest time of his life. In the following year, during all of 1920, he was miserable. He was in love. He followed Shirley like a dog. He was just out of college and just beginning to work, and the comparative independence which followed brought him and Shirley closer. He began to earn money. He wanted to earn money, a lot of money, which was the reason he temporarily gave up chemistry for bonds. He could take her to theatres more often now. But she was very strict about such matters.

"I always pay half, Richahd," she would say. "Remember that, and we don't take taxis unless it rains."

He suffered a good deal and even if it was funny he couldn't laugh. It was not that Shirley didn't care for him—not at all—but that she didn't care for him enough. He found that partial success in love was something infinitely more tragic than blank failure. It was the success which didn't quite come off which was unbearable. He loved her and she *liked* him. That was worse, he thought, than if she hated him. Sometimes he hoped she would hate him. That at least would be a finality. It would end his yearning. He said sullen cruel things, and Shirley only kept on liking him.

Like! Richard writhed.

And it was hard for her, too. She knew a good deal about young men. She knew, for instance, that masculine vanity is infinitely and pervasively more inherent than feminine vanity; she knew how young men in love resembled small dogs; she knew that every young man has a peculiar illusion that he among all the young men in the world is the most ardent. Yes, it was hard for Shirley. She liked Richard. She knew what he was going through. But there was nothing much she could do.

He remembered how she clouded all his days. She was never out of his mind. He was stormingly jealous of the covey of young men still following her, because he knew that she was quite capable, in her detached bored way, of pleasure with them, and he didn't have sense enough to realize any such lapse would be of no real importance in her life or thoughts. But still he listened to her play the piano, and watched her model in clay or plasticine; they walked together and drove in her car; they hiked to the Dunes and listened on Saturday nights to the symphony concerts. And still they were ostensibly friends, but he felt now that it couldn't last. It was bound to snap, some time. He wanted her too much—and she didn't want him at all.

They had one quarrel.

"Richahd," she said one day, with temper in her voice, "you're getting proprietary, and I don't like that."

She was right. He had been a fool. He saw Shirley so much that he wanted to see her all the time. In a way it was her own fault; she didn't altogether realize, probably, how necessary she was becoming to him, while at the same time she tantalized him by withholding herself. And Richard, when other people were around, edged close to her, kept staring at her, and sometimes in mixed company he muttered little references cognisant only to Shirley and himself, so that the party wondered and she became furious.

"Sometimes you come toward me," she said, "as if you were going to envelop me—I can't explain it—you walk toward me as if you intended to *absorb* me—and I want to *scream!* I can't stand that."

He protested feebly, and one afternoon, at a Paderewski

concert, they sat in strained silence, although it was impossible to put in words what was wrong. Richard became aware that everything he did was irritating her, and that she was anxious to avoid him. It seemed to him very silly. He asked her what was the matter, and frankly and openly she tried to tell him. And then again, like a fool, he was hurt.

" I'm not hurt," he kept saying stubbornly. " I'm *not* hurt ! "

And she felt a twinge of pity. But she said :

" You're not hurt, Richahd, but your vanity is—and somehow I don't think that it's anything but your vanity. No, Richahd, *you're* not hurt."

And then, of course, he admitted that he was hurt (after all) ; and if his face hadn't been so tragic she would have had to laugh.

After that he stayed away for several days ; there was once a lapse of four days in which he didn't see her, a very notable lapse, something which hadn't occurred in a year. She had to admit herself a little annoyed. She had to admit she missed him, though she shrugged her head quickly when he came into her mind. When he did telephone, very cautiously, she was glad ; but her tone was cold.

" It isn't important," she said quickly, when he returned. " Don't refer to it, please."

That was the strange thing about that year, as Richard saw it later. Nothing was important. Nothing was significant. Nothing, for that matter, happened. It was just a haze of days, interminably floating past, like a vague tapestry of pain, with rare sudden illuminations of happiness when Shirley smiled ; many moments of pain when she was remote and elusive, with her eyes vague. Part of that remoteness now was defence. Richard wanted to talk too much about them. But there were no angry words or scenes between them. It was just a difference. Their friendship had settled, in a way, to an uneven keel. He kissed her sometimes, and then, because of an obscure psychological necessity, which he couldn't explain, he stopped kissing her. Then it was her turn to shrug.

He stopped kissing her perhaps because there seemed no point in it. Obviously kisses didn't matter to Shirley, except once or twice on supreme occasions. But when he stopped she was annoyed, because it appeared he was weak, afraid to kiss her after once he had kissed her. And this touched her vanity. It was again a nice point, psychologically. Richard refused to move an inch toward her, just because—because—he had a silly adolescent notion of " serve her right " in his head. And that then produced another situation, it produced in Shirley, naturally enough, a physical indifference which turned to slight physical repulsion ; and she got over that only by telling him about it frankly. " I cringe when—when you touch me," she whispered. That almost finished him. Also, and it often happens that way, the fact that she mentioned it helped to remove it from her mind, in fact, after voicing it she forgot it ; but he wasn't wise enough to know that and she couldn't tell him. And so again he was diffident. Again he was afraid.

He hardly felt afraid in any real physical sense. It was simply that he wanted her so much, so much that he turned to water when she was close ; he couldn't touch her hair without going dizzy ; sometimes he felt her arm underneath hot smooth silk, and felt goose-flesh all over him. He was afraid to kiss her because it should mean so much and might mean so little. He was afraid to touch her and yet sometimes touched her furtively ; and that she bitterly hated. And all the time he wanted her, wanted her cool grace and the loveliness of her body, wanted her increasingly, desperately, hopelessly.

Coming home one night from dinner in evening dress,

v

Meanwhile Shirley was working. She was working hard. She had finished two models that spring and was anxious to do one more. Each morning she spent at the Institute with regular classes; and each afternoon she went into the sculpture room and worked. And as she worked, as he worked, still they grew together and still their friendship changed; and there were incidents.

"I'll be able to play to-night," she said, late one afternoon, lying face downward on a couch. She was tired, barely murmuring the words.

"Why?"

"It's in my fingers." She was interested in the idea and she turned to face him. "It's the fingers, Richahd. I'm amazed sometimes. It's almost terrifying." She held out her strong lean hands, with the firm, slightly tapering fingers splayed before him.

"Look, isn't it marvellous, these fingers really have a life of their own. I don't often know what they are going to do. Sometimes they have life in them of themselves. To-day, for instance; oh, Richahd, I worked to-day! And when I can work, when I feel life in my fingers, I can always play."

"Curious," said Richard. "What relation do you suppose that has to seeing clearly?"

"Oh, a great deal. The fingers see."

"Oh, come, I mean by seeing clearly what you meant at lunch long ago; I mean a preliminary survey, an artistic cognisance . . . it's awfully hard to explain. . . . I suppose I mean a directive foresight. And all that must be mental. It must come from the brain, from the soul if you wish . . . from whatever it is we call capacity."

"And not of the fingers?"

"Hardly."

"Well, I don't know," she said dubiously. She was tired and lay with her face cupped in her hands. Richard watched her and felt again that surge of passion. It seemed an old surge now.

"I don't know," she continued. "But there *is* something in my fingers. I do know that. Oh, it's ridiculous, Richahd, but I can *feel* it. And why shouldn't fingers be a part of directive capacity, as you put it? I think they are a part. Why," she said suddenly, "I'll prove it to you."

She got up, walked to the piano and played; she played, not better than he had ever heard her play before, but very well, very well indeed, and he thrilled, listening to the glowing chords of the Tschaikovsky Fifth, the high swoon of the Young Prince And The Young Princess piercing in the top rhythm, sighing in an agony of music. She played slowly, her fingers roamed over the chords; she slipped with her eyes dreaming, and all the time the black bell of her hair swaying over her face, slipped from the quick throb of Debussy and Ravel to the sonorous rhythms of the *Habanera ;* and then back to the Russians again, and the notes dropped like pearls on velvet as she drummed out songs of Borodine and Cui. It was melancholy playing, very beautiful and Richard murmured : "There's something to be said for the minors," and still she played, and then she stopped abruptly with a quick marching Polonaise from Chopin, and she was gay now, laughing, and she turned to Richard, slamming her fists on the final chord with a triumphant :

"See ! "

But he was close behind her; she felt his body close behind her back and she tilted her head forward slightly. And again he was kissing the thrilling black mass of her hair, again letting his lips softly sink into it, as he had done so many years before, so very many moving years before. And this time he was not crying.

" But my fingers . . ." she said, after a slow silent interval.

Another time he met her for luncheon at the Institute, and as they started to swing down the boulevard with the lake, cold and remote, to the right, Richard stopped a second, jumped up a couple of steps, and grasped the bronze tail of the great lion standing before the chasm of Adams Street, guarding the portals of the Institute. He grasped the bronze tail and he twisted hard.

Flushing and apologetic, but with laughter, he rejoined her on the boulevard.

" There's always a chance," he whispered, " that the lion *might* jump ! "

They went on to lunch. He hardly remembered where, but it might have been the Tip-Top, of which they were very fond, or Maurice's, the little French restaurant near Richard's office (such pastry !), or if they had time all the way north to Le Petit Gourmet, or even Baum's, or L'Aiglon : so many neat small restaurants there were in Chicago, and each so distinguished for something ; and they spent many noon-times, while the traffic surged past them, searching them out.

Once after the seduction song of *Samson and Delilah*, at the end of the second act, they were close together in the dark auditorium. They saw the dancers costumed in green and orange sway through the throbbing measures of the bacchanal, and Richard was able to watch. But Shirley felt her eyes fill, Shirley who never cried was forced to blink her eyes slightly, the better to see. She wanted intensely to see as well as hear, while the dancers wavered on the stage, but little tears quivered on her lids, blurring her vision. She was able to see a benediction of white veils hang floating over the dancers and then Anna Ludmilla's entrance in a red costume, like a puff of flame. Tears came again and she shook her head to clear her eyes. But immediately she felt them refill, and

she gave it up, closing them. The shattering curtain fell
as Samson pushed asunder the pillars. But that was
later. It seemed years later. Shirley was overwhelmed.
She stirred from her seat and they walked down the long
dark corridor. She felt she could hardly breathe. But
suddenly she wanted to breathe a great deal, over and
over again, a great deal deeply.

He whispered : " I want to kiss you."

Her eyes still were clouded, and as he bent toward
her she pushed him slightly away in the dark aisle,
and said, whispering : " You will to-night." But
she was as still and remote as the frosty stars as she
said it.

Thus little by little they became closer ; and they
continued to wonder what it was before them.

vi

Just the same their friends were profoundly surprised
when they heard that Shirley had married Richard.

It happened very suddenly. " Suddenly," said Shirley,
" but not impulsively." No one was at the wedding
except Mary Detmers and Mrs. Bowdoin, with Philip
Hubbard as Richard's best man. The ceremony took
place before Mr. Sweitzer in the county clerk's office,
with no flurry, no flowers ; no crowds of well-wishers
trying to masquerade a communion as a banality, no
swarm of drunken stags and maiden aunts. Richard had
always said he wanted to get married like that, if he
married at all, and evidently Shirley agreed with him.
Anyhow, they weren't church people. And anyhow, it
happened. The date was the 17th of September, 1921,
at 4.30 p.m.

" It can't last," their friends said.

But they didn't feel that. They had known one
another all their lives ; there had been the long three

years of friendship and then the awful first year of love, then another year of readjustment, and all the time they were very close, they had been intimates for five years. After all, it was a process of growth. That was why he used to say later it was " inevitable " that they married, and even she said so, once or twice. . . .

But still in many ways it seemed unreasonable. After all, Shirley had no use for Richard permanently. She loved him in her way, loved him as much as she could ever love anyone. But that did not seem quite enough. For Richard, of course, the marriage was a summation, a triumph. For Shirley it was nothing of the kind. Perhaps his attrition wore her out, wore her resistance down : then, too, she did achieve by marriage her first permanency, and even for Shirley permanencies could be valuable ; and she was accustomed sometimes to quote smilingly from the *The Arabian Nights :* " For a girl," quoth Pomegranate-Flower, " there is only marriage and the tomb."

At any rate, they were married. These vastly knowing children, Richard so puzzled by things and Shirley so sure of them, Richard with the first great problem of his life done, his first struggle finished, Shirley with distance in her resolute eyes and the future before her, still as aloof and independent as in the early years, still serene and confident in beauty. At any rate, it was done : and in late September they left for the honeymoon. . . .

That was a happy time. For a time the preoccupations vanished. They spent the honeymoon in Ephraim, a little pine-fringed town in Northern Wisconsin, remote from the grotesque noises of the city, refreshing in calm austerity by the shore of Green Bay. Ephraim was a very quiet little spot : the little harbour faces the placid bay and the cottages straggle downhill to the beach while beyond them the tall pine forests rise and beckon. It

was an ideal place for them. They both thought that
September was the happiest month either ever spent.
They were miraculously, absurdly happy. Forgotten
was that old proprietary attitude of Richard's, forgotten
the occasional sententious indifference of Shirley. They
lived with one another and for one another. Each was
awake to the fierce joy of living. They walked in the
forest of the State park, down avenues of trees on matted
pine needles, and she used to say that she averaged a
statue a mile, and he was quite content just to watch her
face. Few tourists were there as autumn deepened into
the trees and Shirley wore a khaki blouse open at the
neck and khaki knickers and black silk stockings shaping
her legs, with her hair tumbled in the wind and her
cheeks like peach-blow-porcelain awakened to a new flush ;
and Richard loafed in old corduroy trousers and watched
his arms get brown. They swam in water which was
crisp and exhilarating and found a little beach of their
own, where the shadows of purple rocks were deep in the
clear water ; and they swam lazily in sunlight and once or
twice alone at night, when there was a moon and the
village was asleep and the bull frogs and crickets shame-
lessly interrupted the abstract silence of the night. They
were breathless times for Shirley and Richard, breathless,
happy times. The days passed : the days merged into
one another ; and still it was high autumn, still autumn
burned in every bush and tree and flower, while the
crickets hummed and the birds flew north again, and as
they sat on the beach at sunset once or twice they were
even sentimental enough to hold hands, watching the
sun fade in the sky like a purple salute to God, and watching fire from the sun flow into the water. They didn't
talk a great deal these days ; instead there were pauses
and quick appraising understanding, and the long
silences of complete intimacy. It was the only time
they could remember when Shirley did come out of her-

self and forget herself and join him in a perfect equity. It was all very perfect, they kept thinking. Sometimes they wondered if indeed it would last forever, and then they cast that thought from their minds, even Shirley cast that thought from her mind as something quite unworthy. Once they were high on Eagle Cliff, so high above the water that they were quickened, their ears rang; there was a strong wind blowing, a heavy wind in the air, but the water was so far below them that it appeared a sheet of ice, a sheet of blue pathless ice; and the steady lines of whitecaps were motionless from their distance, they were white whipped crusts of foam set in the ice, caught and suspended in some high moment in stillness, frozen by the wind in ridges and flurries to mark the blue. . . . Yes, it was all very perfect . . . perfect. . . . It would last forever. . . .

Later they came back to Chicago, brutal, lowering Chicago, breathing smoke like a bull, turgid with dirt and clamouring, bawling, chanting its gusto to the skies; and Chicago was something of a change.

They took a little apartment on Bryn Mawr Avenue, not far from the Bowdoin home. Richard went back to his office and he earned money, for a young man so shortly out of college he earned a good deal of money. Shirley still went to the Art Institute every day and often worked also in the evening, when he began to potter with chemistry again and set up a laboratory.

And now they decided not to meet for luncheon, because it seemed they were seeing perhaps a little too much of one another every day. They took vast delight in furnishing the little apartment, and wondered, when the first of December came around, whether they could pay the rent.

Also at that time Shirley began her portrait bust of Richard.

vii

They lived together just a little less than one year.

"Richard," said Shirley once, "don't follow me around."

That was it, in a way : he followed her around.

He was hurt then. He didn't understand that even if he were her husband, she wanted often to be alone, very much alone. He had achieved proximity to her ; certainly he was the most important person in her life, and his presence perhaps the most important fact ; but as she came to realize that Shirley resented it ever so slightly. She pursued a quest of loneliness and Richard, hurt, watched her withdraw into that elusion he had known during the awful year ; and he didn't know quite what to do about it. And he followed her around.

And again :

"Richard," she said, "I don't want a sign or whisper of a baby for five years." ·

That, too, was something between them, because he wanted children. He caught himself looking at this stranger in his house, this stranger with eyes distant, far away.

That bust of Richard. It held them together most of their little year. That and the idea they simply *had* to make this thing turn out. The bust was originally called *The Search*, and then Shirley didn't like that title when she couldn't get his puzzled brows in line, and she changed it, at his suggestion, to *The Ultimate Source*, and later when it was exhibited it was simply called *A Portrait in Youth*. It was a heart-breaking job. Richard, as she said, just wouldn't come out. "You see," said Shirley, "I don't want to make a picture of you, anyone can do that, a photographer can do that ; I want to get at the Richard I know ; to show people the Richard I know and *why* I know him . . . and why," she murmured, looking up to his face, " and why I love him."

But that was in the early days.

Even though it was in the early days, she didn't say it easily, that was an awfully hard thing to say out loud—" I love you." It had taken a long time before she could bring herself directly to say it at all, and when she did, even after assiduous practice, it was somehow strained.

And then there was another thing :

" It's this business of fingers," she complained. " It's all in the fingers." She held them out, examined them. " You see, I see something, and I try to see it clearly, and if I see it clearly and honestly enough, why then I begin to feel it, and if I *feel* it deeply and honestly enough, that feeling grows and expands and envelops me, and in the end," she concluded soberly, " I suppose it gets into these fingers."

You see Shirley, too, was very young.

" Anyway," she went on defiantly, " fingers or not— even if it does sound silly—it's I . . . ." she lifted her head so that her dark hair fluttered—" it's I, all I . . . it's *all* I . . . I."

And that, too, perhaps, that incessant inner egoism, was important.

The bust* was finished after Shirley had worked on it three months. Her fingers were sore and her eyes weary. But it kept them happy the first after-months, happy and absorbed. The trouble with the bust was simply that she tried too hard with it. She wanted it for him as her first chef d'œuvre, wanted it in a way to prove herself. Over and over again she worked at the clay, indented, dabbled, modelled the clay with her

---

* It was an excellent piece of work and won a gold medal at the American Exhibition in St. Louis : even though, perhaps, it showed too clearly the influence of the early Rodin, the influence of *The Age of Bronze*.—J. G.

plastic fingers, over and over again she smoothed and cut and built again. They sent it to New York for the casting and waited with fingers crossed. But eventually it was done, with Shirley in high excitement and Richard positively not of this earth ; and in the end she was satisfied.

But as soon as it was done, irrevocably done, she lost interest quickly and he was surprised to see her lose interest ; she was negligent toward it and could hardly be persuaded to exhibit it. In fact, it bored her. Bathetic as it may seem, it appeared some of her love for Richard left Richard himself and went into that statue ; it was a sort of transmogrification ; and when it was done it was as if she had taken everything out of the Richard she loved, as if she had transferred that love to the clay ; and then the clay went cold and dead.

And, too, the trouble was the old fear, the old faltering, which shook his breast ; he worshipped her and worship was no safe basis for marriage ; she took the lead in things and he followed. When they argued, even when he knew he was logically right, he permitted her high scorn to carry her through and he retreated in a blur of words ; and although she partly loved him for his weakness, she came again to be annoyed, annoyed because he didn't have the courage of his intelligence ; she knew often that she was wrong and she *wanted* him to prove himself right against her will. But he never did. And so the pendulum swung back again.

"We're never the same," she said solemnly once. "Always we shift and ebb and flow. And always we know how we are shifting and flowing, and yet we don't seem to be able to stop ourselves. While we *know*. It's a queer thing, Ricky."

"Yes, Shirley."

"I don't know . . ."

And neither did he.

Daily her eyes grew more vague; she was glad now they didn't lunch together; she was preoccupied, her mind soared and her fingers quivered. Also, she wanted to go to Paris to study, but Richard didn't have enough money yet for them both, and anyway he couldn't throw up his job. Paris became a sort of inward obsession.

Yet that mention of Paris is misleading; Richard himself became convinced later Paris had nothing to do with it; he knew that essentially her wish to go abroad had nothing vitally to do with their problem. He became convinced that it was a problem entirely within themselves. That some strange surge of fate swept them together, swept them apart, that it was again like a swing of the pendulum, with a tremendous bond of love between them, and especially a bond of mutual memories; and yet also a stress, a lunge, working like a lever to keep them apart and keep that love fruitless; that if Shirley had never seen clay and Richard never a test-tube, if he had been a chauffeur and she a washer-woman, that same strange mystery within their person-alities would have brought them together, pulled them slowly apart again, brought them closer together and then snapped them—once more then to swing back.

Yet Paris was an . . . excuse. And Shirley—well, Shirley *knew*.

At any rate, their year grew for a while, the reaction set in, the year dwindled in glamour and excitement, the first novelties, the first explorations, paled and wasted; and as Richard's face grew more unsettled, his eyes more sombrely puzzled, Shirley was more preoccupied, her grey eyes vacant and her upper lip sucked between her teeth. They didn't talk about it. They couldn't talk about it. That again was the trouble, perhaps. If they could have said : "Now, look here, Shirley," or "Now, look here, Richard," it might have been very different. But they couldn't, somehow. It was so difficult to put

into words things which were too important for words.
Put into words their values changed.

Besides, Shirley didn't want to talk about it, much.

And so they were constrained ; and so they drifted . . .

One night she came home ; she dropped her gloves
on the table and turned to him very simply.

" I'm going away, Richard," she said, and she hardly
looked at him.

As beautiful and peaceful as a flower she stood, and as
a flower, too, was her face.

viii

She went. It took some while for Richard to get over
it. For several months he had a bad time, and there
was no period of his life to which he looked back with less
pleasure.

When she first went he saved himself by determining
to cast her utterly out of his heart and life, to destroy
this incubus of ten years' standing, to begin anew and
stand on his own feet and see clearly once and for all.

And he succeeded. It was an effort of will. By the
time a year passed he had few regrets and after two
years he felt he had had his lesson and that it was all
over.

Then he came to achieve his third great lesson in life
and love, achieve it honestly : that after all it didn't
matter. It hurt sometimes, but essentially it didn't
matter. And it was done and over, gone and forgotten.

That was why this new and older Richard was able to
detach himself and murmur that it was very amazing
indeed to sit opposite a beautiful young woman at a
more-or-less formal dinner-party and remember that she
had a small birthmark at the end of her third rib.

Chapter Four

CATALYSIS

i

THE morning after Mary's party Leon caught the " L "
at Sheridan Road and rocked down-town to the roaring
of the trains, and in the Loop, just about noon, went
straightway to his favourite stationery store.

Now stationery stores were something of a fetish with
Leon. He was inordinately fond of stationery stores.
If someone had asked him to rank the three great passions
of his life, he would probably have numbered them :
(1) ripe olives ; (2) Doris ; (3) stationery stores. He
roamed in a stationery store with the joy of the aban-
doned, feasting his eye on parades of splendour. Also,
he was a little ashamed of his great unavowed passion.
It did seem rather silly.

A poem was floating in Leon's mind. It would not
quite come out. It was about Doris and only the last
lines were firm in his mind ; he liked these last lines, he
rolled them on his tongue. They were :

> " And your hands like talons,
> Your curved armed fingers like talons,
> Reach out and grasp my heart,
> Compress and squeeze my heart,
> Scratching it,
> Making it drip
> Love
> For you . . ."

That perhaps was not so bad. Leon gleamed.
Inside the stationery store he surveyed lustfully great
snowy piles of paper : typewriter paper, folio paper,

ledger paper, legal paper, creamy deckle-edged manilla paper, heavy drawing paper ; paper in many shades of white, also in pink, cerise, tan, taupe, grey, cream ; delicate flimsy tissue paper and paper as glossy and stiff as armour. With a gathering light in his cold eye Leon passed on to neat ringed notebooks, the sombre velvet of carbon like a pansy's wing, the dazzling counters of pencils and pens, pencils in every colour in the spectrum, pens with stylus points, ball-bearing points, iridium points, tungsten points ; he gazed, his mouth drooping, at inks in rainbow colours, on the soft red and green of erasers (ah, the *feel* of a soft eraser !), on the crumbling piles of art-gum, on thumb tacks, on various fantastic impedimenta of the modern office from great shiny black safes to air cushions for the bony posterior, from calendars to all the useless things, like racks for pens and memory chasteners, letter files and patented memorandum devices. Then Leon progressed to blotting pads and he was voluptuous. He saw also great mahogany desks and tremendous cold glittering filing-cases of green steel, filing-cases with a hundred drawers, of every shape and depth, filing-cases like poems of abandon. He lusted. And there were all the little things, too, pen-wipers of soft chamois, typewriter ribbons, paper clips in fantastic designs, and some great cork pens as soft to the touch as a baby's skin, as light as a wand, and yet substantial, yet tough !

Leon could not resist those pens. He bought one. It cost a nickel.

And then there were the paints. He was ecstatic before colours. He could cry before colours ; he could suffer before savage reds, from blues as pure and dazzling as the north window in Notre-Dame, from tones as darkly purple as the murex. Colours ! Here indeed Leon found his paradise. Here was a pigment the precise colour of crushed raspberries, and here another of that final delicate shading of tan which quivers ecstatically between biscuit colour and taupe, and doesn't quite achieve either, spends its whole life throbbing between two tones. He saw scarlets taken from a tanager's wing, scarlets as cruel and passionate as blood, and also softer reds, reds which drifted toward vermilion and cherry reds that reminded him of holly at Christmastide, garnet reds, ruby reds, madder reds. He saw greens like the new leaves on the trees, darker sombre greens like ilex leaves, shining metallic greens like the rainbow of a pigeon's breast, and oranges, flaming oranges like puffs of hell. And not only these simple colours, not only yellows which paled from flushing chrome to the tart attenuation of lemon, not only blues like Rookwood pottery and Delft china ; rather the borderline shades, the soft violets like a nun's cloak, the fading ecstasy of magenta, the dull pastel ochre a shade higher than tan, pastel blues that were not quite blue and pastel greens that were not quite green, the smoothness of grey and the throb of royal crimson. Leon was in a heaven of excitement. He jerked out a pencil and began to scribble down names of colours, just names of colours, lists of names. He put down :—

Realgar.	Burnt Sienna.	Cerulean.
Afghan Green.	Gentian.	Cinnamon.
Cinnabar.	Maroon.	St. Davis red.
Smoke orange.	Blood tan.	Congo red.
Plumbago.	Saffron.	Yellow ochre.
Citron yellow.	Jasper.	Victoria orange.
Gamboge.	Bottle green.	Saxony blue.
Indigo.	Nile blue.	Puce.
Chrome green.	Russet.	Grenadine.
St. Martin's red.	Apricot orange.	

And so on.

His eyes had something unholy in them. He gloated.

F

He would suffer by colours. He would dazzle his eyes with tingent colours. He would live his life creating colours, listing colours, mingling colours. He began anew to scribble furiously.

ii

"Hullo, there, Leon!"

The boy looked up abruptly, guiltily. He saw Richard.

"Oh, hello!"

He tried to cover what he had been writing with his hand.

"What are you doing, Leon?"

"Well, Richard," he said, a little embarrassed, "I am making a list."

"A list of what?"

"Colours."

Richard began to understand. He, too, knew desire in a stationery store. Besides, he liked Leon, liked him very much. He was interested.

"Colours," Leon repeated.

"Now making lists is a good business," declared Richard. "Whitman and Rabelais and Homer, I may mention as listers. Making lists shows a mediæval type of mind, and that's an interesting type of mind nowadays. But the passion for classification, for category, is also part of lists, and that indicates the modern mind. Science is just that. Making lists. Classifying, aligning, co-ordinating. But then, too, Leon, lists can be dangerous."

"How so?"

"Why, one can be so absorbed merely in lists that nothing else counts. And that is bad, because after all the list itself is but a means to an end; work only

begins after the list is made. The philosophy of lists is
a very queer thing, Leon. I have thought about it a good
deal myself. You see, I make lists, my business is making
lists." Richard paused. "But tell me, why do you list
colours?"

"Why not?"

"Well, yes, but why not as well list the marine crus-
taceans, or the great dates of history, or cosmetics, or
perfumes, or kinds of cigar ash like Sherlock Holmes, or
even food?"

"Food?"

"Just round the corner, Leon, is a food shop," continued Richard. "That food shop interests me.
Heaven knows I'm no voluptuary, I'm no swilling belly-
god; but that food shop not only interests me, it
enchants me. There you can get, Leon, the most
dazzling refinements of food the world can know. You
can get pheasants' tongues and plovers' eggs in jelly."
Richard, in turn, became enthusiastic, but he was
watching Leon closely. "My food shop has no place
for the banal or commonplace. Instead it has Norwegian
anchovies in little wooden casks, it has great kegs of
olives as large as your fist, and it combines the anchovies
and the olives, Leon, it has olives stuffed with anchovies.
It has salmon paste and caviare straight from Archangel,
and pâté de foie gras like cream with fire in it. You can
get there obscure German sausages and also crumpets
from England, and even tanjalo oranges from Africa :
and then there is the cheese department. You should
visit that cheese department : gruyère, brie, roquefort,
port de salùt, cantal, camembert, pont d'évêque, cheddar,
stilton, cheshire, livarot, edam, parmesan, gorgonzola—
and before each great cheese is a tag and that tag tells
the precise day that particular cheese will come to
perfect fruition. The guardian of these cheeses is a
worthy man indeed ; you should see him take care of his

cheeses, Leon, feeding them like children with a spoonful of port each day. And not only cheeses—but sardellan from Sweden, zweibach from the Rhine, gnocchi from Italy and pickled birds' nests from China, stuffed boar's head from Brittany, and, of course, obscure spices from the East Indies!"

"You make me hungry," said Leon.

"Ah!" Richard pounced on him. "You see! That was what I was trying to do. I was making you achieve an emotion, forcing you to achieve it, by listing something quite apart from emotional or æsthetic concepts. You see, my foods can match your colours. You can take your paint shop, but give me my delicatessen."

Richard waited for Leon to recover.

"And meanwhile, we have proved the utility of lists."

"Um," said Leon hungrily.

"Tell me," Richard went on, "do you want *use* from your lists?"

"No, Richard, that is why I shall not list foods; I list only useless things."

Richard smiled. Leon still had a pencil poised in his hand, half concealing the paper.

"Come," said Richard, "come, and I will buy you a worthy luncheon."

"At your food shop?"

"Good Lord!" he expostulated. "No! Food is not to be *eaten* there!"

They left the stationery store and Richard saw Leon furtively cast his eye over the crowded counters of typewriters, cuspidors, paper racks, clips and drills, pens and pencils, soft erasers and the fine whiteness of pulp paper. Leon lingered.

"Tell me," asked Richard suddenly, "have you come any nearer to suffering?"

Leon thought, not for the first time that day, of Doris

and the scene the night before ; his heart shook and he quivered.

" No," he said stonily.

iii

After luncheon Richard said :

" But you are interested in colours. Have you anything to do the next hour or so ? "

" No," said Leon.

" Then come along with me. Would you like to see how colours are made ? "

They walked across the Loop toward the lake there to pick up a bus and roll northward. Richard could never decide how he felt about this noontime walk across the Loop. He didn't know whether he felt that the human race could be exterminated or whether such a demonstration of dynamic frenzy should sociologically move him to exaltation. Sociology was the most fascinating of sciences, because it was fluid, still uncharted ; no one knew just what sociology was ; now was the time to get at .it, before it congealed and atrophied. It took twenty minutes to cross this short stretch of six blocks in a taxi ; with luck one could walk it a good deal more quickly. He listened to the yelp of the policeman's whistle, the distant boom of the trains, the screech of the surface cars jamming the tracks. He saw the motor-cars swarming like ants on a holiday, edging in and out, bumping noses, trucks and taxis and limousines . . . all mad, their drivers with scared white faces watching the wheels. Richard liked to watch the streets, but more often he had to watch his way. People with their faces flung down the wind like scraps of white paper. People were strutting, panting, stumbling, racing along the crowded sidewalks, hatless boys, girls with spider web blouses, old men in frayed hats . . . a convulsive mass of people, seething as the tall buildings at noon disgorged their flood, as the tall buildings in dynamic quietude waited for the return. They reached the lake and the boulevard.

"Whew!" said Richard.

"People," muttered Leon, "I loathe people. I despise people. People offend me."

"Then, young man, you're a fool. I think that . . . hey! our bus!"

They sat on top, took off their hats and coasted through the park to the new roar of the north side, up to Richard's apartment in the quiet side street.

"You see," said Richard in his laboratory, "when you talk about primary colours, why, Leon, you don't know what you're talking about. You say that the primary colours are red, blue, yellow. That's nonsense. I have no intention of going into spectroscopy, but the primary colours,* optically or physically considered, are red, green and violet. It's a question of light, not of palette."

They were in the garage laboratory. Richard had never moved from the little apartment he had found with Shirley. To move merely because it reminded him of her too much would have been a sentimental weakness; also. he had been too busy to look for new quarters; also there was the matter of inertia. It had been small for the two of them, but for him alone, with his laboratory now moved out into the garage, it was quite roomy enough.

He added a little dilute sulphuric acid to a barium chloride solution; first came a hiss, and then a lovely amorphous precipitate, as solidly white as snow, whiter than any snow, settled out as the precipitated sulphate.

---

* I'm not sure of Richard's science here. He knows far more about this sort of thing than I do.—J.G.

" You see," ruminated Richard, as he bent an eager face over the tubes and racks and burners, " you see, I'm not a chemist really. Any child in high school could do what I'm doing. I'm a business man ; you know that, Leon, and I'm a busy one." He chuckled, his face still turned towards the tubes. " And I play with chemistry in my spare time, as all of you play with something or other ; you write, Austin teaches, Mary entertains, Shirley——"

" Shirley ? "

" And Shirley is a sculptor. All of you dabble in what vaguely may be called art, some of you part of the time, and some all the time ; and I dabble because it amuses me, in what vaguely may be called science." Still, he thought to himself, if he got that potash up to $1:33$! " And so it goes. We're all restless, Leon, we're all restless and we play, we dabble, to get rid of surplus energy, to get rid of boredom, to get rid of sex. And this chemistry is only a game. Still "—and he paused, beaming, and held a tube to the light—" still, did you ever see a finer blue ? "

He had added a little $K_4Fe(CN)_6$ to a ferric salt solution while he soliloquized. The resulting precipitate is called Prussian Blue in the drawing books. It hung in the tube, irradiating it, like a drop of melted dark blue sky.

He made a few heavy powdery greens for Leon, and a yellow or two, and even (it was rather a trick and he smiled to himself) the wonderful orange ring of the preliminary antimony precipitation.

" All this stuff is inorganic," said Richard. " No use for dyes. No fixation properties. It's the hydrocarbons, the coal tars, you have to use for dyes. I wish I could do some of them for you. But it takes too long. Those are colours for you ! The pure dazzling radiance of those colours ! The yellow of diphenylamin, or the red of phenolphthalein as alkali touches it ! "

Perhaps, thought Richard, Leon didn't even know the colour change of litmus. He showed him.

" What's that ? " asked Leon, pointing to a heavily stoppered glass bottle off in one corner.

" Not for children," laughed Richard. On the bottle was marked cryptically " KCN." " Not for children. That, Leon, is poison, and it is good poison."

" Oh," said Leon.

But now Richard was thinking of something else. He heated a little potassium chlorate in a tube ; nothing happened. Then he added a dust of manganese dioxide, and the tube spluttered oxygen. Leon watched.

" That," said Richard excitedly, like a child, pointing to a cherished toy, " that is catalysis."

" What ? "

" Catalysis."

" I don't understand."

Richard threw up his hands in glee.

" Is it possible," he shouted, " that this child does not know the meaning of catalysis? Well, I will teach you. I will add a word to your vocabulary. C-a-t-a-l-y-s-i-s. To think," he lowered his voice as if in soliloquy again, " to think of someone ignorant of catalysis ! " Aloud he went on : " Chemistry, like any trade or science or craft, can add, Leon, many useful words to the general vocabulary, words and phrases and ideas, too. Learn any one thing well and it is surprising how much inadvertently you learn about other things. Take the chemical phenomenon of precipitation, for instance. You add one fluid to another, there follows what we call a chemical change, a chemical reaction, a subtle, fascinating interchange of atoms takes place, and a precipitate forms. Isn't that like two people talking and coming to grips? First they feel toward one another, and they reach contact—and bang !—a coalescence takes place, a mingling, an intercourse—and out of it you get something finite

and tangible like that white barium sulphate. And
again, Leon, there is a chemical known as carbon
disulphide. It is a very unpleasant chemical. Here,
smell it." Leon sniffed and made a bad face. " Now
think of that filthy odour, and then listen to what I say,
that the mysterious smell of carbon disulphide is caused
by impurities in it ; that this precise chemical in a pure
state is odourless. Do you see ? Doesn't that remind
you of some personalities you know ? Add a drop of
foreign matter, add an atom of suggestion, and the whole
personality is suffused, overwhelmed, with external
influence. Think how a book critic could use the
symbolism of carbon disulphide ! But catalysis,"
Richard paused. " I started to talk about catalysis.
Well, catalysis is a very wonderful thing. When you
heat that chlorate, as I just did, nothing happens.
Nothing whatever happens. But if you add just a little
manganese dioxide, just a little—why, then, a reaction
takes place—and you get oxygen. Do you see, Leon ?
The chlorate heated alone does nothing, it is inert ; but
when the manganese is added, a reaction thereupon
takes place, caused by the manganese—*but the manganese
itself is unchanged*. You see ? It just helps out. It
does not enter the reaction. It is what we call a
catalytic agent. There are hundreds of useful ones
in chemistry. The process is called catalysis. Well,
that's one word for you, Leon. I could give you lots
more. Hydrolysis, for instance. And the miracle of
capillary action. And the sublime mystery of osmosis—
osmosis ! "

" But about catalysis," said Leon, " that is interestink.
That does have an allusory value for life."

" Of course. Catalysis, for instance," said Richard,
taking a breath, " is what criticism should be. That was
pointed out long ago. Criticism should be a reaction
between spectator and work of art. The critic is the

catalyser ; he himself provokes the reaction, but he is himself unchanged."

" That works, too," said Leon, " with people."

" Of course."

" Mary, for instance, is a catalyser."

" Yes, she brought together Paul and Marjorie."

" She brought together me and Doris."

" You see, then," Richard went on, his face fluid and eager, " how these things work. That's why such a little thing as catalysis can be thrilling. It is thrilling. It is exciting. And it's one of a hundred, of a million things."

" Tell me," cut in Leon, " what about that poison ? "

iv

" Oh, the poison ? "

" Yes."

And then Richard had an idea.

" Why," he asked, " don't you make a list of poisons ? "

" Now," said Leon with enthusiasm, " that *is* an idea ! "

" This KCN, now," said Richard, pointing to the cyanide bottle, " I suppose in a way it's the most magnificent of poisons. It's quick and it's clean and it works. Of course its active principle—hydrocyanic acid—is ten times more powerful, but it's too volatile to keep. Still," and again Richard smiled to the bottle, holding it like a toy, " this is pretty good, pretty good."

" How quickly," asked Leon, with great calm, " would it kill one ? "

" In about five minutes—if you took enough. You see, it affects directly the central nervous system—and after death the odour of peach kernels picturesquely hovers over the body."

" Oh ! " exclaimed Leon. It was beautiful ! Such a death !

" It's utterly beyond me," Richard resumed, " why people continue to kill themselves so clumsily—why they choose painful and wretched poisons like arsenic, slow poisons like bichloride of mercury, dirty poisons like strychnine. It's preposterous. There is," Richard leaned back in his chair, " among the real poisons a substance known as aconitin. That, too, is a magnificent poison. It was the original arrow poison of the East Indians. That reminds me that cobra venom—the venom of Naja tripudians—is probably the most fatal, and most instantaneously and dramatically fatal, of all known poisons, inorganic or animal. Toxicology! There is a science for you, Leon! You must list poisons : belladonna, brucine, wolfsbane, atropine, hemlock, laudanum, morphine, henbane, and then potassium bichromate and oxalic acid, and of course all the corrosive acids—HNO_3, HCl, H_2SO_4—and when you get to gaseous poisons—why, I could give you a whiff of phosgine that would put you out in a second, or of arsine which would shrivel your body, more or less, while you stand."

Leon was excited.

" And then there are the borderline poisons. We hear wild rumours of poisons which simulate disease. I may say that such poisons do exist. Arsenic mimics cholera perfectly ; certain acids produce a replica of eczema and various skin dieases ; the relation between opium and sleepy sickness is well known ; strychnine, if you give it properly, duplicates some of the symptoms of tetanus. This is the golden age of poisons, Leon. The Medici were stupid and blind ; they botched because they had no chemists.

" And there is a poison which kills in a few hours and then turns the body bright blue, a most picturesque poison. And some salts of lead, you know, can produce madness. Did you know that, Leon? Did you know

that *poisons can simulate the symptoms of madness?* *
There's something the mediævalists dreamed about!
One of them is sometimes called mandragora. You have
probably heard of it. Shakespeare talked of it, but he
didn't know what it would do."

" Madness," echoed Leon.

Richard was leaning back over one of his laboratory
stools, enjoying himself, listening to himself talk. He
liked to talk these days. He was a fairly good talker at
times. It was when he talked about poisons, or food,
or modern sculpture, or diseases, or bond house advertising, or comparative theology, that his face wrinkled
up burnished, and his customarily puzzled features
disentangled themselves. He did know an astonishing lot,
in a superficial way. And when he learned more he
beamed.

And this afternoon he talked about poisons for almost
two hours, while Leon listened, entranced.

When the sun slanted more laterally across the rows
of brightly filled test-tubes, across the fantastic cluster
of burners and filters and petri dishes, Erlënmeyer
flasks and pipettes and titration instruments, Richard
stopped : after all, he did have to go back to the office,
even with the day now nearly over. He had work to do.
He rose.

" At any rate, Leon," he said, " you know more than
you did before about colours. And about other things."

" Thank you, Richard. I shall not forget the KCN
nor the mandragora. And I promise I shall use the word
catalysis soon."

" All right. And be sure to make your lists useless.

* I don't know just what Richard meant by " madness." After all, like
insanity, " madness " is one of the loosest terms in medicine. Did he mean
paranoia, or paresis, or katatonia, or hydrocephalic idiocy, or hebephrenia,
or dipsomania, or *folie circulaire*, or melancholia, or even *delirium ferox?*
I am sorry Richard was so careless here.—J.G.

You might put one or two of the chromates in your upper yellows."

" Thank you, Richard."

When Leon emerged from the laboratory he hurried to the street. He recalled he had an engagement, almost for this hour.

He panted down Bryn Mawr Avenue to the drive, caught a bus—one of the big glossy green ones—and scurried toward the near north side and the Loop.

v

Leon suddenly forgot his colours, his lists, the poisons ; he forgot suddenly everything in his heart except an ache. And as he went up the steps of the little flat just north of the river with the sun gilding the narrow pavements and dusty leaves rustling in the gutters, his heart began again to shake in his breast.

He rang the bell. A voice answered him.

Yes, Doris was at home.

Chapter Five

RICHARD'S THIRD SURPRISE

i

LATE that afternoon Richard returned to his office to find a telegram on his desk. He opened it:

FLUNG SPRAWLING SIXTEEN HOURS ACROSS FLAT SHINING GLOBE WHILE EBON GOD GRINNED I WILL BE HOME FOR LUNCH TO-MORROW PHIL.

Richard laughed. The idiot!

"I'm glad you're still here, Miss Cade," he said. "Please take this memorandum, will you?"

He began to dictate to Miss Cade, Agatha Cade, his secretary. He liked to work in the office late in the afternoon or early in the evening when the Loop was quiet and his only companions in the great office building were char-women and a few elevator boys. He found Miss Cade waiting. He hardly looked at her as he continued to dictate.

"My *God!*" breathed Richard, as he finished his memorandum. "What bilge! No, great heaven, don't put that in! That will do, Miss Cade. Type it out for me if you have time, will you, please?"

In his tone was a wealth of mental gesture. He was a little tired and somewhat bored, but also, on the whole, rather sceptically amused. Perhaps it was just as well his work was of this kind. It kept him busy. Besides, it earned him a living, a good living, and he appreciated that. He was advertising manager of Stern, Maschwitz, Goodwin & Stern: in five more years, still considerably under thirty-five, he would be a director, in five more a partner. It was a good business. Ten years more, then . . . hmmm . . . a little under forty. Then, thought Richard, he would have his million and he would retire : whereupon the real business of life would begin.

" Still at it, Northway ? " sang out a voice.

It was the voice of Mr. Stern, the vice-president. Mr. Stern served to reinforce Richard's faith in the eternal humours of life. He was a small man, very alert, who could do nothing without making a noise : and he rushed away every evening, always in a fussy hurry, to what he considered also the real business of life, which was Japanese prints. Mr. Stern was an amateur at Japanese prints and was writing a book about them. He often talked about Kose No Kanaoka and his marvellous *Wa-Gwa-Ryū*.

" I don't know what Noguchi will say," Mr. Stern puffed over his shoulder, " but I have totally disposed of Hirogishe in the new chapter—totally ! "

Richard didn't know what Noguchi would say and he didn't much care. But he was very polite to Mr. Stern, who had almost reached the elevator now, treading on the balls of his feet with his knees rigid. He called " Good night " after him and then bent to his desk again. Mr. Stern's electric footsteps disappeared in the whir of the elevator, and except for the distant rattle of Miss Cade's typewriter, Richard was alone.

He liked to be alone in the building at night. His building wasn't a skyscraper, properly considered ; it had no tower and it rose above the street a mere twenty stories, a mere 550 feet ; but it contained thousands of offices, it contained during the day the population of a fair-sized town. But at night, except for the char-women swishing their mops on the marble floors, it was deserted. There was something fantastic in a civilization which could produce such a phenomenon, thought Richard. This marble palace, this shining thrust of steel and ferro-concrete, all compact of steel and stone and the glitter of frosted glass—used eight hours or so each day, when it buzzed like a great metal hive—and for the rest was as silent and deserted as the caves of Kôr. In that building, Richard knew, in that one building, a man could live all his life and find no need to emerge. He could eat his breakfast, buy his cigar, have his hair cut, open a bank account, visit his attorneys, take his gymnasium exercise, play tennis on the roof, telephone his friends, do the work of the day, command the attention of a hundred people, hire anyone from a bricklayer to a philatelist, publish a paper, rent a flat, make love to a thousand stenographers, eat again, drink again, have a manicure, buy flowers or stationery or morris chairs, take an afternoon nap, or visit a library. And Richard knew there were dozens of buildings like it in Chicago alone. Amazing! Epochal! He knew because he had done all these things—except the stenographers.

"I've finished, Mr. Northway, and I do hope I can go home now, because I've missed my dinner already."

It was Miss Cade's voice.

ii

Agatha Cade, thought Richard, was a very unpleasant girl. But she was an extremely efficient secretary.

"Oh, sorry," he said, as he turned in his chair. "It was only a few minutes. I had no idea you would miss your dinner."

"Well, I did."

"In that case," said Richard quietly, "here are two dollars. Go out and buy one."

She looked at the money crumpled in his hand, a little hungrily.

"That's too much."

"Oh, come," he said, "it's not too much, and you know it. If you insist it is, go buy yourself a sandwich and save the rest."

"It's all right for you to talk, Mr. Northway; you're rich, but us poor girls—we can't spend two dollars for a dinner."

He was just a little bored. "Good Lord," he thought, "I don't care *how* much she spends on her dinner." But he didn't say it aloud. He was very gentle with Agatha. He liked her ominous unpleasantness, sometimes.

"Why," she continued, "our grocery bill for a week isn't much over two dollars."

"Please," he said wearily, "forget it, then."

Agatha wore her hair brushed straight back from her head over her small ears and had fine, sharp teeth which clipped off her words. She was a damnably efficient secretary. It was a pity that she had fallen in love with him. Richard had never made the slightest advance to her, but he knew for years that she had been in love with him. She never said so, Heaven knows. But occasionally he intercepted her looks in his direction, he overheard her pronounce, "Mr. Northway says this," and "Mr. Northway says that," to the other girls, as if she might be quoting Lâo Tsze; he noticed her furious efficiency when it was particularly addressed to his desk, as if she were saying: "There! Find another girl who could do *that!*" Richard was genuinely sorry for her. It was pretty awful to be in love in such a position. Love was bad enough anyway, but worse when you were in a glass cage. Like a goldfish, inarticulate, watching . . .

He drummed his knuckles on the table. "Look here," he said quietly, "I do wish you wouldn't bother so over little things."

"I do my best, Mr. Northway."

She stood before him, her upper lip quivering and the lower one slightly between her teeth. She was getting

G

indignant, thought Richard. What a shame, that people ever got indignant. It was the most unbecoming of all human emotions.

"Of course you do," he said with a faint gesture of impatience. "I know that." The two dollars were lying on the desk. "Here now—take it—and don't argue. I *order* you not to argue—and eat a chop for me at the Drake."

"It's all very well for you to talk about places like the Drake, but do you know, Mr. Northway, I've never even been in the Drake ; I've never been *inside* the Drake . . ."

"Good Lord," thought Richard ; "what next ? " Aloud he said : "Well, you will some day and you haven't missed much anyway. Now run along, that's a good girl. I want to work."

He noticed that Agatha was looking at the picture of Shirley, with soft high lights on the lovely oval face, which he had always kept in its thin silver frame on his desk.

"It's girls like that who go to the Drake," said Agatha, suddenly pointing.

And now indeed Richard was becoming bored.

"That's my wife, Miss Cade," he said quietly.

"Oh, I know it's your wife, but she ran away from you two years ago ; the whole office knows that, Mr. Northway ; I know it, too ; it's your wife all right, but she ran away from you two years ago, and I'm sorry, but . . . "

"*Please*."

Agatha saw his face. His face was burning. She stopped.

"Oh ! " she said. "Oh ! "

He leaned back. After all, it was no use to say anything. What could you say ? Poor girl ! And what could you *do* ? Her restless suppressed speech—the rare times she did speak—her small glittering teeth and

the mousy hair brushed straight back over her ears—
wondering, yearning—perhaps she too was trying to
see clearly, perhaps she too . . . "Hell!" thought
Richard.

"Now why, I wonder," he said with a faint ruminative
smile, "why did you say all that? What did you mean?"

"Nothing," she murmured dully.

"I don't mind in the least, but I'm interested in the
why of things, and I want to know *why* you wanted to
tell me the whole office knows that my wife ran away
from me. You see, Miss Cade, I knew that; you can't
believe I didn't know that. But *why* should it mean
anything to you?"

"I didn't mean anything, I guess," she shrugged.
She looked at the picture again. "She's not like me.
She's beautiful."

"Oh, come," said Richard, "now you're tantalizing
yourself by inverting your own vanity and jabbing it.
There's no sense in that."

"I don't know what you mean when you talk that
way."

"Well, then, I'll talk another way. Do run along
home, I've got to work; you know that I like to work at
night, and this is the first chance I've had for a long time.
Here's the money for your dinner. Good night."

"Can I stay and help?"

Richard sighed.

"No, I'm afraid not."

"Please let me stay."

"But you missed your dinner once."

"Maybe I can get out the typing on those Xb121
forms."

"No; I'm sorry. Better wait till to-morrow. *Good*
night."

Richard shifted around in his chair and turned
resolutely to his desk.

He saw Agatha powder her nose before the mirror and slip on a little cheap fox choker around her neck ; then he heard her footsteps toward the door and the slamming of the door. He drummed a second on the table ; and already she was out of his mind. He thought of Mr. Stern playing, like a child with stamps, with his Japanese prints, of Mr. Maschwitz, the other vice-president, out continually on lecture tours for the Association of Commerce. It was a strange business. In a way it was as enchanting, as alive and dynamic a thing as chemistry or love. Business . . . ten, twelve years more. . . . He hunched his shoulders and got to work.

"Now," he said, "those Piedmont 6's."

Then he saw that Miss Cade had not taken the two dollars.

iii

Later, in the vault, he was looking over the memorandum she had typed to his dictation, checking up some of the material from the files.

He was very fond of the vault. Ostensibly it was no more than a smallish steel room, very bare and grey. But somehow it meant a great deal to Richard.

Leaning against the filing case in the vault, he glanced through the memorandum. It was a circular about bonds. It was full of pretty words like " amortization " and " fee-simple " and pretty phrases like " Bonds callable on 30 days' notice on any interest payment date at 102 and interest," and " Price par and accrued interest to yield 6¼."

How delightful if Agatha had made some mistake and his former words " What bilge ! " should appear neatly at the end of the memorandum, at the end of the printed circular. He thought it would be almost worth getting fired for.

He leaned over the grey filing case in the vault and got

out the maps and survey which were the basis of the circular, which needed careful checking.

Working in this cloistered silence was *fine!* His big red fountain pen scratched along.

Treading on the stone floor of the vault with the steel ceiling above was like groping in the interior of a gun-turret, like living in an iron cave. The silence! The steel beams, the bolts abutting like those of a steamer's engine room, the massive triple door, the lock that weighed a ton; and yet so sensitively balanced a child could swing it closed. He always slid into the vault quietly. It was a furtive and mysterious sort of place. What strange manner of things might happen therein! He paused a second, to rustle and turn over some papers. And he remembered, too, the great bank vault down-stairs, forty times as large as his little one, where the grey-haired guardians sat in slippered feet all day, never talking except in whispers, never walking except on tip-toe, dressed in grey uniforms and watching, watching. *That* was a scene for a drama! And even his little vault, with its grey steel shadows, might be something of a stage. He thought of Leon and his pen paused in its flow, for he knew that Leon could find here some sort of ecstasy. Imagine, for instance, a young man and a young woman, locked in together for a night. The echoing caresses in these remote walls of steel. He smiled. Ah, here was a place for romance, the romancers had forgotten and overlooked it, a steel vault! No flowers, no moonlight, none of the pettifogging orna-mentalia of the cheap romancer, no lanterns swaying in the breeze or soft ripple of water or spring buds in bloom—none at all—instead only grim silence and triplicate doors!

"Now," thought Richard, "if I were one of those story-tellers, I should write a story about *that*."

He stopped. Wonder if any of the office people had

ever thought of all this? Anyone could get in the vault. Some of the pretty stenographers, perhaps, and the young accountants—all night listening to themselves kiss in the whispering silence. . . . Even Mr. Goodwin, perhaps, who had a taste for such things. The vault was open all day. The last person in authority to leave the office at night swung shut the massive door.

" Hmmmmm," thought Richard.

But he walked absently from the vault later when he finished his work. Back in the big chair before his desk, he sat and scowled at vagrant memories : his face puckered a little when he thought of Shirley the night before. He looked at her picture and a glimpse of pain crossed his eyes. Then he turned to work again and worked steadily for an hour. When he finished cleaning up the papers on the desk he thought of Miss Cade and the two dollars.

" Well," he said absently, " guess I'll have to fire her."

Damned shame !

iv

" I might as well," he thought, " go home."

That was a little later again. It was about eight o'clock and the streets were dark. He was tired for some reason and felt like working no longer. He was irritated also and kept rapping on the glass top of the desk and scowling. For no reason he could call to mind, he was nervous. Well, overwork. His spinal cord was putty and he had rheums, catarrhs, distempers, vapours, malaises, in his soul. He rose abruptly, slapped a pencil on the desk and shrugged. What was the matter ? He *was* nervous.

" Yes. Might as well go home."

Richard walked across the Loop again, but now it was a silent, almost a lonely walk. Now it was deserted, such a difference from the walk with Leon a few hours before. He stopped for a moment at Dearborn Street at a coffee shop for a sandwich, one of those great red-hot smoking sandwiches of roast beef and rye bread one can obtain everywhere in Chicago, but nowhere else, apparently, in the world. That was his supper. He reached Michigan Boulevard, took a taxi, and rustled swiftly north along the lake. At his house he paid the driver—the fare was just two dollars—and thought again of Agatha's dinner. He gave a quarter to the driver, climbed the stairs fingering for his key, and paused a second to see if any mail were stuffed in the letter-box. He continued up the steps to the second-floor apartment. At the door he drew back in surprise. He had had several surprises in the last few days, but this was the greatest of them.

The door was open.

Richard stared.

Chapter Six

MASTERFUL LEON

i

AS LEON walked solemnly in, Doris thought somehow he was attractive in his lean oblivious way. " I don't know," she said quietly, " just why you wanted to see me to-day. I should have thought, Leon, that last night was enough."

She was standing against the windows to the east, half-standing rather, for one knee rested on the window-seat. She held out her right hand lightly to Leon as he entered, the other was hidden a little above her head, grasping a handful of curtain. It was a pleasant frame for beauty, a pleasant little picture, and she knew it. The tuft of gold over her right ear was dull, in shadow, it was like amber, but over her left ear the sun shone, glinting the fluff of gold, patterning it with flying motes of gold.

" I should have thought," Doris continued tentatively, " that last night was enough."

" There is somethink between us," said Leon. " That somethink we must clear up."

He was standing in the centre of the room awkwardly. She told him to sit down. He did sit down, uncomfortably, with his knees close together, facing her. She continued to stand before the curtain with the curve of her arm over her head.

" So far as I know," she said, smiling down at him, " there is nothing between us that really could be called important. Perhaps you are looking for something between us, perhaps you want something between us to clear up."

" No," he said, " but I am thinkink of leaving Chicago, and I wish to be clear in my mind about you first."

" Leaving Chicago. Why ? "

" Chicago is too brutal a city. It is too tense a city. One can do no work in Chicago, not if one really feels. Chicago is like a dynamo. It is too big for one. And," he continued, perfectly seriously, " it is æsthetically too young. There isn't a single rose window in Chicago ! "

" Good heavens, Leon ! " interrupted Doris. " A rose window ? What on earth do you want with a rose window ? "

He shrugged. In his pocket, he could feel it, was a copy of *The Brothers Karamazov*. Alyosha would have understood.

" It does not matter," he went on. " That was only an illustrative example. But Chicago has no artistic soul. It has no artistic consciousness. It has no soul at all."

" But do you think, Leon, that it is necessary to live in some place with a soul in order to write—should not your own soul be enough ? "

" Ah, but I am not lookink for a place in which to write. I am lookink for a place in which to suffer."

" So," said Doris. " So." The conversation was, she saw, about to become more intimate. As soon as Leon talked about suffering, then he was thinking about love. She dropped the flood of curtain and sat down before the window, sat back deep in the chair. She could still watch the smooth swell of the lake a few hundred yards off. The trees were bending with new green leaves which whispered among the branches. Doris took a long deep breath. She almost sighed. She stretched her legs out luxuriously, in the chair, then pressed them together. While she did it she watched Leon watch.

" That reminds me," she went on, " that for twenty-four hours, I think, I promised to be in love with you."

"I had forgotten that," said Leon.

"Not," she proceeded, "a very gallant remark. You had forgotten my close cup of golden hair . . ." Doris pointed, mocking ". . . and my still blue eyes . . ." and she pointed, still mocking ". . . and my lips, Leon, my cruel red lips?"

"I had not forgotten," he said, "your hands. Your hands are like little white talons." He recalled his poem and decided to work off the few completed lines in conversation. "Your hands are like little white talons, so smooth, so sharp with the fingers inwardly bent and the nails glistening, and your hands reach out to grasp my heart, to grasp and squeeze it . . . making it . . . drip . . . love . . . for you."

"Bravo, Leon!" cried Doris. "Bravo!"

He smiled very simply.

"I think," he said, "that I shall make a poem out of that."

"Bravo, Leon, *encore!* By all means make a poem out of that and then give it to me. And then, Leon, perhaps I might be in love with you another twenty-four hours . . . or so . . ."

She was lounging curved in the chair, her body outlined under glossy silk stretched tight across her shoulders.

"I want you," he said cautiously, almost whispering in her ear as he bent forward, "I want you, Doris, to teach me somethink."

Oh! That was it. She leaned back again and pursed her lips. At first, because she knew what he was about to say, she was simply going to reply: "No, Leon," but she reconsidered a second, with her hair shining in the lathe of sunlight, and she said, very directly, baiting him:

"What is it you want me to teach you?"

"You know perfectly well, I think."

"But," she said, sailing widely, "I want you to tell me . . . in words."

He faltered. He couldn't. He couldn't look into her eyes when she stared coolly in that way.

The girl, he thought, should be torn apart with bare hands, savagely ripped limb from trembling limb.

And Leon thought of colours suddenly.

"I think," he began, "I think . . ."

He thought of his favourite exhibit in the Field Museum. He retreated in retrospect. The exhibit was enclosed in glass, a tableau built up with sticks and moss and little wooden figures, to represent an Indian ceremony of sacrifice. A girl stood at one end of a little hollow in a wood, stood very erect and brave, with her head high and her lithe body straight and perhaps quivering. Leon, at least, thought she was quivering. At the other end, a simmering fire. According to the neatly printed card before the case, she was a Sioux girl, captured by Pawnees and used as a human sacrifice to the crops. Two days before the sacrifice she was led from wigwam to wigwam, accompanied by the whole council of chief and warriors, after she had been well treated in captivity for six months. At each lodge she received a small billet of wood and a little paint, which she handed to the warrior next to her. In this way she called at every wigwam, receiving at each the same present of wood and paint. The next day she was taken out to be sacrificed, attended by the warriors, each of whom carried two pieces of wood he had received from her hands.

"What do you want me to do?" asked Doris.

Her body was then painted half red and half black, like a pierrot. Here, when Leon read the card, his eyes dimmed and blurred, and he could hardly see. She was attached to a sort of gibbet, and then was pulled slowly apart, the red leg pulled from the black, the body splitting lengthwise, the red part of the abdomen away from the black. She was then roasted for some time over a slow fire and then shot to death with arrows. As he read, Leon looked from the card to the glass case, and it seemed actually that the figures had movement. The chief sacrificer then tore out her heart and devoured it. While her flesh was still warm, it was cut in small pieces from the bones, put in little baskets and taken to a neighbouring cornfield. There the head chief took a piece of the flesh from the basket and squeezed a drop of blood on the newly deposited grains of corn. His example was followed by the rest, till all the seed had been sprinkled with blood; it was then covered up with earth. According to one account the body of the victim was reduced to a kind of paste, which was rubbed or sprinkled not only on the maize, but on the potatoes, the beans, and other seeds to fertilize them. By this sacrifice they hoped to obtain plentiful crops.

"What is it you would have me teach you?" repeated Doris, as she saw Leon's eyes glaze in memory. She was still looking at him coolly and appraisingly and she wondered what he was thinking so intently.

The red leg, torn from the black, torn, the red half of the belly from the black, torn . . .

"I want you to teach me somethink about love," he whispered, quivering forward.

"It is true," she meditated, "that I am in love with you."

"And, Doris, Doris," he said, as he rose in excitement, as his voice choked, "I want you, I must have you . . . there is somethink between us . . . I must have you, teach me . . ."

" No," she said abruptly.

His words trailed off into incoherent emotion. He stopped, haggard.

" No ! " she repeated.

" But *why ?* " he went on. " But why then do you lead me on this way ? Is it that you are just playing with me ? No, Doris, you must not do that. Teach me."

" No, Leon."

It was too pitiful, she thought. She was thinking that the unluckiest creature in the world is a love-sick youth who plays only in words, like Leon, an inhibited boy who was tortured by his own self-doubts. If only he would *do* something !

" Please," he whispered.

" You are a coward, Leon," she said suddenly, and leaned forward a little in her chair, stirring her breasts. " You are a coward ! "

" What ? "

In the grip of an overpowering emotion he rose ; he rose and grasped her, grasped her arms ; and for a moment it seemed to him that the cool grace of her body was painted in red and black. He grasped her arms, tore at them, pulled at them, pawing, panting. Doris was amazed. She was dumbfounded. She was too dumbfounded, at first, to struggle. Then she did struggle, violently. She pushed his face away. His face was coming toward her and she felt wet smudged kisses on her shoulders, her cheeks, her face. And all the time he was tearing violently at her arms, wrenching them. She panted, pulled herself away, and Leon, his emotion ending suddenly, fell backward and toppled into a chair.

She breathed a moment : her eyes were still amazed and her beautiful arms were red, pawed ; and then she said slowly, deliberately :

" You dirty Jew ! "

ii

Her face slowly relaxed to composure. She looked at
Leon. He was not looking at her. He was thinking. It
was true, he knew, that he was a Jew, but it was not true
that he was a dirty Jew. He was used to be called a Jew,
but hardly in such circumstances. Leon once said that
all intelligent Jews, if they are young and sensitive,
have an inferiority complex based on their Judaism;
and it was more peculiarly true of Leon, perhaps, than
of many others. Anyway because he was a Jew, he had
an initial capacity for suffering, he was sensitive. But
he was not a dirty Jew. " I think," he said, and his
voice sounded crushed with fatigue, " I think that I
shall go now."

" I wish you would stay."

He looked at her and shrugged.

" Why ? "

" Because," she said seriously, and although his little
bout of emotion had exhausted him, characteristically to
Doris it was a spur, " because I want to talk to you."

She was indeed interested now. He *had* done something : she leaned forward.

" Why did you call me that ? " he asked.

" I don't know."

" I'm curious, because people always call me that, or
somethink like that, when they are angry with me,
unintelligently angry. It is a weak and vulnerable point,
I suppose, for I have no defence; and people always
see it."

" You mean that when they can't attack you intelligently, they simply retire and sneer, and call you a
Jew ? "

" Yes."

" Well," she said kindlily, " I shouldn't let it bother
you. I think you pay too much attention to people and

what they think and say. To hell with people, Leon. That's what I say, and perhaps you would be happier if you said it also."

" I have no wish to be happy."

" That," she said, " is pose, and you know it."

" I do not think so. Genuinely I have no wish to be happy. I was not born for happiness. Only vacant fools like Hubbard are happy. Really, Doris, I want to be unhappy. I want to suffer."

" Have you ever thought," she responded, " that you might suffer just by being a Jew—that being a Jew might cause you sweet and lonely suffering ? "

He paused in surprise. Now, that was something of an idea. Curious, he had never thought of that before. It was the lot of his race to suffer and he should suffer too, just because he was one of that race. His eyes lit.

" Excellent ! Thank you, Doris," he said. " Like colours."

" What about colours ? " she asked.

" I list them. Let me show you." He pulled out the paper from his pocket and showed it to her. " Gamboge, indigo, cinnabar, Afghan green, lapis lazuli . . ."

She looked at the list and was puzzled.

" Vermilion," he continued, " smoke orange, velvet grey, citron yellow, azure, magenta, puce . . ."

" Leon," she laughed, " don't be silly."

He thought then when she laughed of two other colours, of red and of black, the colour of red and the colour of black, torn ; and something came into his eyes.

" What is it, Leon ? "

" I was thinkink," he said, " of you."

And Doris, too, was thinking of him. Somehow her respect for Leon had grown since he had tried to attack her in that way. " It was exactly," she said to herself, " as if he tried to tear me apart." She was impressed.

Her mind worked curiously, and she was much fonder of him, he had a much greater chance of achieving her, now that he had brutally assaulted her in that fashion. " Like being ravished," whispered Doris to herself. Suddenly she decided that it would be rather fun to be ravished. And Leon . . .

But he didn't know she was thinking of these things. He was playing with his colours.

" Remember," she said finally, " that our twenty-four hours are nearly up."

He looked at her in amazed surprise.

iii

But then he remembered. He decided to teach her a lesson. In his mind slowly formed an idea, a plot; in his mind was wary action.

" Yes," he said slowly, reverting back a few sentences, " I was thinking of you."

" And just what were you thinking of me, Leon ? "

He smiled doggedly, complacently, and told her in detail of the Pawnee sacrifice ; how the body was red and black, how it was pulled apart.

" I see," she murmured, with lips pressed tight, for in a way, so lustfully did he describe the ceremony, she was shocked. " I see. You think perhaps I ought to paint myself that way ; and then you could . . ."

" It would be a sacrifice," he continued, " to love."

" And to your education."

" Yes, to my education, Doris, and my education is important, not only to me, but to you also, because always the teacher gains more than the pupil, always the teacher is enriched."

She was suddenly bored. She didn't want to hear Leon, with his cold eyes burning, mutter apothegms. It was very true, perhaps, what he said ; in fact, it was

well said ; but she wasn't interested, she didn't want to
talk . . .

"Look at me, Leon," she whispered, curling against
the chair. The faint sunlight glinted in her hair, just
behind the powdery gold of her hair where it faded in
a blur to her white neck. "I want you to look at me . . .
just look at me . . . and don't talk . . ."

"I will talk," he went on stubbornly. He would teach
her a lesson. He would wear her down. And then . . .

"I will talk about anythink I wish," he proceeded.

"Then talk about me."

Leon paused. Well, he could do that. But he must
play for time.

"And what shall I say about you ? " he went on
cautiously. "That you are beautiful ? But you know
that already. That I love you and want you, and want
you to . . . teach me ? But you know all that, too.
What shall I say about you ? "

"Did those lists of colours," she whispered, "make
you think . . . of the red and the black . . . and of
me ? "

The sacrifice was a somewhat startling idea, Doris was
prepared to admit.

"No," he said ; "I got that from the Field Museum
and *The Golden Bough*."

She was disappointed. Why didn't he say the right
and graceful thing ? Really, universities should give
courses in elementary seduction. She was getting a
little tired of this, of being *humiliated* . . .

"But still, Leon, you thought of colours, and then
you thought of me . . . and you kissed me."

"Yes, and when I kissed you, you called me a dirty
Jew."

"I did, Leon, and I told you I don't know why.
But I'm not sorry, and if you tell me by calling you a
Jew I made you suffer, why then, I shall be glad."

H

Clever Doris! She smiled herself at that.

"That is good of you."

He was sarcastic. He could pull it through now. Teach her a lesson. And then . . .

"If you kiss me again," she murmured, "what shall I call you then?"

That was the greatest advance Doris ever made to Leon. But he did not take advantage of it. No, he would wait, he, masterful Leon, would wait: he knew this girl was within his power: he would dally with her. And Doris, watching him, was annoyed, her vanity was hurt. She saw his eyes fade and realized he was not thinking intimately of her. And he answered:

"I do not know what you will call me. But I suspect it will be something unpleasant."

Masterful Leon. Gamboge, indigo, Turkey red, cerulean, delft blue . . .

"*Will*, Leon?"

"Yes," he said boldly, and stepped forward to kiss her. He said "Yes," and decided that now she had had her lesson. But as he reached for her lips and tried to grasp her arms again, she withdrew, she withdrew harshly; she pushed him away with a gesture of distaste: he was too late.

"No," she said abruptly. "Not now."

She pushed him further away.

"Doris! I do not understand."

"Ha!" she said scornfully. "Ha!"

"Doris!" he pleaded.

And now it all flooded back into him.

"Doris," he cried, "I want you, Doris! I must have you!"

"No."

He made again as if to advance toward her and she looked at him this time with something more than cool appraisal in her eyes.

"If you touch me," she said intensely, "if you *touch* me, I shall throw myself out of the window."

He looked at the window and the street below, and looked at her standing there, indignant, taut. And then he shrugged. After all, it was no use. Who could understand such a girl? Who could even talk to such a girl? He withdrew. Then she said, very slowly and deliberately smiling a little now:

"Coward!"

He shrugged unhappily. He prepared to go. He found his hat, turned near a plate of flowers, and sneezed. She saw him to the door. She whispered, just whispered the words so that they barely formed from her lips: "You . . . Jew!" and then laughed harshly. He looked at her in sick amazement. She kept on laughing. He went out. She closed the door and was still laughing.

Later she drifted out of the hall into the big room again and looked absently in the mirror as she crossed the room, and saw her face in the mirror and smiled at the beauty of her face. It was all gold, old powdery gold, the red gold of gold-foil and the pale whipped gold of sunlight. She surveyed herself a long time. Then she moved suddenly, with a strange swift gesture; she moved to the glass and kissed the glass quickly, a shy, direct childlike kiss, kissed her red parted lips in the mirror. She drew back. The glass was cold. She laughed a little, quietly now. She looked at herself a long time. Probably she had what the Freudians call a narcissus complex.

iv

As he trod down the steps, weary and heartsick again, Leon had an idea, a sudden illuminating idea. He gasped and then almost ran to catch a bus to his favourite stationery store.

He had been there that morning. How long ago it seemed ! What was Richard doing now ?

Leon entered the store just before it closed ; he had time to buy a small can of black paint and a small can of red, and to address them to Doris ; he did address them to Doris and saw them sent off, and he somewhat bitterly smiled.

Chapter Seven

THE RETURN

i

SHIRLEY had been in America now about ten days. She arrived on the *Berengaria* on April 29. She waited in New York only long enough to clear her belongings through the Customs and catch a train which brought her to Chicago late on the 30th. From the La Salle Street station she went home. Her parents were somewhat surprised. "I *don't* understand!" said Mrs. Bowdoin, and "if you had only told us!" puffed Mr. Bowdoin from his cigar. She didn't tell anyone she was back in Chicago for the first few days. Instead she walked quietly down the boulevards, occasionally wondering if she might see some friend of former days, observing the changes of the city in the two years she had been away—the brilliant challenging monument of the Tribune Tower, the growth of the buildings north of the river, the new museum shining in white marble on the lake front, the atrocious statue to Theodore Thomas in Grant Park. She paused before the Art Institute portals, and thought of the hundreds of times, in so many varying moods, she had entered them. She went to one concert at the Auditorium. She shopped at Field's and decided that after all Field's was the greatest store of any kind in the world, better even than Harrod's in Brompton Road. She watched the noontime rush of State Street and the slow green movement of the dirty river. She inspected the chasms of deep buildings down La Salle Street, listening to the screech of the trains as they hastened past. After a long drive in her

car, she decided that the Midway campus with Frank
Lloyd Wright's gardens at one end and the old crumbling
amber pile of Columbian building at the other, was one
of the most beautiful plaisances in the world.   She
bought anchovies at Tebbett's and Garland and first
editions next door at Kroch's.   She watched the brave
sweep of the boulevard along the lake level to the four
towers commanding the river mouth.   Occasionally,
when the wind was from the west, she smelled the Stock
Yards. She dined at St. Hubert's grill. She saw again
the lake front lacerated by railroad tracks, the parks
slowly eating out into the water as the city grew, the
cribs like forts on the blue horizon, and the noise and
bluster and gloom of the districts smothered in smoke,
beyond the west branch.   She enjoyed architecturally
the cylindrical equipoise of the gas tanks. She ate at
little old favourite restaurants like Frascati's, Wurtzen-
zepp's, and Julienne's, and the Armenian hovel on East
Chicago Avenue opposite the police station.   She
enjoyed the smart parade down Michigan Boulevard.
She heard the scream of wheels, the hoarse shouts of
angry policemen, the quivering jam of brakes.   She
admired the new twinking signal lights.   In a word,
Shirely was fond of Chicago and she was glad to get
back ; and she spent a few days, after her long absence,
just in getting acquainted again.

Finally she decided to telephone Mary, and she was
a little excited when she rang the number. Mary was
excited too.

Mary insisted Shirley must come out that very
evening for dinner.   She said she would have a surprise
for her.

The surprise was of course Richard. Shirley fancied
it would be. She didn't mind. She had not been thinking
a great deal about Richard one way or the other. She
knew that sooner or later she would see him ; she had no

intention of avoiding the meeting, but, on the other
hand, she didn't contemplate going out of her way to
search him out. When he came, however, she was glad
to see him, genuinely glad. She was sorry that her
return evidently hurt him. She had no fixed intention,
that evening, of disrupting his life again, although she
knew that her return in any case must have a certain
influence on his affairs. When she thought of that,
and was sure of it, she was glad somehow that he had
never divorced her. For a time in Paris she hoped he
would ; she didn't want to *belong* to anybody and she
watched the incoming mails for a time, hoping to be
served with divorce papers, but they never came, indeed
no word from Richard ever came, and she only wrote
to him once, a tiny slip of a note, impulsively jotted down
from Bellagio, when she happened to think how he
would have loved the view of Como and Lecco spread
beneath the terrace of the Villa Serbelloni. He never
answered that letter. Later, in Paris, she drifted through
a couple of vague love affairs, studied at the Beaux Arts,
drank coffee at the Dôme, learned something of Paris
and art and life (though not at the Dôme), and Richard
faded in the distance, although he never faded completely.
He remained definitely a figure in the background of
her life, but in the end she came to acknowledge intimately neither the background nor the figure. That
lasted a long time. The fact of her marriage was utterly
apart from the daily routine of her life. She continued
to call herself " Shirley Northway," but only because
she liked that name. But when she did return to Chicago
she returned with new thoughts of Richard in her mind.
She did want to see him, she did want to be friends with
him again. And she wondered how he had changed,
whether he too had outgrown that old pang, whether he
could still be absurd enough to be hurt. More than
anything she was *curious* about Richard. After all, it

wasn't every day in the week one returned to exchange
formalities with a former husband.

And then came Mary's dinner and her two conversations with him thereafter. And after the dinner, conversation with Mary about the years she had been away . . .

Before she settled down in Paris she spent a few
months roaming in Italy, where she saw the lovely grace
of the Donatellos in Florence, the sagging white beauty
of the Michelangelo *Pietàs*, and in the Lorenzo
Chapel the cool splendour of his chiselled tombs. Back
in Paris again she went to the Rodin Museum, and then
remembered the Pope Julius figures in Florence; they
amazed her in retrospect, as they amaze most students
of sculpture, and she thought, smiling slightly, what a
pleasant little essay might be written of Rodin's influence
on Michelangelo. But she was not writing those days.
She was working. She was not playing with words.
She was playing with clay. She was successful. Her
second year she had a bust, a self-portrait, exhibited in
the Salon (1923); she was accustomed, like most of
her Paris friends, to sneer at the Salon, but she was
pleased.* Her *Mariposa*, too, was successful, and
also *The Mystery*, which was a cool subtle rendering
of a mother looking at her hands, and also her
Bacchante, a trim little figure which was one of her
first ventures in terra-cotta, and also *Blue Moons* and,
too, *The Infant Sprite*, this last one of the most successful
of all her child figures. Shirley was very popular in
Paris. She greeted her popularity coldly, and when it
became pressing, she moved suddenly from the Rive
Gauche and took a little studio at the other end of the
city on the Rue Victor Massé under the Butte. There
she worked. She worked alone. The only love affair
of any importance she did have was with a Spanish boy

* She called it, vainly, *Pleasantry*. Later it was bought in Washington.—J. G.

named Ramon Sanchez, and it came to very little; she
forgot him in three weeks. She continued to work. Her
old tranquillity was untouched, she was the same grave
fresh little child with the thick black bobbed hair : but
the tranquillity became mature. Her deliberate remoteness was lost and she became instead serene; she was
cool and untouched and serene.

It was rather fun telling Mary about all these
things . . .

" And how about Richard ? " asked Mary.

" I don't know," said Shirley gravely. " I think he's
still in love with me, and I'm sorry for that." She
paused. " I suppose I should be sorry, anyway."

She decided to stay the night with Mary after the
party, and now, talking to Mary, she couldn't help
thinking of Richard pretty intimately again.

" He has grown a great deal," murmured Mary
judicially. " Dear, dear, how long ago it all seems.
But then, you've grown too. I wonder what you and
Richard are going to do ? "

First Shirley was going to answer " Nothing," and then
she decided to be candid, and she said : " I don't know,
I don't know."

" That's a dangerous symptom, Shirley ; I do think
you're still in love with him," said Mary. " Maybe
differently, maybe not enough, but you still love him."

She turned in surprise.

" Of course I do," said Shirley. " I thought you knew
that."

ii

The afternoon following the party Shirley went
north to her home. She was talking to her brother.
This was something she did very rarely. She did not like
Jack. She ignored him. He had grown into a nuisance.
When he came back from Yale on his holidays, his talk

was a continual chatter of neat little women and hot parties and she was a sweet little baby by God.

"Say," he asked, "is it all true what they say about Paris? And is it true that the girls in the shows . . ."

"I suppose so," said Shirley. "You see, Paris is a place for grown-ups."

"Oh, Shirley, stop kidding. But tell me . . ."

She was bored and found it easy to deflect him into conversation about the latest little hot sketch he had found, a yellow-haired girl about whom he was very mysterious and about whom he had been talking as she came in.

"But, say," he continued, edging back toward Paris, "that was a swell statue you did, the one called Mari—— Mariposa. There were lots of pictures of it in the papers. How did you happen to do it? And what does Mariposa mean?"

"Butterfly."

"Who was the model, Shirley? My God, what a build! Where'd you get a girl like that, and, say, do men and women all together . . ."

"I modelled it from myself."

He stared.

"What?" he exclaimed. "*What?*"

Shirley laughed.

"You?" he queried. "*Yourself?*"

"Yes—models are expensive, you see, Jack, and a mirror is cheap—and I'm very nice, you know," she continued deliberately, "very nice, and . . ."

"My God, Shirley!" he cut in aghast.

To Jack, as he rushed off to meet his little yellow-haired friend, Shirley's performance savoured of the immoral. It was excessively immoral. He was profoundly shocked. It was an epoch, in a way, in the life of his imagination. His sister, modelled that way, for everyone to see . . . Of course, everyone didn't *know*, but still . . .

"Those artists are all queer birds," thought Jack. "I gotta tear now," he said aloud.

"Good-bye," said Shirley. "Run along."

Her brother!

She closed the door in relief. She wondered who the blonde hot sketch could be.

All that day an idea had been cloaking her mind. Somehow, returning to Chicago had intensified the bond with Richard. Perhaps it was the revival of old memories and old associations. In Paris, Richard had been little more to Shirley than a dream, all in all rather a pleasant dream—but a dream from which she had awakened. Here in Chicago he was a person. He counted again and he was on her mind. She wanted to see him.

"I think I still have it," Shirley muttered to herself.

She went into her old studio-room where she had worked so hard before she married him. She had returned thither just one week between the time she left him and sailing for Europe. She rummaged in the desk and found it, dusty and forgotten, wedged in a drawer. It was a key. Also in the drawer were other reminders of that old, forgotten life. She smiled a little wearily as her fingers played with a handkerchief of Richard's, a silk handkerchief in which she had embroidered his initials; a couple of old theatre ticket stubs (so many times in those days she had taken him to the theatre), a powder puff frayed and forlorn ("I wonder," mused Shirley, "when I ever used *that*?"), and then something which brought her heart to her breast, three little shrivelled bittersweet berries, rolling in the drawer like ghosts of a deserted passion, three tiny berries, still brilliant red-orange, still flushed with autumnal colour —berries they had picked that autumn, alone in the forests near Ephraim.

"*Dear* Richard," said Shirley aloud, suddenly, and then in the mirror above the desk she was surprised to see her face; her face was shining warmly, with her lips apart in a tentative, reconsidered smile. She looked at herself again, in slight surprise, shrugged quickly—and put the key in her pocket-book. Then she snapped the pocket-book open again and tossed the key out. It was better not to go. But the key fell on the desk top amidst the red berries. She smiled faintly, scowled, and then scooped up berries and key and inserted them again in the purse.

"We're old now," she was whispering to herself. "Old . . . old . . . we're . . . twenty-five . . . twenty-six . . . oh *Lord !*"

How long could she be beautiful, she wondered?

Then she started. Her eyes widened.

That would be a good idea for a statue—a *good* idea— the face of a woman, with level knowing eyes, staring out of clay at the moment she realized she was no longer beautiful. What a tragic figure such a statue could be. Oh, she would do it right away. It would be heart-breaking, an intolerably poignant thing. What an extreme pathos there might be in the realization in a beautiful woman's eyes that she was no longer beautiful . . . Shirley became slowly excited. Her eyes were afire. She paced the room, with her fingers stroking her chin, with the other hand clenched. She looked at herself and saw her lips apart. It would be a master-piece. It would be *her* masterpiece. She would do it !

After all, that was the most intolerable thing in life, that people grew, grew apart and astray, as rankly as sere weeds. Think of her own lovely body, for instance. Some day she too might be fat, she too might see her ankles oozing over her shoe tops. She might harden, desiccate, decay; and then she would remember wist-fully the promise of her lost youth. She thought of old women she knew. In a way, she loved old women. And to think that each one had been as lithe and firm as she was in this her youth, to think that hovering through the years was the spectre of age, to think of parading through the years as age crept closer, watching, waiting, seeing—to *see* that metamorphosis hover nearer, approach, see it flowing over her body and vanquish her body. Age! And to think that every woman was beautiful . . . once. To think that every woman owned *youth* in body and gesture and mind . . . once.

" I'll be beautiful till I'm thirty-five," she said aloud suddenly.

And then she added : "When I want to die, I *shall* die !"

Later she thought of that statue again.

It was the kind of sudden, illuminating, overpowering idea which came to people very seldom. It was, she thought, triumphant. It scared her. She ran away from it a little and tried to survey it coolly. It was the best idea she had ever had. It was . . .

But she couldn't do it now. She didn't know enough. She couldn't do it for years. Besides, she didn't *feel* it now. No. She looked in the mirror again. No. For some reason it seemed she saw her face distorted with joy. She saw herself in the glass proud and beautiful. And then she knew suddenly that she *did* want to see Richard, that she wanted to see him right away ; and with that queer revelatory intuition she had, she knew, just because she was perfect to herself in the glass, so she would be perfect to Richard ; she knew from the way she felt, watching herself, that she must mean something to Richard, something not only important, but inevitable. It was in her. It was in *her*. It was the way she looked. Shirley was astonished to find herself in the grip of this surge of emotion. She was inclined a little to resent it. " Hell," she murmured to herself. But no. She *knew*. She looked at herself and smiled a little wearily again, but then tossed her head decisively and lifted her chin.

On the table was a heavy parcel. She picked it up and put it under her arm. Had she told Richard she had a present for him ? No. Why had she forgotten that ? Oh, because he had been so cold, so brusque. Well, he wouldn't be brusque now. He couldn't be. She wouldn't let him. She wouldn't let him be anything but the Richard she loved, the Richard she wanted. " I do love him, I suppose," she said to herself. " After all these years. . . ."

She slipped down the stairs and found her mother in the drawing-room.

" And now, Shirley," said Mrs. Bowdoin, " I do hope that to-night we are going to see something of our daughter."

" Why no, mother, I'm sorry, but I'm going out right away."

" But your dinner, Shirley."

" I'll have a bite at Sally's. I'm not hungry." (Food !) " I'm sorry. Tell dad I'm sorry. But I *must* go—right away."

Mrs. Bowdoin sighed.

" I should think, just after you've come, that you might give us a *little* time. After all . . ."

" Yes, mother dear, but don't you see, I'm in a hurry. I'm excited—it's Richard—I must run along. There, mother, be a dear ; I'll feed all right, and tell father . . ."

" Richard ! " echoed her mother aghast.

Shirley was already down the steps.

" And will you be home to-night ? "

She turned suddenly. She stopped.

" No," she said.

iii

She dropped off for a bite at Sally's—she ate a waffle
and bacon—at about the same time that Richard was
eating his sandwich at the coffee shop. Neither of them
was much of an eater, they were spare people. Then
she hailed a cab, settled back comfortably, and drove
to the old apartment. There was excitement in her
breast. It seemed very strange returning to that old
address—619 Bryn Mawr—how many times similarly
she had returned so long before! Walking up the steps
she felt an almost intolerable emotion in her heart. It
seemed such a *return!* Once Richard had carried her
up those steps. Once she had slipped and almost sprained
her ankle on that treacherous dark curve near the bottom.
She remembered each light fixture, each spot on the wall.
How many times she had raced up those steps after a
day's work at the Institute, with words for Richard on
her lips; and how many times, preceding him, she had
heard his dark step on the stair! She wondered this time,
as she reached the second floor, whether he would be
home. In a way she hoped not. She was almost scared.
She knew how he liked to work late, and she pictured
him returning at eight o'clock or so, just as the soft
spring dusk was settling over the city, and she would be
waiting for him, sitting facing the window in the old
chintz-wrapped chair they loved; it would be rather fun
to precede him and hear him open the door, sitting
quietly and watching his face as he saw her, watch his
face widen and flash up in surprise . . . or distaste . . .
or pleasure. She wondered which. Shirley turned the
key in the lock, very quietly . . . yes, she remembered
that, a little turn to the left and then completely around
to the right . . . and slowly, cautiously, she pushed
the door open. Silence. The hall was dark. She tiptoed
within, shut the door quietly behind her, and listened.

She bent her head, listening. She could hear her heart beat. Yes, that was the old mirror opposite . . . she could just see her face poised floating in the cool glass . . . and there the hat rack, there the umbrella-stand, all unchanged. She saw an old grey slouch hat and she remembered that hat. "Richahd," she said quietly. "Richahd." There was no answer. Well, he was still at work. She was suddenly angry with herself for useless absurd imaginings. What nonsense, she had lived two years without worrying about Richard. And now! Somehow it was all changed, back in Chicago. Her heart was tingling. She saw a splinter of sunlight bisecting the greyness of the floor, a long V-shaped sliver of sunlight quiet on the rug of the front room. She could see the pattern of that rug; she remembered it. They had bought it, just after the honeymoon, at Colby's: it had been their first really ambitious purchase. She remembered perfectly its colour and design as it lay shadowed in the furrow of sunlight. Into the room she tiptoed further. She discovered that she was breathing cautiously, as if afraid to disturb the velvet silence, afraid to shatter with the cool pebbles of her voice this pool of stillness. But in the front room she whispered again: "Richahd!" and then called slightly: "Richahd!" No answer. She pushed an electric-light switch—she felt for it on the wall and knew exactly its position as her finger reached it. Such a *lot* of books! Good heavens, Richard *had* been reading. Books were piled in built-in cases from floor to the low ceiling. That old parchment lamp they had built into the ceiling did shine nicely. Shirley remembered the designs she had painted on it and she looked for them, smiling. The piano had been moved to another corner, to make room for a new bookcase. That was almost the only change. She was still breathless. After all, two years is pretty long. Over the piano was her first successful adventure in the delicate business of staining batik, a long scarf. The batik was flowing in deep purple and on it was one of her first little busts—of a child—and also her fanciful *Icarus* of which she was still very fond. She remembered the parcel still in her hand and she put it on the table, settling it carefully between yet more books. She noticed together on Richard's work desk Bertrand Russell's *Mysticism and Logic, The Golden Bough,* and *The Dance of Life.* Heavens, it was just as if she had left two days ago, not two years. Except the piano. The piano bothered Shirley. She looked again at the room, saw the old chair, in chintz to match the purple batik, waiting for her, the old chair like a faithful servant waiting for her; and then she passed quickly into the other room, for a quiet tiptoeing survey of the kitchen and pantry, even the closets. She reflected quickly as she saw the kitchen where Richard doubtless washed the dishes once a week. In their old bedroom she saw the great Moffett portrait of her, with her face level under the black hair, the portrait so often reproduced in *Vanity Fair* and other magazines, still unmoved, still on the table in its fine silver frame. She stared at the bedroom a long time, and touched gently with her finger-tips Richard's pillow. She drew the finger away quickly—sentimentalist!—and scowled, an energetic scowl. Then she tinkled with laughter.

Back in the front room again, although she knew he wasn't home, she whispered again: "Richahd!" And then in the old chair, cautiously still, she sat down. She sat down and found she couldn't sit quietly. Her heart was beating. Silly! She mastered herself. Again she looked at her face in the cool poised reflection of the mirror, swimming with high lights. She *was* beautiful. She was glad she was beautiful. Back in the chair, she picked up a book and started to read it, when she discovered it was a volume of Spinoza and that she was

I

holding it upside down. He always did have the most
absurdly esoteric books. How the backs of those books
faced the walls ! Long lines of books, red books, blue
books, buff books, yellow books—of every shape and
size and form, piled on the window-seats, stretched
on the tables, marshalled in long lines on the shelves.
She sank back in the chair and then she rose to turn off
the light. She closed her eyes. " Richahd," she said
again. She left her eyes closed. Peace flowed into the
simple little room. The faint darkness was comforting,
soothing. She lay back with her heart only faintly
stirring her breast. Home again after all these years
. . . Home. And Richard, Richard . . .

Shirley prepared to wait for him.

iv

He came in at about half-past eight. She heard his
step on the stair—so like the old days. And she forced
herself to remain quietly in the chair. Then she sensed
his pause, as he discovered the door open. She waited.
The pulse was strong in her temples. Her first glimpse of
him moved her, with his hat close over his eyes, papers
under his arm, and a puzzled wonder wrinkling his brown
face. She watched him with surprised eyebrows look
into the hall, peer down the hall. He also appeared to
move cautiously.

He was pausing before the mirror, just as she had done,
listening, listening to the close filtration of the silence.
His face was as if caught and transfixed in a moment of
aware surprise. She looked again and could hardly wait.
He advanced cautiously into the room, his hat crooked
still over his eyes, and said :

" Hullo ! "

" It's I, Richahd," said Shirley.

Mechanically he took off his hat. It rolled over

round and about the old situation : she had run away
from him, he had reconstructed his life, and now she had
come back.

When they got that far, she did say one thing that was
important.

" Richahd," she whispered, " it's just your pride again.
I deserted you and just because of the fact of that
desertion you're afraid to welcome me again. Pride,
Richard ! "

He knew that. He said, rather cruelly :

" Wise Shirley."

After that though she was a little weary they talked
again. She was surprised that his " Wise Shirley " had
hurt her. She was glad, too, in a way. It was good,
actually good, to know that she could be hurt again, that
someone in the world was vital enough to hurt her.
And her sentence had hurt Richard. It hurt him
chiefly because he knew she was perfectly right. The
fact of desertion was what mattered. But he did not
want her to go now—he wanted her again. He knew
he wanted her and the old flow surged into his breast.
She knew that too. She watched and was serene as she
watched, because she was pretty sure how it would come
out. How she loved his severe flushed face ! Richard !
Richard !

But he sat there doggedly talking while she waited.

" I love you," he was saying irresolutely. " Lord
knows I love you. There isn't any doubt of that. I
love you ; I've always loved you. And I always will . . ."

" And yet," whispered Shirley, " you haven't told me
yet that I . . . I am beautiful."

He jumped up.

" That's not fair," he cried passionately. " I told you
last night you'd do that and it's not *fair !* "

" I wonder," she smiled, " if this is fair, dear, *dear*
Richahd " ; she opened her pocket-book and turned out

the three tiny orange pips, the bittersweet berries ; and she saw him flush, saw that he remembered. And suddenly she was sorry that she had done just that. Somehow that, too, was unfair ; worse, it was cheap, it was a gesture and a cheap gesture. She stretched out her hand and cried :

" Sorry, Ricky ! "

But he remembered. He retreated almost grimly and sat back ; whereupon she pressed her lips together and leaned over and traced deliberately with her finger the long gnarled outline of one of his brown fingers as his hands were stretched on the chair, traced it from tip to knuckle, from knuckle to the strong square back of the hand. Then she rose abruptly and walked to the window.

" Don't you see ? " she said quietly, " that I *love* you ? "

She waited. She didn't hear him move. Then she heard him speak.

" And I love you, too," he said. " May God damn your soul ! " he repeated. " I love you ! " He measured the words, continuing : " I say, may God damn your soul and your body, may God damn them—I love you ! "

After that came a long pause.

" Is it as bad as all that ? " she whispered.

v

Later, a good deal later, he said moodily :

" The whole trouble is, if we do join hands again, it won't last."

" I think I know that."

" Then why do it ? "

" Because I want to," her voice rose suddenly. " And I forgot this," she continued. " Look." She was unwrapping the parcel. " Did I tell you I brought you something from Paris ? I do hope you'll like it. I'm willing to forget the *Mariposa* and the *Spring Flight* and the others, but I *want* you to like this—look— see——" and she held it up.

It was a plaque in clay. Out of the clay came her face. The eyes were level, her nose turned up gently at the tip, her straight little mouth with the short upper lip was like a child's, her hair, her heavy bell of black hair, just cupping her face, danced a little over the ears, with a severe part, a most severe part, in the middle.

" Do you see ? " asked Shirley.

" I see," he said. " I think I remember, too." It was that old visualization he had of her face, that old picture he had tried to draw so lamentably. " I remember it and see it . . . very clearly."

" And Richahd," she was continuing, " this afternoon, just before I came, I thought of a *good* idea—the best idea I've ever had and I can do it some day, some day when I know enough—the face of a beautiful woman caught just at the moment she discovers she is no longer beautiful. Isn't that glorious, Richahd ? Just think, *if* I can get it—*get* it . . ."

" That's a good idea," he said.

" Yes," she went on, " and if I can get that—it'll be awfully hard—why then, I'll be a great sculptor, not just a ' promising ' one, not just an ' interesting ' one— and *then* we'll see, *then* we'll do things—Richahd, I want to start on that bust to-morrow, but I can't, I can't do it until I see myself grow old . . ."

" Old ? " Richard was smiling. " Old ? "

" Oh, yes, I will, some day," continued Shirley rapidly. " I'll be old and desiccated and maybe oozy and— oh, *drawn*—or fat or something," she went on en- thusiastically. " And you'll be old too some day, you'll be old sooner than I, because you think so much, you furrow your old brain so much—we'll be old . . . old . . ."

Her voice dribbled off. They were both standing now and Richard leaned toward her.

" I adore you ! " he whispered.

" I want," she said suddenly, " to play the piano. And why did you move the piano ? But I'm glad you kept my picture, my picture is still there, that was nice of you, sweet of you, Richahd. But I want to play the piano—that batik *did* come out well—I want to play."

" Fingers," said Richard quietly.

" Yes," she said, " fingers."

She played. She played a long time. She roamed over the chords and he thought that she herself was like one of her arpeggios, her face had a living harmony of its own. She played through the minors they loved, Rach-maninoff and Debussy and Borodine and Rimsky-Korsakoff, and then a few gay pieces in the old manner, like the Just-So Stories, and than back again to the weary chant of *Les Sanglots Longs* and then, in sentimental reversion, even to Lehmann and Friml. She played with luxurious abandon. It seemed as if she hadn't played for years. She turned to Richard as he watched her and her smile was brilliant. The chords sprinkled down the scale like the tinkle of harps. They boomed toward the bass of the keyboard and murmured softly at its top. As she played she decided finally they would be happy again. . . .

" Fingers," said Richard.

vi

" Good God ! " he suddenly expostulated.

" What is it ? " said Shirley, barely turning her head.

" Oh Lord," he continued, " to forget *that !* " He grimaced. " What a fool I am. As if I were a damn . . ."

"Such vile language," she remonstrated. "What's the matter?"

"Hell!" he said. "I forgot to lock the vault door."

He explained how it came about. It was absurd of him, ridiculous. It was the most careless thing he had done in five years of that office. "That's what you do to me, Shirley," he laughed.

"Oh, forget it," she said, still playing with chords.

His brows wrinkled. "No," he said, "I'll have to go down."

She wheeled on the piano bench.

"Then, Richahd," she said, "I shall come with you."

He suddenly jumped as if struck. That bank vault. His early thoughts. The great door, triply made of steel, folding slowly shut . . . the tomb-like emptiness . . . the velvet grey silence . . . Good Lord!

"Anyway," he said, chuckling to himself, "we're married."

"What?" asked Shirley sharply.

"Nothing," he said, and reached for his hat. He half pulled her from the room. She held back, protesting faintly, surprised before his hurry, slightly puzzled at his excitement.

"*Come along!*" commanded Richard.

Thus ended the second day of these adventures.

Chapter Eight

CONVERSATIONS

i

RICHARD, Leon and Philip Hubbard, several days later, were gathered in the little Bryn Mawr apartment, drinking whisky and talking.

"Look," said Leon, as he entered, "I have been planted."

His hair was falling over his forehead and his blond face was beaming.

"What do you mean, planted?" asked Phil.

Leon uprolled his shirtsleeves. Tiny pricks shone on the slightly swollen surface of his upper arm.

"That red spot is strawberry," he pointed out gravely. "This one, ragweed. The one near the elbow, golden-rod. The one near the shoulder, horse-dandruff. There is also grass pollen, hay and marigold. I have been inoculated against hay fever. My arm is a flowerink garden."

Richard took another drink and laughed.

"If it is a garden on your arm, Leon," put in Phil sardonically, "what, may I inquire, is on your mind?"

"Well," he began cautiously, "I have just written the first chapter of a book."

"Ha!" muttered Richard. "Tell him, Phil, why writing a book is like falling in love."

"I know that already," said Leon.

"Impossible," said Phil. "No one knows it yet but Richard and me. I have just told it to Richard. It is an astonishing idea. The analogy between composing a novel and falling in love is complete. First one makes a contact, it may be with a person or with an idea, this first contact gives way to explorations, exchanges, investigations, and then, both in love and in writing a book, there follows an absorption and an excitement. The early struggles and efforts and frustrations are similar, the gropings toward climax and the compelling sense of rhythm and flow. I suppose one loves because one feels deeply enough, certainly one writes in the same way if one feels deeply enough. In any case, if the real urge is there, absorption follows the first contact, while a variety of emotions may follow absorption. A lover loves his mistress no less than an author his budding book. Sometimes it is an incubus, it rides his dreams, it frustrates his aspirations, it makes him a fool. It is also often enough a solace in weary hours, a spur to the mind, an engaging food for the soul. Perhaps that explains why one should love and write in solitude."

" What is the name of your book ? " put in Richard.

" I am thinking," said Leon solemnly, " of calling it *Orgasm*."

" Perhaps I am wrong," continued Phil, who was stirring round the room restlessly. " Perhaps I may change my mind. People may write books for the same reason they drink whisky. It is a form of self-expression. It is a kind of self-indulgence. It is a sort of release and, after the release, an outpouring and a catharsis. The germ cumulates within, it grows and develops and gathers unto itself fruits. When it is ready it pours out. Art, too, is like a fœtus. You, Richard, you in your laboratories, have seen little wrinkled fœti pickled in alcohol and labelled on shelves and catalogued nicely. I have seen them too, and I know we agree. Works of art are processes of conception and growth and birth as surely as those fœti, and there are many abortions and many miscarriages. But wait : I have another idea. I have been talking about art in general, now I am talking about great art. Great art is always scatalogical. Great art is a sort of sublime defæcation of the soul. The accumulation is within and then gradual emergence and then a final outburst. But what did I say about whisky? It seems to me I started by talking about the self-expression latent in whisky. Well, that is an artistic impulse, too. All indulgence is an artistic impulse."

"Well, have another drink," laughed Richard.

"I should prefer," said Leon, "to have hay fever."

Leon told Phil about his quest for suffering and he scoffed. Leon told it to him because he knew Phil would scoff. That was a curious phase of Leon's experiments in personal contacts. He felt (quite unjustly) that Phil didn't like him, he felt that he irritated Phil slightly, and in the strange manner of irritant personalities, when he talked to Phil he deliberately sought to increase the irritation. It was as if he took a delight in trying to make his friend dislike. him. But Phil did worse: he paid no attention.

"Sit *still*," commanded Phil, for Leon was wriggling nervously in his chair.

"I am always self-conscious before inferiors," responded Leon loftily.

Richard wasn't talking much. It was more amusing to listen just now. Besides, his mind was far away, his mind was with Shirley, and he kept half an eye to the clock, wondering when she would come in. She was out shopping. On sudden curious impulse he left the room for a moment, to go to the bedroom and look at her picture. He smiled to himself, a slow smile turning inward, irradiating his heart. But he couldn't help laughing from the other room at Phil's voice as it rose above the drone of conversation to pronounce:

"Nevertheless, I assure you Anatole France first had intercourse at the age of nine."

Richard returned to pour out more whiskies, and they

sat down leisurely, Leon wriggling a little, and began to talk in earnest. . . .

ii

It was several days after Shirley's return. On Sunday she had formally moved in. Richard was very happy. At first, though, he had been furious, immediately after the vault episode he found himself tense with an unreasonable resentment. It was not an emotion he could easily explain nor an emotion he was proud of. And it passed very quickly. It was all gone now. He wondered if Shirley knew how inwardly furious he had been. It was such a *submission* on his part. . . .

"But it's over," murmured Richard. "We're together. We're happy. I'm happy."

So far this afternoon he had had no chance to talk alone to Leon. He rather shirked the chance. It was an unpleasant sort of thing. Shirley's little brother had confided to him, the other day, his affair with the little blonde, and Richard was enormously shocked to discover he named Doris. He had no interest in Doris himself —far from it—but it might hurt Leon. And he supposed Leon ought to know.

Richard listened. Phil was saying something about God.

Phil, too, had just returned. He was a newspaper man and had been out of town a few weeks on assignment. He was Richard's closest friend. He had something of a capacity for friendship. Friends succeeded themselves in his life like suits of clothes. But Richard stuck. In a way they were foils to one another, Richard with his intent puzzling grasp of things, Phil with brilliant intuitive readiness. Also, Phil had once been in love with Shirley; that is, he had been one of the young men swarming near Shirley in the early years. In the interesting way such things sometimes come about, he and Richard, even when they were rivals, became closely fond of one another. They took to one another their separate woes each about Shirley. Besides, Phil fell out of love with Shirley very quickly. He never did last long with women. He was in love with Joan Tilford now.

What was the idiot talking about ? God ? What God ?

Phil was tall, angular and dark ; he had long dangling legs, and he was intensely restless in speech. He talked swiftly and Richard liked listening to him. But now Richard was almost ready to take part in this conversation himself. Still, he ought first to deal with Leon. And when was Shirley coming in ?

" God ? " Richard inquired quizzically.

" Yes, I repeat anyone *must* believe in God who has seen the ordinary beef tapeworm, the tæna solium : that tapeworm is surely one of the most marvellous, one of the noblest works of the Almighty."

" I," said Leon indignantly, " know nothing of either tapeworms or God."

" I am willing to admit," said Richard slowly, " that God is something of an artist . . . in His way."

" And you a scientist ! " exclaimed Leon severely. " I knew it, I knew it. Richard, my faith in you is shaken."

Phil stirred in his chair and rebuked Leon with a long stare.

" Yes," continued Richard. " Only a day or two ago I was naming colours for you, Leon ; any chemist can do that and make such colours and many others. I think I boasted about my colours. You should have rebuked me. Because no chemist and no artist ever painted as clear and thrilling a yellow as the yellow of a Protho-notary warbler's breast : and no painter or chemist ever devised a red like a poppy wading flame-like across the grass."

" These nature lovers," scowled Leon.

" Let him alone, child," remonstrated Phil. " Let him talk."

" But seriously," proceeded Leon remorselessly, " do you *believe* in God ? "

Now Richard was a little bored. He had outgrown adolescent discussions about the nature of deity. Discussions of God seemed almost as remote in his past and in Phil's past as aone or postage stamps or shooting craps. But he was a little amused and Phil caught his eye to egg him along.

Leon repeated his question with brows stern.

" What God ? " asked Richard.

" God."

" *What* God ? "

" Why, God," insisted Leon.

" There are several."

" But you know the one I mean."

" Not at all." Richard paused for breath. " What God ? Do you mean Jesus or Jehovah ? Do you mean Horus, Rê, Amon, Isis, Osiris, Neith, Ashur, Ishtar, Zeus, Apollo, Poseidon, Lakhmu, Anshar, Kishar, Eä, Bel, Baal, Marduk, Jupiter, Janus, Mars, Varuna, Mitra, Indra, Prajipati, Yama, Civa, Allah, Lâo-Tsze, Buddha-Gotoma, Brahma, Hermes, Ares, Pan, Dionysus, Methra, Anahita, Ahura Mazdu, Angro Manya, Hera, Demeter, Artemis, Hekate, Astarte, Aphrodite, Kojiki, Sin, Ramman, Dua, Al-Lât, Al-Uzza, Plouton, Saturn, Neptune, Volcanus, Mercury, Quetzalcaotl, Mungan-ngaur, Ukkö, Olerun, Keb, Nut, Rangi, Tano-Makuta, Tien, Shang-Ti, Fu Mu, Manibosho, Arno-Tsarchi, Vishnu, Manu, Hanuman, Apis, Qat, Koevasi, Gilgamesh, Qamata, Xosa, Moruno, Melkart, Nabū, Ashar, Eshmun, Skin-To, Chkaī, Tapío, Hillero, Ahto, Tengri, Zi, Potina, Levana, Juno, Ceres, Vesta, Diana, Minerva, Venus, Yahweh, Jahvah, Sūrya, Shamash, Helios,

Shinto, Baiame, Daramulun, Bunzil, Supu, Kane, Tangaloa, Tapa, Obatala, Oki, Kiehtan, Okaba, Adüm, Eberebo, Chemoch, Vohu Mano, Avolokiteçvra, Tupan, Juropari, Set, Sa'd, Rūda, Manāf, Maāt, Metis, Themis, Tashmit, Zalencus, Lanàpé, Savitar, Tistrya, Hopp, Mumbo Jumbo, Thor, Balder, Freya, Odin, Shiva, Krishna, Juggernauth, Asteroth, Ormuzd, Zoroaster, Moloch, Osnodeus, Lilith, Ninib, Cybele, Eros, Fum, Silenus, Thoth, Fafnit, Joss, Ito or Ffa ? " *

Leon was impressed.

Phil, enchanted, leaped in his chair and smote the low ceiling upward with his fists.

iii

" Richard, I am subdued," said Leon, when they had settled down again.

" The only trouble," chanted Phil, " is that your list is not long enough. Give me a dictionary, quick. Let us have more gods ! More gods ! "

" Seriously," said Richard, " I assure you that every God I have mentioned was once a real God, worshipped of many thousands and in some cases hundreds of thousands of people. Every God I have mentioned was as real once as Christ is real to a Holy Roller, and in many cases a good deal more real. My Gods were veritable. They were omnipotent, they were personages. People bowed to them and armies chanted their glory and their temples saw bloody sacrifice. I repeat, each of these Gods once held very powerful suzerainty in the kingdom of the heavens. Many of them were very much more powerful than the Christ-God has ever been in His meagre two thousand years. And now all of those Gods of mine, nearly all of them anyway, are dead. They are as dead as Cheops. They are forgotten in dust. Base

* I am inclined to think Richard invented some of these.—J. G.

your theology on that, Leon. Tell that to your next pastor."

" Richard, I am impressed."

" It is just a demonstration that celestial mutability is as certain as human mutability."

" But," shrugged Leon, " granting the omnipotence and now the oblivion of all your gods, let us go back a bit. How about my first question? The conventional god of our fathers? You talked about ' God.' And colours. I don't know what God you mean, but you must at least remotely touch the Christian God. Do you believe in Him? "

" N-no," admitted Richard.

" But you do believe in some God? "

" Of course."

" A personified God? "

" N-no," hesitated Richard.

" Well then," went on Leon, and he was very stern, " it is my turn to ask : ' What God? ' "

Richard paused.

" What God? " repeated Leon.

" Did you ever hear of the Periodic Law? "

" No," said Leon. He had never touched science in his years at the University.

" No? Well, it's a hard thing to explain, but maybe it will answer your question. It answers it for me."

" The Periodic Law? "

" Yes. Well, now, the Periodic Law is much more exciting than catalysis or osmosis. It is—it is the most exciting thing in life. Largely considered. It is a rather terrific thing. It is like Einstein : if you believe it and know it you must believe in some God."

" What? "

" Well, now," hesitated Richard, " take the periodic. It is the most immense thing in life next to reproduction. The most marvellous thing. You know that all matter

K

is composed of elements. Carbon and potassium and silicon and copper and so on. Each of those elements cannot be subdivided or decomposed : it is rock-bottom stuff. There are about ninety of these elements."

"As many as that ? " put in Phil.

"About ninety. Well, take these elements. Each of them has what is called an atomic weight. It serves to define and place the element and is mathematically ascertained. The atomic weight of the element is as near a fact as we ever get to facts in this world. It is mathematics pure and simple.

"Well, take all the elements and arrange them in series according to their atomic weights. Just list them, the element with the lowest weight first. Then a funny thing happens. You find that the elements behave like well-trained dogs and automatically adjust themselves into families. There is an inner relation between them, an inner pattern. They compose all life and they indicate all life is a pattern.

"For instance. The element with the lowest atomic weight is helium. Next comes lithium, next beryllium, next boron, next carbon and so on. The elements arranged in that order show a very peculiar rhythm. They develop into one another as yellow grades into orange and then into red and then violet and so on, and yet they remain perfectly distinct.

"Well, that's exciting enough. I won't go into detail. It is very exciting that the properties of each element, as we say, are dependent upon its atomic weight, upon its place in the general scale, upon its part in the big-pattern. By properties I mean what it looks like and how it smells and its solubility and so on.

"But that's only the beginning. As I say, there are about a hundred of these elements. Well, when you finish listing the first eight or so, then you find that *the second group forms a new series analogous to the first series.* That is, you start over again with number nine, which is neon, and you find neon almost identical in properties with number one, which was helium. Both are inert gases. And number ten (sodium) is almost precisely similar to number two (lithium). And number eleven which is magnesium corresponds exactly with number three which is beryllium. Do you see? Each group runs its gamut, shades from the one end to the other, and then *repeats itself* in an ascending order.

"I speak, of course, very loosely. But you must see what I am getting at. Anyway, when you get all the elements lined up you find them arranged in families both ways—up and down the pattern. Each element has a particular place in the scheme of things. Each element has its fore-ordained nook and cranny. You can't move it. It fits. It fits there mathematically.

"Isn't that *superb?* Don't you see, it shows that all matter—everything in the world—*belongs* somewhere, fits in its place in the scheme of things. No one knows why it happens that way. No one can know. It just is. In a perfectly mystical way each element, and thus all matter, finds its position and stands there like a good soldier—for eternity.

"And that isn't all. When Mendeleef announced the law some elements were undiscovered. The pattern was not complete. There are still some elements not discovered for that matter. But before the elements came to light Mendeleef was able to predict what they would be. He filled the gaps in his chart with hypothetical elements, and after his death these same elements, just as he predicted them, were discovered.

"I think that's the most stupendous thing in the world. I think it is somewhat frightening. To think of elements of matter, unborn, so to speak, waiting for the day of their emergence, waiting patiently, and all the time, though we can't find them, can't isolate them, we know their names, their weights, their properties, even their colours.

" It is like a vast and thrilling battle. We on our side wait because we know some time that element must come out of hiding and take his place with the rest and fit in the supernal pattern which is ready—and on the other side the elements also wait, they hide deep in ore and crust and earth and defy us to prove that we are right, that we know better than they. They are unborn, but we know they must be born and finally they come.

" And all the time the pattern is complete and every unit—*including the undiscovered ones*—is at work. . . .

" Well, now," concluded Richard somewhat lamely, with a shy laugh, " that's why I suppose I must be honest and say I do believe in some kind of directed force which, if you want to, you can call God. But call it anything you like. I want a drink. And, Phil, give me a match."

Leon and Phil were silent for several minutes.

iv

Later. They had become livelier. They were talking about chastity belts, the pithecanthropus erectus, and the marvellous poem by James Elroy Flecker called *The Old Ships*. But Leon in a corner had picked a sharp paper-knife from the table and pricked his finger. He was admiring the red dripping bubble.

Thought Richard : " Shirley is a little late."

Leon held up his finger. He was impressed by Richard's gods and also by his God, and he was wondering if he couldn't work them into his next chapter somehow. Have his hero in a long soliloquy address the unknown forces of evil, have him . . .

" Good Lord, what have you done ? " broke in Richard.

Phil, too, looked and saw Leon's hand dripping blood.

Leon drew back and was slightly ashamed.

"Red," he muttered, "is the colour of blood."

"Fool!" uttered Richard. "Why did you cut yourself?"

Phil shrugged.

"I admire," said Leon gravely, "the colour. Look. Isn't it lovely?" He held up the finger and a slow globule of crimson trailed down to his wrist. "There, Richard. I admit you are right, there is a God, only God could make a colour like that."

"Don't be an ass," said Richard shortly.

"I should like," commented Leon, "to bleed to death."

"Oh, nonsense," said Phil. "The age for bleeding to death is over. You can't cut your veins in an alabaster tub with fans waving over your head any more. Give him cyanide."

"Cyanide!" said Leon.

"Give the fool cyanide." Phil turned to Richard. "But don't let him spoil my drink dripping that way like a bloody stuck pig."

"Ha!" said Leon. "Yes! Give me cyanide."

"Not until you prove to me you have some real reason to die," laughed Richard. "Here—take this handkerchief—clean up the filthy mess."

Leon mopped.

"The real reason to die . . ." ruminated Phil. "Now there you touch something, Richard. What a charming idea! And how charming it would be to know the exact moment when death would most completely recompense the lack of further life. You see what I mean. If one could plot out life and seize the point of climax and then be able to make a choice. Then indeed we should have a self-determinate civilization. I am wondering if it would not be worth trying. Catch the rhythm, you see. Think: one could balance putative future with positive past, find the exact point of contact between them and then choose. There, Richard, I bequeath the idea to you. Trace the current of life and watch carefully for the moment the ebb tide begins to swell and then cut it off. Trace the rhythm of creation and watch for the moment of supreme antithesis and then weigh the fading years ahead against past glory—and decide to die. That would be a reason for death! But it would be a death for philosophers only. If all of us could learn to live and die like that your long list of gods will have to turn tail and hide in clothes closets."

The bleeding was subdued. Leon surveyed his finger critically.

" I am reminded," said Richard, " of a phrase, a notable phrase, which says that life belongs to the benevolent marble-heart, the world belongs to the enthusiast who keeps cool."

" Death," interrupted Leon, " is a very beautiful thing."

" Nonsense," said Richard.

" Death," said Leon again, " is a very beautiful thing."

" What do you know about death? " queried Phil.

Leon reflected that he knew very little.

" Have you ever seen a person die that you should think death beautiful? "

" No," admitted Leon.

Richard was thinking that the conversation had run true to form. It reminded him of Green Chalybeate days. Always the same full circle : love, sex, art, God, death. Always that five-pointed star of the adolescent crown.

" Well, anyway," said Leon, " it would be pleasant if death were a beautiful think. It would make people suffer. Now death is only surcease. But if people could be convinced death was beautiful, then perhaps they might suffer more when dying."

" Shut up," said Phil in disgust.

"That is nicely put, Leon," said Richard, "but it doesn't mean a damn thing."

"Nevertheless," shrugged Leon, "I am convinced it is good to suffer. Myself, I shall be a great sufferer. Death or no death, a *great* sufferer."

Phil had to go shortly thereafter, to chase a story. Richard promised to meet him for lunch on Friday. Leon made also toward the door, but Richard said : "Just a moment, I'd like to talk to you." Leon retreated, holding his bandaged hand, and Richard saw Phil down the darkish stairs.

Richard sat down, crossed his legs, and began.

"I've just heard, Leon . . ."

But at that moment there was a slight stir at the door and Shirley entered. Richard felt a quick relief, not because he was afraid to talk to Leon, but because he wanted to see Shirley, he wanted every moment of Shirley, he resented even this her afternoon's shopping tour. He and Leon rose at her cheery, "Hullo !" and Richard turned to find her poised on the doorstep, poised in the pool of light before the mirror, with her face outlined in dusk and a full smile glistening on her red lips.

Chapter Nine

i

THAT same day, Wednesday the fifteenth, Austin Devery walked slowly across the campus toward his class. He was unpopular with many of his students, who distrusted his precise fastidiousness and his lack of interest in their affairs. But he was by way of becoming a very successful young professor. Old heads on the faculty grimaced somewhat about rumours concerning Austin, but they all admitted he could teach French. His courses were not desiccated romance language affairs, with all the romance eliminated. Instead, by teaching a language he tried to picture a civilization. This day, for instance, he reached the rostrum, surveyed his class with mingled boredom and disdain, and began :

" As I recall yesterday we were talking about the wines of France. To-day I should like to discuss the liqueurs. It will be necessary also to mention the liqueurs of other lands, but I trust only in passing. The best liqueurs are as follows, and I should advise all of you to take down the list :

" Fleur de Cassis (de la Côte d'Or) Rouvière Fils, Dijon.

" Crême d'Allash.

" D.O.M. Benedictine Veritable.

" Crême de Mandarin. Huyens et Cie, Bordeaux.

" Rhum St. Georges (Marque deposée).

" Van der Huym.

" Cognac Pêche. Nuyens.

" Crême de Cacao Chouva.   (Parfumerie à la Vanille).
" Cointreau Triple Sec.
" Eau de Vie de Dantrich.
" Apricot Brandy.
" Anisette Rose. Fockinck, Amsterdam.
" Crême de Menthe Glaciale. Cusenier.
" Kummel-Wijnard. Fockinck.
" Crême de Menthe Verte.*

" Of course, in addition there are the fines champagnes known commonly as brandies. These we shall discuss by themselves another day. The best years, I might remark in passing, are 1848 (brown), 1875 (pale), 1900 and 1904. Veritable spiritus vini gallici of pre-Napoleon date is now very rare.

" You will notice that I have not mentioned chartreuse, neither the green nor the yellow. That is because I do not like chartreuse."

From this point Austin's lecture proceeded. He was very grave ; he thought subjects like the wines of France merited gravity. As he talked about infusion and distillation, viticulture and essential oils, he did not smile. This class was his chief interest of the day : it came at 3.30 in the afternoon and academically it finished his day ; he had good students and he liked his subject, French Contemporary Civilization. He began, as a rule, with Gambetta, curiously surveyed politics as far as Caillaux and Briand, and then, with this background, proceeded into the economic and social fabric of French daily life. He talked about the capital levy, petty mountebanks like Tristan Tzara, Jean Cocteau, and Guillaume Appolonaire, obscure idioms in French slang, the cigarette taxes, the murder of Calmette, the social ritual of Deauville, the hobos of the Seine, the best restaurants in Paris, the claims of the present Duc

* I must say that I should quarrel bitterly with several items on Austin's list, as well as with several of his omissions.—J. G.

d'Orleans, *Du Cote de Chez Swann*, the Chateau de Madrid, early plays by Henri Becque, and the Quatz' Arts Ball. This last subject, always given a lecture by itself toward the end of the quarter, was a campus sensation. It was proposed one year to hold it in Mandel Hall and charge admission. But the deans frowned.

Austin finished his lecture.

" I have forgotten," he said, " to take the attendance. I shall take it to-morrow instead and then immediately dismiss the class. As I recall, the inter-collegiate tennis matches, by an unfortunate coincidence, are being played the same hour as this lecture. It happens that I should prefer to watch the tennis. I trust my predilection in no way interferes with your plans. For the present the class is dismissed. Good day."

He picked up his hat and notes and turned away. His students filtered out till only one of them remained. He had rather expected her to remain and he stepped off the rostrum to greet her. It was Doris.

She smiled.

" Well ? " she asked.

ii

I think I have forgotten to mention that Doris was a student at the University at this time. And this quarter she found herself in one of Austin's classes. Occasionally she attended : when she did, she enjoyed his détached insolence and the controversial manner of his discussions. But since the night at Mary's party Doris held a slight grudge against Austin. It would be amusing, she thought, to pay him out.

This day she was wearing a purple hat to heighten her colour. She loved purple, anyway, and tried to choose clothes running from imperial purple to faint wistful violet, with mauve, lavender and magenta particular favourites. These colours became Doris. They softened

the brilliance of her hair and made dramatic the small
face disdainful under arched golden brows.

Doris was feeling well because she knew she was
looking well. She said: "Pretty, aren't they?" and
pointed to her fingers. Austin shrugged as he looked at
her short white fingers and observed that in submission
to the current fashion she had rouged her nails, rouged
them a little, just a tinge of shining pink at the tips.
She smiled at her fingers and then drew down her brows
as she reflected it was Austin to whom she must direct
her attention.

The class-room was empty.

"Have you," he inquired, "yet reached the proper
number entitling you to confession?"

"If I had you'd be the last person I'd tell," she
replied.

"Pretty," he said. "I am glad I stung you. I am
glad you have sense enough to be stung."

This was not at all the way she had envisaged the
conversation. But Austin kept on directing it.

"Then let me vouchsafe you a further word of advice.
I noticed you talking with young Leon. I should advise
you to make no pathetic miscalculation regarding the
age of consent."

"Brute," said Doris, pouting.

She suddenly remembered Leon and determined some
day to rouge her nails for him. She thought of his
ridiculous poem about her hands, and she decided that
he would approve of her nails pink and rouged. It
was queer how she kept thinking of Leon. He hadn't
appeared since the adventure of the red paint. But
he would come soon, she was sure.

"However," went on Austin, who was in conversational mood, "I daresay you wished to speak to me with
an eye to prosaic affairs. Well, it is about prosaic affairs
that I must talk to you."

"Now," she said, "I know you are going to lecture me."

"I am merely warning you that inasmuch as I never give a really beautiful girl anything better than B—in any of my classes—it would be wise for you to attend occasionally if you wish to get even that."

"Austin," she said. "You're not going to say I have to study?"

"I should never ask you to study because you are, I fancy, incapable of study."

He was standing beside the little rostrum, tall and polite and mocking : she was sitting against his desk, swaying slightly. She took his hand suddenly and clenched it, whispering :

"Austin, you *fool!* Don't you *see?*"

A faint ironic smile turned his lips, not up, but down, as Doris in irritation pushed the veil from her face.

"Of course I see," he said. "And that is why very deliberately I shall disengage your hand."

He did so : he picked her fingers apart from his wrist and removed her hand with a faint wrinkling of his nose ; whereupon she was annoyed.

"I should advise you to be careful," he said, "when playing with grown men."

Austin, it may be interpolated, had no faintest interest in Doris emotionally. He was not fond of children. And he detested the obvious advances she had been making to him during the week. She directed them with one aim only, he was pretty sure : she wanted to pass his course.

"I should think," she began on a new tack, "that you would get sick and tired teaching this rabble."

He shrugged.

She pointed vaguely to the empty desks and went on : "They're all such hopeless asses. Why do people come to college when they'd be so much happier selling millinery?"

" I am wondering," he uttered, " what this change of mood portends. Doris, you are bad enough with your banal patter about amour. When you turn to serious business you are hopeless."

" I'm glad," she said after a pause, " that you enjoy being rude to me. Frightfully rude. Myself, I'm not sure it doesn't cloak something deeper. Perhaps you are concealing something, Austin. Perhaps you are in love with me."

" Have you learned anything new lately about love ? "

" Y—yes."

" What is it, may I ask ? "

" I shouldn't dream of telling you. In fact, I don't think I shall talk to you any longer. I think you are boring me this afternoon, Austin ; in fact, I am sure you are boring me."

He bowed ironically.

" When you fall in love," he said, " be sure and pick someone who can support—what shall we say ?—your physiological indiscretions—in the matter to which doubtless you will become accustomed."

" You *fool*," she said again, and her lips turned. " Austin, you disgust me. Shall I tell you what I really think of you ? "

" Do."

" I think that you are the vulgarest, cruellest, filthiest wretch I have ever met."

" Precisely."

" You are a cad."

" You honour me."

She shrugged her shoulders in sudden disgust and stopped speech. The lazy sun dappled the rows of scarred desks before them. It illumined her close-fitting suit of fawn colour. She stopped speech also because Austin had leaned over and kissed her. He laughed. She struggled, but he held her close. She wrenched herself free. For the second time that afternoon she uttered the single word :

" Brute ! "

Austin was still laughing. After all, it was Wednesday.

" Come with me," he finally said. " Come with me, and I will show you those Von Bayros prints. Come, and I will show you other things."

She looked at him in amazement and then demurely smiled.

They sauntered off together.

iii

When he left his flat to keep an appointment Austin was mildly disgusted at his behaviour ; but he shrugged, after all it didn't matter, and Doris was a very pretty girl. It was a substitution in his routine and that was about all. And she had enjoyed those prints. He smiled precisely. Also, she was callipygous, and that was a fine thing in a woman.

" Syzygy," muttered Austin.

He was rather late, but he did not hurry. He never hurried. He stopped, in fact, to chat a moment with three colleagues he met as he crossed the campus back of the library. They were Professor Graveson of the English department, and Professor Crabtree, who taught hydraulic engineering, and Dr. Coniver, who was a specialist on Volhynian folklore. Each was a comparatively young man, each a superb example of the young academic type. Each was very much on his dignity and sought to emphasize in his demeanour, all at once, solidity, erudition, poise, humour (but not too much), gentility, character, resourcefulness, tact and charm. Austin passed them, and in his frosty smile there was something of contempt.

Also, he thought he saw across the campus Doris's father. He pursed his lips. That was a funny thing.

Many students passed him. There were young men from the fraternity houses wearing tight-fitting coats, enormously baggy trousers, soft collars buttoned down on white shirts, and Oxford brogue shoes. Passing him also were girls who were amazing: girls often pretty and always smart, excessively smart in their brief skirts and close-clipped hair, glittering and shining in the sun. They shone with youth and disdain and a casual knowing confidence. Although it was late in spring, many of them still wore huge fur coats just cupping their small faces, and unbuckled goloshes defining trimly their silken brevity of leg. So fresh and young and brave and knowing, these hundred of girls. It was a pity, thought Austin, that they drank so much.

He saw the grey towers of Mitchell and reflected grimly that what the University needed was a Loop skyscraper.

Broadcast lectures by radio. Cafeteria culture complete. Put a nickel in the slot and get out peptonized learning, neatly wrapped in glazed waxed paper.

Hutchinson, ahead, was a good-looking building, he thought. The ivy was close on the walls and the gargoyles pleasantly mocking. Pity they copied it from Magdalen. Pity they had to use it as a restaurant.

As he reached the lag end of the campus his lips were still amused by the rabble he passed. Not only the girls and the pretty young men in their flopping trousers. The law-school crap shooters and the ancient schoolmarms and the brand-new Ph.D's, already bald. The "bibs," as he termed divinity students, and the Jews from the commerce school, and the English department people writing theses on the use of the comma in Chaucer.

Austin nodded to the registrar in passing. That man knew a lot. But chi non sa niente, non dubita di niente.

Courses offered in Pali, Lithuanian, Icelandic, Wilson and the World War, Syrian Literature, Elementary Sumarian, Roman Sepulchral Poems, the Pseudo-Cædmonian Legends, Hermitician Matrices of Positive Type in General Analysis, Stratigraphic Palæontology, General Morphology of Byrophytes and Pteridophytes, Horseback Riding . . .

Amazing place ! Very Chicagoan . . .

He emerged into 57th Street and walked toward the lake with slightly quickened steps. He was late. He was on his way to be cleansed. Every Wednesday afternoon at this time, Austin went down-town on two errands. The first was to see a lady. He saw her, always within the same hour, each Wednesday afternoon, and then progressed to his magnificent Turkish bath establishment, there to have his fantastic bath. This afternoon he would omit the lady. Doris had upset his routine.

This routine had persisted for about two years. In his immediate circle it was well known. Richard knew it. Mary also knew it and so did Leon, which was one of the reasons Leon didn't like him.

Austin didn't mind. It was part of the ordered routine of his days. He taught three or four hours a day, lectured several, ate three times, and slept ; on Thursdays additionally he studied the comparative philology of the Roman tongues, on Fridays he swam at his club, on Saturdays he worked on his monograph on the Provencal etymology of the Chansons de Geste, on Sundays he played golf at Meadowbrook, on Mondays he did special tutoring, on Tuesdays he dined with a few friends, and on Wednesday he went to see a lady and be cleansed.

Austin reached the I.C., caught an express, and went down-town. He was beginning to regret Doris. Well, next Wednesday he wouldn't be interrupted. At the portals of the hammam he sighed, and after a slight pause entered. He did hope that fellow would get the steam hot enough this time.

iv

Austin had had his cleansing and was now on the I.C. bound for the campus again. He was thinking about Mary, for it was Mary whom he was on his way to see.

He had come to a decision in regard to her since her party, and it was to voice and confirm this decision that he wanted to see her.

He jumped off the train and turned toward the sunset at the end of 56th Street. In the distance the University towers beckoned and he could hear the chimes ring out from Mitchell Tower.

He was a little tired. The water had been very hot.

He wanted to see Mary. He wondered if Mary wanted to see him.

L

Chapter Ten

CANDLE-LIGHT

THAT evening, after Phil and Leon went home, Richard and Shirley dined alone by candle-light in the cream-coloured, low-ceilinged room. Shirley was quiet and serene in her acquiescence to happiness, and Richard, too, was happy, but he was not serene. He was never serene, always he questioned, always he had doubts. But now the glow of the candles and the marvellous clear light of Shirley's face momentarily washed these doubts from his mind, and as he watched the ivory sheen on her arms and shoulders he felt himself indeed poised in some veritable pool of tranquillity. She was in blue velvet, with a deep oval cut at the throat and a string of gay crystal beads looping to her breast. Ever since she had arrived when Phil and Leon had been talking so absurdly, she had been lovely, extraordinarily lovely. From her shopping she had brought candles, great marbled candles in black and gold and also small slim dark-green candles like wax jade. " Candle-light, that's for us, Richahd," she said.

In candle-light then they dined over the little table in the corner. He drew the shades and in the warm lustre of the candles the room was close and familiar, with the tall shelves of books frowning amiably and a wide white cloth glimmering on the table. Over the ceiling were flung pulsing shadows as the flames sank steadily lower like tapers, making of the table an altar, of the room a glow of shadows. After dinner one candle burned down, the little fan of flame guttering out with a hiss ; they watched the tiny puff of black smoke emerge upward and join the phantoms clustering in the corners of the room. Richard had been smoking and the low ceiling was festooned with smoke, hovering over the blur of light from the candles. They said very little. Shirley was amused by Richard's brief account of the afternoon. But for the most part there was no need to speak. They had established, somewhat precariously, an equilibrium which at all costs must be preserved. For three or four days now it had persisted, and each of them was breathing a little easier. But Shirley feared moments of moodiness in Richard, and he feared moments of abstract determination in her, and with good reason, because he knew to what lengths she could go under the spell of abstract determination. Looking at her now, quietly smoking across the pool of light, he wondered what she might be thinking, and it bothered him that he did not know : for with that smile assuredly she did know what he himself was thinking. That was the dangerous part of it : the whole basis of their relations was wrong, because their days together were essentially a submission on his part, and that also she knew. But if it crossed his mind like a cloud it crossed Shirley's like a dream. "Dear Richahd," she murmured, just opening her lips, and it was only by watching her lips that he saw what she was saying. Then she said it louder and he bent over the white shining table top to kiss her finger-tips. She drew back and slightly shivered : what was this mysterious business of love that could make her tingle all over if one man touched her hand? It was a nuisance, a bother, an insanity, but she accepted it.

And she also accepted Richard. Through the candles she saw his queer moulded face just touched with high lights and it gave her a peculiar sense of warm satisfaction that his face was hers, not merely in substance, but hers in spirit as well : with her fingers she could outline it, model its curves and planes and lines, emphasize the

strong line of the nose and the upward rise of the brows,
with her fingers she could know his face and possess it.
She was happy at this realization. That had been part
of the realization these three or four days, days which had
merged smoothly into one another, drifted to form one
long day and night. When would they awake and know
it was a dream and that this happiness had ended ? Both
of them deep in their minds recognized that problematical
end, both of them knew that all good things must be
ended, that in such a concept of finality arose the most
bitter poignance of life. But she felt no outward fear.
The three or four days had flowed past them so smoothly,
she didn't know if it were actually three or four : time
had disappeared into a brief eternity. The day after her
first return Shirley had formally moved in, collected her
bags and trunks and things from the Bowdoin house and
shipped them to the Bryn Mawr flat. Richard was
excited. That had been a Sunday and they had used the
whole day for this new beginning. It was a new beginning. Over the mass of bags she had smiled at him the
question " Scared ? " Her face was alight under her
black smoke of hair and he said : " Damn right I am."
Then she moved her head slightly so that her throat
swelled out and her smile was a caress as she said : " I'm
not ; I'm happy," but that was something of a lie
because she was a little afraid, tremulously afraid, and
they both knew it, even if her eyes were resolute.

The flat was in disorder and they dined in a little
north-side restaurant near the Edgewater Beach, partly
because she wanted to watch the lake. Before them
for long miles the lights in spring mist were floating
like bubbles. After dinner they walked, like children,
hand in hand ; people stared while in an utterly
absorbed way they were unseeing. They whispered a
little, and once in the shadow of a tree he leaned over
and brushed her hair with his lips ; she was, of course,

bareheaded; she loathed hats. They felt like children,
like Paul and Marjorie, and it was their great happiness
that they were genuinely able to feel deeply within
themselves with the divine simplicity of children. Back
in the apartment, they were confronted with trunks
and paper and scattered ribbon. " Scared ? " asked
Richard this time. " I am now," said Shirley. And
so that first day passed. Then other days passed. Three
of them. Maybe four. They were dream days. And
now they sat by candle-light and wondered how long it
would last.

    She got up suddenly, blew out with a quick whiff
another candle, and in sombre darkness they stood
silent together. " I'm going to work to-night," she
finally said. He very quickly realized he didn't want
her to work, but he said nothing. What could he
say ? It was like those painful days so many years
ago, before their marriage. He had lost the faculty of
argument in those early years : she had extinguished
him : and it had taken him a long time to reassert
himself after she had gone, to rediscover himself, to
return to his own values. And now was all that to
happen again ? " No, Shirley, don't work to-night.
Let's drive up the shore and watch the lake." He wanted
to voice that appeal, that wish to drive and watch the
lake, but he decided not to say it. After all it was her
job, her job to do and do well. (He was too confoundedly
considerate !) " But I don't want to work," said Shirley,
with a nervous little laugh, " I want to be just with you."
" By all means go ahead and work," replied Richard,
cursing himself. She looked at him and he said whisper-
ingly : " Why don't you look at me when you talk ? "
because now she often averted her face when she talked
to him, and she replied : " My dear, my dear, if I looked
at you I couldn't talk at all." And that was the sort of
thing Richard could never answer, he could never talk to

Shirley when she spoke that way : he could reply in only one manner and he did reply in that manner. He took her in his arms and kissed her. In the far corner now the candles were glowing. Later she said : " Damn it, let me go. I want to work ! " She was almost on the point of beginning that statue which was to mean so much to her, the statue of a beautiful woman caught at the moment she realized that she was no longer beautiful. She had a title for it now, she was very particular about titles, always she tried to find names first ; and the afternoon before, when she dropped into his office to take him to tea, she had said : " I have a title, Richard, a good title, *La Désenchantée.*" " Good," agreed Richard. Shirley had only casually mentioned her statue. She thought it would be more fun to tell him later, perhaps some day at his office. In a way she liked to drop in at his office, because he loved so much to see her there : and also because she was sure it ever so slightly annoyed him. She had never met Agatha and wanted to see her. Agatha was very polite and precise when Richard introduced them, but her lip trembled. " No, I won't have to fire her," he thought. " Poor girl," said Shirley, later. " Well, I don't blame her, falling in love with *you.*" She added very wisely : " But I know that kind of girl pretty well : she'd fall in love with anyone she happened to work for ; she'll fall in love with the next person she works for."

Richard was surprised and then realized Shirley was quite right. Maybe that was the reason she might not be a really great sculptor, she was too sure of things. She saw things too clearly. (Seeing clearly !) " Well," Richard smiled to himself, " I've not improved in that direction." Shirley saw him smile as they stood together before the window, with the blur of candles to one side, and she, too, smiled. In a way it was infuriating, because when his face became alight, smiling, then she too had to

smile, always, and sometimes she didn't want to smile.
Oh, it was good to be back, good to be back with Richard
she loved and always would love. That is, so long as
she felt like it. That statue now. Well, the first job
would be to block in the head a good deal more carefully
than she usually did block in heads. The forehead
especially must be carefully done. Why was it that people
never paid the least attention to foreheads : always they
gabbled about eyes and mouths and noses, whereas every
artist knew that the forehead was the most important,
the most revealing fact in physiognomy, the forehead
was the base, the key to the whole thing. Forehead first
and cheek-bones afterward. If you got your cheek-bones
right the other features just naturally plopped into line,
rightly and inevitably. But in *La Désenchantée* the set
of the eyes was going to be a job, that was going to be a
tough job. Perhaps she couldn't do it, yet. Well, she
would do it, in the end, if it took ten years. Meanwhile,
it might be fun to do another portrait of Richard. He
had changed. Oh, he had *changed*. She looked at him,
as he watched the silent street, and saw how his face had,
so to speak, distributed itself, how it had become finely
and firmly organized, a finished job and a tempered one.
God was a pretty good sculptor too, at least with people
you loved. Richard felt her looking at him, and he
didn't turn, for a moment. When he did he was choked
with some unreasonable kind of emotion. It seemed to
nullify all the things in his inmost heart he wanted to do.
With Shirley looking at him like that, it was no use, it
was no use ! She alone mattered. She alone was the
world. She saw Richard breathe deeply. Her Richard !
Then she saw a cloud pass his eyes and heard him say :
" I didn't tell Leon." She pursed her lips and said :
" Of course not. It's impossible to tell Leon. One
can't hurt people like that and go on liking them."
" What was that ? " asked Richard. " Haven't you dis-

covered that? " said wise Shirley. " Hurt someone and
you'll never forgive *him* for having hurt him." That
was a queer and important and usually true thread in
the maze of human nature, she reflected after she said it.
It made her glad to say it. She had often thought of it,
but she had never articulated it before, never put it
into words. Such discoveries gladdened her. They
refreshed her own confidence in her intelligence and made
that intelligence tangible to other people. Richard was
appreciating it now. Look at Richard. The *dear !* Shirley tingled all over. Then he said: " But what are
we going to do about it? " " Nothing," said Shirley.
But it was a miserable business. Her brother and *Doris*.
Shirley had never met Doris till Mary's party and she
hadn't liked her then. (She didn't like other girls, as a
rule.) And it was worse for Leon. But after all she was
right, there was nothing they could do about it, things
like that just had to adjust themselves. " My God ! "
said Richard suddenly aghast, " Leon may be my morgan-
natic brother-in-law or something." Shirley chuckled
and then said: " Don't laugh. Poor Leon. How did
he get on with Phil? " " Oh, as usual," said Richard ;
" I did most of the talking. Got all excited about
God and things, and gave them the piece about the
Periodic." Her face quickened. " Please do it over
for me." " Never," said he. They had slipped back
toward the table in the gathering dusk and still the
candles like captured stars shone. For some reason
they found they had been whispering. People always
did whisper in dark rooms. How pleasant it would be,
thought Shirley, always to live in comfortable dusky
rooms, with voices never strident and light never obtru-
sive. She was bending over the table to clear away the
dishes and Richard drew back at the lovely curve of her
breast. It was the most preposterous, the most insane
thing, that the nonsense called love could make him

quiver all over just because one woman moved her body. It was unfair, in a way. It made people too dependent. He touched her and felt her quiver. And Shirley had been the most independent person in the world for years and years. Now he knew she felt his finger with every atom of her body. Queerly, as she grew older, she grew more dependent : as he grew older he became more independent. Still—if she should move suddenly and kiss him, then again, as in the old days, the lights would begin to sway. He was poised over her and he wondered if perhaps she read his mind, if perhaps she would twist up and kiss him. She did know. But she withdrew. " Must clear up this mess," she said. " Then I shall work." Pause. " But I don't want to work." " I'll work, too," said Richard. He knew he wouldn't, and he knew also that unless he did she wouldn't either.

That sudden realization, as he still refrained from touching her, gave him a rare exhilaration. Almost for the first time in their long relationship he felt himself dominant. He knew that dominance and he exulted. He had not forgotten how furious he had been with Shirley directly after her return—she had beaten him— and not until this moment in the candle-light did the ramifications of that fury leave him. But now somehow he could always beat her. She had come back, and by putting herself at his feet had also put him at a terrific moral disadvantage. But now curiously that was all over, and Richard realized that Shirley was indeed his. He could do with her as he wished. She would kick and scratch and bite, no doubt, but his was the upper hand and he would retain it. Richard exulted. " Damn her," he said to himself. Then, still amazed, he very slowly said aloud : " Damn you ! " and reached over to take her to his breast. She was surprised and he could see also as her eyes were suddenly liquid that she was glad. " Damn you," he repeated, and almost choked her with kisses. She said, " Don't," and " Stop," but Richard didn't stop, and if he had stopped, it flashed through his mind, he would have to begin all over. He might never again be able to reassert this ascendancy. He kept kissing her till she was amazed at his passion. " You are not going to work," he said, while her head was in his hands, an oval of soft gleaming light with her throat swelling out. " You are *not* going to work ! You are coming with me. I don't know where, but you are coming with me, anywhere, *anywhere*, maybe to the movies ! " And then he released her slightly and laughed, for now it was safe to laugh ; and she laughed also, rather proudly.

Chapter Eleven

MARY

i

MARY DETMERS stood* with her eyes puzzled before the new chintz curtains in purple and orange she was hanging over the white wide windows smiling to her lawn : her eyes were puzzled because she wasn't really thinking of the new chintz curtains, she was wondering why it was only unintelligent people were happy.

She took that statement, for what it was worth, to be true. Did she know any happy people? Well, ye-es. But for some reason they were also very dull. They were charming and pleasant and attractive (in a way) and sometimes decorative—and also very dull. She thought of faculty wives she knew and of alumnæ lately married to bond salesmen, of undergraduate council leaders and ladies in the women's clubs. Yes, they were happy. Mary was glad she didn't know any of them very well.

She stood with arms akimbo and her head gently tilted to one side, surveying the curtains. Shirley would approve of those curtains. Richard and Shirley, now. Mary wondered about them and was quite sure they were not happy. At least they could never be happy permanently. They were too sensitive and too intelligent. Things counted too much for them. They thought too much about little things. They watched for undertones and overtones and in a youthful way they had subtile minds. No, they could never be happy.

" Leon," she thought suddenly, her arms still akimbo, " is the only one with wisdom. He doesn't want to be happy and he doesn't try."

* This was the same day.

" What did you say ? "

Mary had quite forgotten that little Marjorie was beside her.

" I was only saying," she came to attention, " that the curtains are very good now, but if anyone whispers they will be very bad."

" I see," said Marjorie thoughtfully. Marjorie did not see.

Mary started to think about Marjorie. Paul and Marjorie, now. They were delightful children. So content within themselves, so mutually adoring. They could not but be happy, always. They knew it and Mary knew it too. Every once in a while the Lord God appeared to bend low smiling, and introduce two people whom only God could introduce. They fell in love, married, bore children, bore more children, raised families, grew fat, played bridge, joined clubs, married off their children, paid the rent, listened to the radio, withered, decayed, and died. It was divinely organized. The Pauls and the Marjories had no questions to ask. They never suffered and they never thought deeply. They never searched for deep things. They were just healthy children made for one another. Mary always wanted to introduce them as : " This is Paul and this is Marjorie they are children in fact they are stupid children who will never praise God grow up they are imbeciles but charming."

" I think they're quite good," cut in Marjorie critically, staring at the curtains with her pink child's lips puckered, and her tumbled head nodding.

" Oh dear, I suppose they will be right enough," Mary replied, in her best helpless manner. " However, I *don't* see how we are going to get Richard and Shirley out for dinner if the dears just *refuse* to leave their apartment."

And herself, now. Perhaps her unhappiness was a

survival of those black days when her husband died.
It seemed spiteful on someone's part. Struck down
when they were together, more vividly alive than ever
before, struck down by something cruel and unknown.
Dr. Detmers laughed at a headache one afternoon and
the next day he was in bed. He died three days later.
Because it didn't manifest itself until the very end, because it was painless and concealed till the very end,
it was much more terrible for Mary, much harder to bear.

"Brave Mary," her friends said.

It did seem rather a stacking of the cards. She shrugged
slightly before the new curtains and shook her head
nervously, as if to rid herself of the memory of that old
dynamic brilliance, the thin beard and the waving
hands. And she so much younger. She shrugged again,
smiled a little, and thought that after all it was part of
the game. Like Richard and Shirley and Doris and
Austin, she was part of the game. Austin, now. (And
Paul and Marjorie remained outside.) It was a game,
and some people played with loaded dice, that was
all.

She enjoyed how her friends marvelled. Brave Mary.
She hadn't cried, much. But she smiled when people
said tragedy had made her warm and mellow. It was
queer, how she liked to keep real things to herself. She
knew well the ironic circumstance of her own mind
—except over little things.

Mary turned suddenly because with her quick apper-
ception she realized something froward had clouded the
little room. She looked and saw Marjorie with head
turned full away deep in her hands : she saw Marjorie's
little white neck bent forward with the blond hairs
shaved down to the whiteness so trimly. She inquired :
" What's the matter ? " and Marjorie turned, and Mary
saw that Marjorie was crying.

" I'm so unhappy ! " wailed little Marjorie.

ii

But at that moment the maid announced Austin.

Marjorie raced out of the room, shaking her head violently and sobbing. Mary looked after her and then, deciding to let the child fight it out for herself, she advanced to greet Austin. He was bowing. He looked polished and shining, so efficacious had been his pre-prandial cleansing. In fact, although he was somewhat constrained, he beamed. Mary greeted him rather absently, her mind still with Marjorie, and wondered a little, for Austin of all persons she knew was not one to parade his emotions.

" Marjorie announced a moment ago she was violently unhappy," said Mary, " and burst from the room crying. Whatever shall I do ? " (She knew exactly what she would do.) " Sit down, Austin, and tell me what I shall do, or at least explain yourself. I haven't seen you since dinner last week."

" I have been busy," said Austin.

" Lecturing to your chosen numskulls ? "

" Exactly."

" Dear, what a nuisance it must be for you, Austin, you with such a superior mind."

Sometimes, Mary thought, her irony did shine through her conversational mask. But Austin only bowed and smiled.

" I'm really worried about Marjorie," Mary went on. " She has just announced she is unhappy, and I fear she may be intelligent after all. It is such a disappointment. Paul and Marjorie were a divinely appointed pair."

" Mates," said Austin.

" Yes, and now Paul has forgotten to send some flowers, or didn't 'phone on the stroke of the hour, or perhaps didn't want to go to the theatre to-night, and poor Marjorie is crying."

Austin sat down and dabbled with a cigarette. He watched Mary. She talked and it occurred to both of them she was not particularly interested in what she was saying. He lit his cigarette. He puffed. Mary reached for a cigarette, dabbled with it, took a light from him, and she puffed. They looked at one another. They both puffed. Then she tinkled again with laughter.

"Is it possible," she asked, "that there is something on your mind?"

"Yes. Something important."

"Dear, dear, it must be something dreadful besides. Austin, do you wrinkle your face that way when you talk to your classes?"

"I never say anything of importance to my classes."

She sighed. What was the matter with him? Austin, now . . .

He rose abruptly, pushed out the cigarette.

"Why do you keep talking such patter?" he asked sharply.

She shrugged.

"I am very serious," he went on. "I want to ask you something." Pause. "I want to ask you to marry me."

Mary was stupified. She was blank with the kind of sudden amazement which washes clear the mind and leaves only an insecure sense of shock. She looked at him and saw that he was not drunk. That was her first thought: "He's drunk." But he was sober. He was very sober. He was leaning near her and she came to an abrupt decision that she didn't like his face. It was leaning a little closer now. She was still too surprised to speak aloud. But it leaned closer still and she tilted her head to one side with her hand up and said sharply:

"Don't."

"I want you," repeated Austin slowly, "to marry me."

" Dear, dear," said Mary, almost to herself. " I may say, Austin, you have surprised me. Do sit down, please. I think . . ."

" Don't talk like that," he said.

" But I must talk like that. I always talk like that. And as you say this is a *very* important occasion. I feel . . ."

" Mary," he leaned forward again, " please do answer me."

Somehow her mood settled back to herself—she had been talking to gain time—and somehow Dr. Detmers was in the foreground of her mind. She felt emotion surge through her breast. Her pulse quickened and she felt she might choke. She remembered their courtship —those were the times when people had courtships and became engaged—she remembered the tragedy which had stamped itself so unreasonably, so cruelly, on her life ; she remembered the old companionship and the quick vivid days which now seemed a living shadow of the past. Austin saw the change in her face and mistook its meaning entirely. He leaned forward again. Then Mary saw him and spoke clearly : she spoke a natural and inevitable command which came within herself ; she hardly needed look at him as she said :

" No."

There was a long pause and Austin lit another cigarette.

After that they talked, quite unimportantly, for a few moments. After a few more moments Mary was laughing in her quiet cheery way. " Austin, you *goose*," she said. " Really, and a man of your age and station ! "

" I am glad," he said acidly, " that you consider it a matter for humour."

" Bravo, Austin ! " Now he was in a class-room again and he was all right. " Do run along now, because I have a domestic tragedy upstairs to straighten out. Will you come for hot dinner on Saturday or cold supper on Sunday? Good, Sunday then. We shall all be here."

She pressed his hand warmly and felt his friend again. She did like Austin. Now perhaps she would like him better. She was glad he sought to muster no anguish. He was abstractedly smoking again, with the old sardonic smile just turning his lips. She was also glad in the certainty he would never again impinge in any important way on her life or consciousness. She shivered slightly.

" You're a dear person," she said, as she led him to the door. " Do run along now and we'll expect you on Sunday. Eight o'clock." She opened the door and smiled cheerily. " Good night. *Good* night."

He looked a last time at the big room and saw the new curtains.

" Very nice," he pointed. " Next time do them in grey."

Austin disappeared.

iii

Mary sighed. What an astonishing afternoon! She was about to run upstairs to see Marjorie when the door bell rang again : she opened it herself and stepped back before Paul. He was very black and she reflected he made a rather good face all by himself.

" Dear, dear," said Mary. " My child, what *is* the matter ? "

He was solemn.

" I can't possibly tell you," said Paul. " It's pretty terrible. I can't possibly tell you."

Mary looked at him with his lips drooping and woe in his eyes.

" Oh, come," she said, " if it was as bad as all that you wouldn't even be here."

That impressed Paul. That was a good idea.

" You're right, Cousin Mary," he said. " You're

M

quite right, but just the same, it *is* something rather awful."

Probably, thought Mary, he *had* forgotten the theatre seats.

He smiled a little, as if it were not every day he could report an event rather awful. He was looking at her with desperate earnestness. She wanted to hug him. This *boy !*

"Well, you know, Paul," she said, "it's rather nice sometimes to have awful things happen. It helps you, you know. It helps you to see clearly." (That was Richard's phrase, she remembered.) "It's only when something awful happens that you can see how fine happiness is. It gives you perspective. It helps you give a value to things and nothing is worth much unless you have a scale of values for things."

"That's very true, I know," he said solemnly. "But I'd like to see Marjorie right away, because it is rather awful."

Mary had difficulty in concealing laughter.

"Are you sure ? " she said, " that Marjorie wants to see you ? "

This was a new thought. Paul paled.

"I'm not sure," Mary went on, "that you haven't been cruel to Marjorie. And I *know* "—she was very sober—" that Marjorie isn't feeling very well."

"Not feeling well ! Oh ! Do you mean . . . she's *ill ?* "

"Well-l-l-l-l, perhaps not exactly ill. The trouble is, Paul, she is upset, you understand, emotionally upset. Emotionally, you know."

"Emotionally," he repeated.

"And, of course," she proceeded, "one must be very careful of such disorders. Marjorie is very young. You, of course, are much older. I know you love Marjorie, Paul, but you must be very gentle with her also."

He nodded eagerly. He was, of course, much older
than Marjorie. Ridiculously older. He was twenty-one
years old, and would be twenty-two January next. Paul
straightened. Yes, he must be very gentle with Marjorie.
Mary had a way of understanding these things. Of
course, Mary was ancient—good Lord, she must be over
thirty—but anyway she was still a good sort and surpris-
ingly good-looking. He straightened his lips again.

" Can I go up now ? "

" Yes, I think you can go up now."

Mary watched him take the steps three at a time.
She sat down, rather weakly, and laughed. She looked
at her curtains. She was not thinking of her curtains.
Outside a yellow warbler was diving like a top through
the trees.

iv

Paul and Marjorie returned downstairs together and
both were a little red and mussed, and both were smiling.
They had decided, they said, to go out for dinner. Mary
deprecated this suggestion. They pleaded. In the end
she gave them permission and they walked across the
lawn toward 57th Street. She thought how good it
was to see youth in brave display saunter hand in hand
down the dirty streets of life.

(She never did find out what the something awful
was. With the quarrel over, she didn't want to awake
the issue, and she never asked. Paul and Marjorie though
forgot it in a day. They forgot things quickly. Children
. . . children. . . .)

Mary rose abruptly in an aimless fashion, and looked
around the great wide room with the dusk now floating
through the white windows. She picked up a magazine
from one chair and emptied Austin's cigarette stubs from
an ash tray to a waste-paper basket. Austin ! Had she
dreamed that ? It was too preposterous. She discovered

it made her a little angry. But she shrugged and he disappeared from her mind. Around the room aimlessly she walked, tidying it. Suddenly she realized she must dine alone and that the evening was empty. Brave Mary, as her friends said. Mellow Mary. Out of the window she could see Paul and Marjorie reach the corner; they stopped and hailed a taxi; the boy handed her in. They looked very fresh and charming, Paul in grey flannels with a ridiculous striped tie and his hair slicked. They were both hatless and Marjorie's hair shone gold in the dying sun. She saw Marjorie smile, saw a smile glisten on her puckered little pink lips. Children, children. . . . And they were going, going. . . . Mary suddenly discovered she was lonely.

In the middle of the room she stood, in her familiar capable helpless way, her hands poised, half-raised, before her. She looked about her. There was nothing more to tidy. The dusk was deeper now, but she decided not to turn on the lights just yet. It was too pleasant, alone in the house, with the shadows beginning to sprawl in long plumes over the floor, and the fading light to lie dappled in the corners. She moved to the window again and saw that Paul and Marjorie had disappeared from view, and she felt for some ridiculous reason tremulous. She was trembling. She paused by the window and saw that lights were beginning to float down the long silent streets. Mary laughed, a little weakly. Then she bit her under lip. When she sat down, still aimlessly, it was a surprise to discover that she had begun to cry.

Chapter Twelve

THE EXQUISITE SENSUALISTS

i

RICHARD was shaving. It was a few mornings later and again his thoughts had undergone change. As he slapped the clean-smelling lather to his cheeks he reflected that there was only one thing which was a greater nuisance than love, and that was shaving. Some of the lather plopped into the wash-basin as his fingers searched through the white foam, rubbing the beard : it plopped with a wettish sound and flattened out, and Richard thought it was something like a snow-man's tears : that is, if a snow-man ever cried. He stropped his razor and began to shave.

He had a tough beard and was one of those excessively unfortunate individuals who must shave twice a day to remain presentable. Richard often thought that a man who shaved twice a day must have an outlook on life completely different from lucky fellows who had only to shave once. He knew his double shaving had been of immense importance in shaping his attitude to the innumerable petty burdens of life. It had given him fortitude and also many new oaths.

" Richahd ! "

" Yes ? "

" Come here a moment, please."

" Can't. Shaving."

" But I want you ! "

" Can't help it. Shaving. Hey ! " He paused and grinned at the door. " Did you know that a man who shaves twice a day is immeasurably superior in moral discipline to the man who shaves only once a day ? ”

“ Fool,” called back Shirley gaily.

But now the lather had hardened and Richard had to begin all over again. He grunted as the razor slipped. He finished one cheek until it was glistening and glabrous, and then bent his head in the light toward the other. Wonder what Shirley wanted. Hardly anything important this hour of the morning. He spotted a puff of lather over a doubtful patch, the treacherous region under the ear. That finished, he turned with new energy to the chin. The lather dribbled off tinged with clipped bits of hair into the basin. The chin was the difficult part. Under the chin and over the chin and along the lips. Richard finished. He washed his face and rubbed it till he shone.

Then, in his bath, he was glad he belonged to the second of the two great schools of masculine thought, the school which never bathes before shaving, but always shaves before bathing.

Shaving was an economic sort of process and ugly. But the bath was an altogether different affair. It was in his matutinal bath that Richard for the first time each day began to have conscious and intelligible thoughts. Every man is in a bad temper or at least a negative temper while shaving, but in his bath Richard whistled. He laved the cool water over his skin and leaned back to relax. The water filled his pores luxuriously and he felt caressed. But Richard was no voluptuary. His bath was not a rite because he liked it. He had too much good sense for such sophistry. He bathed every morning for one reason only, and that was because he liked to be clean.

The shower of bitter cold water spurred him pink, and he towelled himself red and was dressed in three minutes.

"What did you want?" he asked Shirley, as he arrived for breakfast.

"Just had an idea," she said. "I'm glad you wouldn't listen, because it isn't the kind of idea one shouts."

She was fresh and supple as a flower and some of the ideas Richard had been assembling turned cart-wheels in his brain.

"What's the idea?"

"It occurred to me we are exquisite sensualists, you and I, Ricky dear."

He was startled then to discover he didn't like that. They might be exquisite sensualists all right, but surely not before breakfast. Words paused on his lips, but he didn't utter them, and his face became puzzled. Shirley looked up and saw his surprise. Then she saw also that he appeared annoyed. He hadn't the remotest intention of being an exquisite sensualist before nine o'clock in the morning. She looked at him.

"Now," she said, "you're being a pig, and I don't like that."

He shrugged in protest, but still maintained silence.

"It seems to me," said Shirley, with her eyes slightly narrow, "that you've been rather a pig several times lately."

"Please," said Richard.

"I don't like it," she went on dangerously.

"But, my dear," he protested, "what on earth is there to quarrel about? I'm not being a pig. I didn't say a word."

"Exactly. That's just it. You didn't say a word."

"But . . ." he wrinkled his brows, trying to explain. "You startled me—you see, Shirley, you startle me a lot, even now—and I was just trying to figure out what you meant and whether I did like it or not, when suddenly you call me a pig and start to quarrel."

"Oh, all right," said Shirley.

Quite solemnly, feeling a little ridiculous, they began to eat toast and poached eggs. Quite silently, with little grimaces, because the eggs were hot, they continued to eat toast and poached eggs. Quite remorsefully, with the uncomfortable feeling that the day had begun wrong, they finished eating toast and poached eggs. Shirley was a good cook, but it didn't seem to improve the meal.

Richard gulped a last mouthful and said:

" Forgive me."

" Oh, it's all right," said Shirley, but it was easy to see she was still annoyed.

Now he began to see that it was his fault. When she said something like that which was meant sincerely to interest and charm him, it was up to him even if it was before breakfast to make some sort of reply, to play up to it. But the way the conversation had turned was a curious illustration of the turn in their relationship. In the old days, even granted she would have said anything like that, Shirley would have dropped the subject at the rebuff ; it wouldn't have mattered and she would have shed his piggishness with simple scorn. But now she bridled and quarrelled. It was very strange. He reflected that there was a third progression possible, when she might be hurt. That progression he decided must never come.

Shirley was surveying the debris of the eggs, her lips rather tight and her shoulders ready to shrug. He saw it was a dangerous posture.

" Come to think of it," Richard began with deliberation, swallowing his pride and going to it, " that *is* a good idea, an awfully good idea. We *are* exquisite sensualists. I do know, I think, just what you meant. You didn't mean sensualists like Gilles de Rais. You meant sensitiveness to light and mood and colour and phrase, to music and art and ideas."

Shirley looked at him quickly. His grave face was deep in earnest.

"Richahd," she said, "don't be an elaborate ass!"

Then she got up from the table quickly and crunched her napkin.

"Pardon," she said, "must go bathroom a second."

He looked after her in blank amazement. He had seen a new Shirley these last few days. But this further manifestation was a surprise. Cool, imperious Shirley! He was incredulous and his eyes were startled and wide. He was a little scared. He followed her and found her in the bedroom looking stonily out of a window.

"I wish," she said, as she heard him enter, "that you'd get out of here."

"Shirley, I'm so awfully sorry. Please pardon me for being a pig and a fool and an ass and lots of other things. I had no *idea* . . ."

"Oh, I forgot all about that long ago."

"But you haven't forgotten it. That's the trouble. Shirley, be reasonable. Look here, I've *admitted* I was an ass. Now let's just be *sensible*."

Richard was getting just a little nettled, partly because he had been so obviously in the wrong.

"Whenever," she said bitterly, "a man offends a woman and hurts her vanity and is utterly in the wrong and then she's fool enough to make an issue of it and make a scene, always, *always* he turns to her and says, 'Be sensible.'"

He looked at her still amazed.

"But I told you," he said, "that I was sorry and I am sorry and that should end it. As far as I'm concerned it does end it. And it's late, Shirley; I've got to go. I'm going. G'bye."

"Don't go."

"All right. I won't go. But I don't see any sense at all in talking about this nonsense and keeping on quarrelling. And really, Shirley, I've got to go."

" It wasn't nonsense."

" Do you want to have breakfast all over again and start from the beginning ? " he said impatiently.

" Richahd ! " warned Shirley.

There had been an edge to his voice and now there was an edge to hers also.

" Richahd," she went on, " I don't want to hear you talk to me like that. I don't like it. I'm not cowing you or bullying you, and I don't like it." She looked at him closely and her eyes were liquid. " Don't you *see* ? "

He took her in his arms and kissed her. She let her head fall against his shoulder and then arched against him. She didn't move for a long time. Neither did he. With slow lips he began to kiss her hair till she moved away : then he also withdrew and looked at her at arm's length. A queer crooked smile came over her mouth. He leaned forward to kiss it straight, and as she closed her eyes it was as if she felt the taste of dust upon her lips.

" We're pretty deep in it," she said quietly.

" Yes. My dear, my dear ! Don't you see, I adore you, I *adore* you. You must know that, you must *feel* that. I adore you. . . ."

" Yes," she said, " but I'm not sure it's nearly enough."

ii

Richard turned to the garage, got out the car, and started the trip down-town. At the corner of Broadway and Bryn Mawr he paused each morning for a second to get his paper. At the corner of Sheridan Road and Bryn Mawr he turned into the searching flood of traffic. It was about six miles to the office and he usually made it in forty minutes.

He was glad he didn't have to gobble breakfast and

hang on a strap in the screaming elevated trains. After all, he was a lucky person, everything considered. He lit a cigarette and narrowly missed colliding with a bus near Wilson Avenue. Yes, he was lucky, lucky. . . . But he was late. He must hurry along.

Richard had seen his mind change slowly in the past few days. The quarrel, ending in Shirley's submission in an assertive sort of way, had served to emphasize it. When he first discovered his ascendancy in the moment in candle-light, it had shocked and exhilarated him : but later, because his mind worked queerly with such things, he felt sorrow, almost remorse. He felt as if he didn't want to be dominant. His dominance was a cenotaph to the past. For a day he searched about vaguely trying to define his feelings and then did discover something which delighted him : he discovered what he wanted to do was erect a monument in his heart, so to speak, to her capitulation. He did. It was an easy thing to do. Shirley saw and was silent. She knew that public comment on such strange masculine monuments are unwise. He could see her smiling and knew that she knew. It was a good thing.

Richard was crossing the link bridge now and his car struggled through lanes of traffic. He watched the dirty green flood of the river insanely flowing backward like some monstrous abortion of nature. For the Chicago river does not empty itself into the lake : it sucks water out of the lake, and flows perversely, a stream of sewage, toward the Mississippi. Richard watched for a few seconds the strange, unnatural flow, dipping past the canyon of buildings toward sun and prairie, slowly regurgitating its own viscid flood. He crossed the bridge and swarmed with the other cars into the Loop.

At the office he found it difficult to work. He found it difficult to concentrate on even the simplest tasks. He snapped at Agatha and snapped at his boy. He was openly inattentive when Mr. Stern rustled near to talk of Japanese prints. At eleven-thirty he sent a telegram to Shirley, reading : " This exquisite sensualist is having a bad time." At twelve he sent to the bootleg parlour upstairs to have a drink. He was thinking of Shirley and she was bothering him. He had come to a conclusion during the early morning, and it scared him. He refused to admit that conclusion for an hour, and then realized it was inevitable. With this realization, because he was fundamentally a person of good sense, he dismissed it from his mind, and until lunch-time worked hard to make up for a bad beginning. He gave his boy a quarter and smiled at Agatha. He went into Mr. Stern's office and asked him a question about Hishigawa Moronobu. He emerged half an hour later. At one o'clock it was time for lunch and he went to Emil's and there chatted with Phil.

After luncheon he returned to his office and found on his desk the memorandum for another of those bond circulars which at times particularly enraged him. He dabbled with it half-heartedly and turned instead to a calculation of small-issue advertisements. It was a mean sort of game, wheedling money out of other people, however legitimately, so that he might have the things he wanted. Later he sat back alone to face squarely the idea which had arrived to shock him early in the morning, shocked him so much that he had run away from it and camouflaged his own emotions (believing momentarily in the camouflage) by silly telegrams. That was the best way to deal with an idea : run away from it, quite honestly dissipate its implications, turn round cautiously from a distance and see it in perspective, survey it warily, explore its causes and ramifications, and then decide. Size it up and decide. Well, that was what he had done. He had come to his conclusion. His conclusion was that Shirley bored him.

`He was very quiet and intent for a few moments.

"That's an extremely unreasonable idea," he muttered to himself.

He drummed on the glass top of the desk and fiddled with a pencil.

But it wasn't unreasonable at all. That was the bad part of it. Unreasonable, he could dismiss it; reasonable, it remained. And it often happened that way. Always, in every love affair, there is one who must give and one also who must receive; only once in a million years did you have a perfect equilibrium and then you had people like the Brownings. But in the ordinary run of human affairs it was simply Mendelism expressed emotionally: one factor was dominant, one recessive. You could almost chart it biologically and speak of extrinsic factor x and intrinsic factor y. Anyway, it happened. It was that business of rhythm again. Once Richard had bored Shirley. That at least was one reason why she had run away: he hadn't been vital enough, or strong enough, or big enough, to hold her: it amounted to the same thing, boredom. Well, now Shirley bored Richard. Bored was too strong a word, perhaps, but it summarized everything neatly, it blanketed an emotion. He drummed on his desk with a fixed clarity in his eyes. And what could he do about it? He could kill the boredom and settle back into the old relationship. But did he want the old relationship? Did he want her back, now that the first flush of greeting was over? He didn't know. He hadn't been able to answer that question when she first put it, at Mary's dinner-party a week before, again when she asked him at the flat; and he couldn't honestly answer it now. He didn't know. It was a full stop. It was a stalemate. He had found Dead Sea fruit.

He thought of Shirley with her brows taut and her black hair tumbled before the clay, and his breast twinged.

But she bored him.

That is, using boredom as a generic term.

Richard sat moodily before his desk and his severe puzzled face was less severe, perhaps, but infinitely more puzzled, than Agatha, who was watching him, could ever remember having seen it.

Then he began to work again.

iii

During the morning Shirley was busy. She sketched various plans for *La Désenchantée* in charcoal on creamy paper. She was happy now. Even while her mouth pouted concentrated malediction on a bad line, she kept humming. The scene with Richard was forgotten. It had nevertheless been an extraordinary scene for her, because so rare. Not three times in her life had she ever unreasonably lost her temper like that. But it was over and she didn't permit herself the luxury of remorse. "Occasionally one regrets things which in their importance to others become distasteful," she murmured. She was much more emotionally detached than Richard, and such a flurry departed from her quickly. Perhaps it was because she felt things so intensely—at moments —that with such facile ease they slid off her back and were soon forgotten. With her fingers smudged with charcoal she went on with her work.

She looked at her fingers. Some day, she supposed, her thumbs would be flat, like the thumbs of most sculptors. But now they were supple and capable. Her fingers smelt slightly of wax, but in the little garage studio she had to use wax, regular mud clay being too much trouble to handle. Mud clay in any quantity took too large a clay-bin and too involved a water apparatus. Besides, wrapping the cast every night in wet rags was such a nuisance. On the other hand, clay was fun because it washed off the hands so nicely. Shirley had a superstition it was good for her complexion.

"I wonder," she said to herself, when another attempt at a sketch was discarded crumpled on the floor, "I wonder if Richard knows just what *is* troubling him."

She paused : and her fist went up to her chin.

"Well, I can't tell him."

No, she couldn't tell him. That was sure. It was the kind of thing he couldn't accept from anybody ; it had to come from himself. Words just interfered. One called in the old banalities because there were no other words when conversation became really intimate. Words were a nuisance. Bad nuisance. Good luck she wasn't a writer. Richard, he would be a writer some day and maybe a good writer, and it was lucky he didn't know it yet.

She began sketching again, but it didn't work. Still, sketching of any kind was easier than modelling of any kind. It was pretty wearying to work on large pieces, when you had to keep the arms up and usually extended almost to their full length. But it was fun. And what fun it would be some day to work in marble ! That reminded her, she *must* see about getting that cast of Richard's wrist.

"Fingers all wrong," she said.

She passed her hands over her forehead to brush back her hair and smudged her forehead too with charcoal. She laughed. Richard should see her now. Bother him, he *was* on her mind.

She always worked in overalls—it was one of her very few outward eccentricities—and she was sorry on such occasions no one was apt to see her. "I look a darling," she laughed, under her shaggy bobbed head. She kicked off her slippers and walked back and forth before the easel in bare feet. Without high heels she felt absurdly small and childish. "That's why women wear French heels," she murmured, "it gives them a sense of moral superiority." She looked at herself in the glass and chuckled like a child in delight. So small she was and so tousled and smudged. She reached for a handful of hair and mussed it, pushing it over her eyes and because it was so stiff making it stand in queer angles and directions. . She chuckled again and surveyed with chin on breast the blue denim of the overalls and her peeking bare feet. "I *do* look a darling," she laughed. She kept on drawing.

Shirley was surprised, not unreasonably, at the turn affairs with Richard had taken. She had returned to him, as she told him, on one of those sudden desires which are not impulse, but which nevertheless may be overwhelming. It was partly Chicago, partly old memories, partly physiology, partly a gesture within herself, partly her growing years, partly him. Well, a good deal of it was him. She must admit that. Scientifically, however, she couldn't explain it. It was one of those things which just happen. Certainly in Paris she had not missed him. She thought of Sanchez. And when she left Paris for Chicago, certainly she had not the remotest intention of ever seeing Richard seriously again.

But granted the fact of the return all the rest was easy to follow. All the rest was strictly in order. Except, perhaps, things like that scene this morning. Well, that was just nerves. Her lip curled. It would not happen again, or if it did would happen differently. As for the rest, it was clear sailing. First his surprise and then his first fine burst of feeling; then his fury and then his slow, half-unwilling acquiescence, always a battle with pride; then an exaltation and a happiness. This Shirley knew must come and she welcomed it. She genuinely welcomed it, because she wanted to be taken, she wanted to be taken and dominated just for a few moments or months of her life: it was a sort of laziness, a sort of submission. Let it happen once. She knew what she was about. She had laughed, rather proudly.

And with all this in mind and the scene in the morning what would happen next?

" The strange thing is," she ruminated, " I can go on thinking and analysing this way and yet I suppose I love him."

Again :

" It's different when he's near and I see his face. I can't think so clearly then and 'specially I can't think back."

And again :

" I don't think he really loves me any more."

Shirley pursed her lips at that and perhaps her lip slightly trembled. Then she shrugged. Well, too bad. Couldn't be helped. It was all in the game. With serious face and brows a little weary she began again the slow round sweep of charcoal which outlined a head. She worked slowly now, carefully, with her eyes intent on the paper. Beneath her the bare feet were curled excitingly, but she had forgotten them. From time to time she pushed back her busy hair from the forehead. She sketched with lips compressed, earnestly. It was coming now. It was a serious business. She mustn't stop : if she stopped she'd lose it. That was the trouble with all artists : they stopped. Then they discovered they had pencils to sharpen and a desk to clean and old letters to read and a telephone call to make and then the morning was over. Some of them never even started. They began with the pencils and old letters and things. Inertia. That was a strange thing about artist people. But Shirley didn't pause and these thoughts hardly eddied the surface of her brain. She worked. The head was blocked and shaded in, till she had on paper the rough outlines of forehead and cheek-bones. The eyes were vague, but they could come all right later if the

N

rest were good. Half an hour later she paused and found her fingers were tired. She got up, stretched, and surveyed the sketch from across the room. Yes, it was good. *Quite* good. Well!

Shirley took a long drink of water and then drifted back to the flat. She found Richard's telegram and laughed a little. Then she took another drink of water, and, resting, lay full length in her overalls on the bed.

Exquisite sensualists. H-mmmm.

She wondered again if Richard knew just what was bothering him, and reflected till she opened the telegram she hadn't thought of Richard for quite half an hour. Did he know?

"Of course," she said to herself, "it all rests on the fact that I *did* leave him : and he'll never be happy again as long as he lives, I suppose, for fear and humiliation that I might leave him again." She paused. Yes. That was it. That was the whole thing. "Always it will be something hanging over his head that I *might* leave him again, and if I left him again he'd have to kill himself."

Yes, that was it.

That was it, all right.

Well, she couldn't tell him. He'd have to fight it out for himself, and she knew that there was only one cure. She hoped he wouldn't take that.

Shirley rose and made herself luncheon. The luncheon was a tomato sandwich. Then, because she was tired, just physically tired, she slipped into bed and in two minutes was very peacefully, very sound asleep. Her breathing was regular as a child's and her lips were smiling.

iv

Richard arrived home toward six o'clock and found Shirley in a tea-gown of orange and dull green. She was very beautiful. He damned himself as he saw how beautiful she was and how it made his heart tingle. As soon as he stepped in the room he saw as far as she was concerned there was no tension between them : she had made up her mind, in whatever direction it might be, and was calm and aloof : she seemed the old Shirley again, the high-chinned indomitable Shirley, and because there was something in Richard's blood which must meet that appeal, his decision of the afternoon, however right, seemed useless, he was turned to water, to water and to fire, the tremendous physical power she exerted over him reasserted itself. She looked at him tentatively.

"Pretty dress," said Richard, shortly. "Get it in Paris ? "

It was a strange thing, but after their first few breathless exchanges of information, they had talked very little about her years in Paris. She kept them very much to herself. She had nothing to conceal—in other words, nothing had ever happened to her she wasn't at any moment willing to tell him—but some inhibition kept her from talking. And he wasn't curious. Of course, often enough she was reminded of things, how she dined at the Chez Francis and ate peaches burning in kirsch, how the only reason for staying up all night in Paris was the opportunity it afforded to ride at dawn in the Bois, what a jolly restaurant was the Petite Biche, and how gay the parties at the Bal du Printemps. But that was about all. That and how cheaply you could buy clothes.

She showed him the drawing which had occupied her most of the morning and he liked it. "Soon, Ricky, just as soon as I get this thing started, let's go to work on another portrait of you." He nodded and told her of a lunch with Phil. But he wasn't talkative. He proceeded to wash and shave and then they sauntered out quite casually to dinner.

"That telegram," said Shirley. "You're an awful idiot, Richard."

"Sorry," he laughed. "I had rather a stupid day. I shall clear out of that office soon."

This was another decision he had been slowly reaching. He had no business earning too much money writing advertisements. Chemistry was beginning to occupy him urgently again. That and many other things. There was so much he wanted to do. (And he hadn't been in the laboratory for a week.) But first something was a necessity. Settle this Shirley business first once and for all.

Then it happened she began to lean over the table toward him with one fist to her chin and started settling it for him. She had decided to talk, in spite of her earlier decision.

"You know, Richahd," she said, "I worked a lot this morning and worked well, but I did some thinking, too. I had another idea."

"Like the first one?"

"N-no." She smiled a little. "No. The only similarity is that they're both true and they both concern us. I think we should do something about us, Ricky."

He nodded, puzzled, and the planes of his face shifted.

"Isn't it extraordinary?" he asked. "It's almost impossible to trace what's happened in these last few days, but something *has* happened. Between us. Pulling us apart. And I want to know what it is."

"It's that you're afraid of me."

She looked clear across the table at him and he couldn't but admire her direct courageous mind. He knew it wasn't easy for her to say that. To him when he was in this mood. She did have guts. And he knew what she said was true.

" Granted," he nodded.

" You're afraid," she went on, and now her voice lowered almost to a whisper, " that some day I might leave you again."

There ! Out !

Not very long before she had thought she couldn't say that to Richard. It was an awfully hard thing to say. But it was necessary now. Something was necessary and something was necessary quickly if they weren't to topple. She felt a lot better having said it. And she saw he was intelligent enough to grasp it quickly, and honest enough to admit she was right.

" I'm glad you said that," Richard whispered. " Very glad. It's quite true. I suppose I never thought of it before that way. Of course."

Now he felt if Shirley could say that it was up to him to be frank and say something.

" I've been thinking, too, along the same lines. In fact, what I was thinking was this—forgive me—I was thinking that just as I bored you so long ago, now you might perhaps—oh, just a *lit*tle—bore me."

She shook her head gravely.

" N-no," she said. " Not bored. Not quite that. But I think I see what you mean. You mean that you want other things more. And it's the same thing. You're afraid of my staying with you and my loving you, all because once I left you. And you're afraid I might do it again."

" Granted," repeated Richard.

(Why did his heart behave so ridiculously when he talked to Shirley this way ?)

" And I've been thinking," she went on quietly, " what possible cure there can be for that state of mind."

(Why didn't he help her a little bit ? As if it were *easy* to talk like this !)

" You see," she went on, the words barely emerging from her mouth, she talked so slowly and so quietly, " the trouble is, I can't say that some time . . . I might not leave you . . . again. I don't *think* I ever shall. I don't *think* so. I love you too much, Ricky, I need you too much—really I do. I don't *think* I can ever go. But that's not very good security. You see, I'm trying to be honest. I'm trying to clear up this mess. But you know it's not very good security. I *might* go. And what then ? "

He was playing very carefully with a spoon, balancing it on his little finger. He stared at the spoon although her eyes were clear on his face.

" Of course," he said, " that's just it. I don't think you'll go either. As you say, I don't think you can go. I love *you* too much. But you might. And that's a hell of a sword of Damocles to be living under, it's an *impossible* thing to live under."

Pause.

" If only we weren't so honest," said Shirley bitterly. " If only I could swear to you I'd always be with you and always faithful to you, and you could believe me. . . . But we can't do things like that, somehow, we're better than that. We've *got* to be honest."

He brought his jaws together and discarded the spoon.

" I'm glad anyway you said it all," said Richard. " I don't think it will do much good to talk about it any more." He paused and smiled very crookedly. " Anyway, let's make the best of it. Maybe it isn't quite as bad as we think."

" Yes."

" Let's see it through and hang on anyway."

" Richahd," said Shirley, with a rare wide smile, " I *like* you ! "

" Let's fight it out then somehow. Waiter ! "

The waiter brought the bill and Richard paid it. He

looked out at the assortment of thumbed bread balls
before him and he laughed a little. (It was good to be
able to laugh!) "Let's get a taxi," he said. "I want
to kiss you, to kiss you hard." "Very hard," said Shirley,
and with his hand firm under her arm grasping her
forearm warmly they left the restaurant. They were
rather grave. After all, they had done something to
clear it up. "Sorry I was so brusque about the dress,"
said Richard. "I was just afraid of how beautiful
you were." "Of course," said Shirley, "I knew that."
They stepped to the kerb and entered the cab almost
solemnly.

"Dear . . ."

"I adore you!"

They groped for each other's arms . . .

Chapter Thirteen

THE NATURE OF JUSTICE

i

"I THINK," said Leon to himself triumphantly, "that I have epilepsy."

He was on the way to see Doris. He was very happy. He had been sleeping badly, and the night before, in that strange haze between consciousness and sleep, found himself suddenly stretched taut in bed, the action of his heart apparently suspended in a tonic contraction of all his muscles. At first he thought quite seriously he was dead. Then his heart released itself with an alarming thud and his nerves twanged free like piano-wires. He felt unable to move, but with a prodigious effort twisted himself out of the choking catalepsy. He relaxed to freedom, twitching in every part of his body. Then he slept. In the morning he rushed to an encyclopædia, and in the article on epilepsy found his symptoms almost precisely described. He was transformed with delight. It was just that which had struck down his beloved Dostoievsky. This was a new way to suffer. This was much better than hay fever.

Leon was so delighted he broke into meditation in Russian,* something he did only on rare occasions :

"В этом последнем обстоятельстве между прочим заключается и причина «несовременности» музыки Рахманинова. Будучи благозвучной, она недостаточно интересна гармонически (в смысле пользуемых в ней звукосочетаний); будучи полнозвучной, она иногда мало подвижна в модуляционном отношении и в смысле."

* I do not vouch for the pertinence of this matter.—J. G.

arrested. If he took his clothes off on the beach and then dived in, naked, even more surely he would be arrested. Everything was a frustration. He walked along the beach, scowling. Well, there were other ways to die.

He would discard the beach and the grey water, they were not worthy of him.

He walked further. He turned northward.

And what was Doris doing, and what was Doris thinking ?

Leon groaned aloud and thought : " Impotent ! "

No more in his mind were carefully articulated poems, and no longer reminiscences of literary Russia. As he forgot even his newly discovered epileptiform delusions, Leon realized somehow that at last in a fashion he had come to grips with life. All his paltry doubts were washed away, and he collided blindly with a Fact. The Fact had beaten him and it was within him. And it suddenly occurred to him what suffering was. Leon discovered as he walked in humiliation that suffering was not pleasant.

" It is an awful think," he worried.

But his more reasonable side thought :

" It is not permanent."

Anyway, it was something furtive and horrible, like dreams by Karamazov. It was the kind of thing which might happen to Aloysha before Aloysha turned to the devil. And there was nothing he could do about it. He must wait and suffer. And he could never see Doris again. He realized that he did really love her when he remembered her " *Please !* "

But that was not the real Doris. That was because she must have been deeply hurt and humiliated too. And what would it do to *her ?* Leon cringed because he saw it must mean for her other men. He held his lips tight and gritted his teeth. He remembered her

amazed scornful eyes and the slope of her shoulder.
He closed his eyes and stumbled northward.

She had asked him to away, and she had uttered the
word " Please " in a way he had never heard it said
before.

Please.

Oh, God !

" Somethink," muttered Leon, " must be done."

He neared his apartment still walking, and then
decided he couldn't go in. He must keep on walking.
He must walk unto death. Death ! Yes. For he didn't
deliberately approach the idea of death in self-pity : it
was simply death had arrived to his mind and enveloped
and clouded and seized his mind. Death. Yes ! He
could not stand this suffering. Death. There were
many ways. He kept on walking.

He thought of Richard suddenly, and his eyes lighted
and he went faster.

Chapter Fourteen

RICHARD WALKS ALONE

i

INTO the silence of the city Richard Northway walked. The city was asleep and the streets empty as they stretched their interminable miles. He reflected that he, too, should be asleep, but it had been necessary to him to get away, to walk alone and try to think. He had slipped away very quietly. A late omnibus whisked him down-town. Sitting high on the bus top he found his way bound by the great silver lamps sliding past his elbow. Before him the street was paused taut between the burning lamps till it dissolved far ahead in the night mist. He ducked a few green branches and felt the swell of the lake curving slowly to the left, with the lights of great hotels defining the sweep of shore. Down-town he disembarked from his bus, cut westward over the silent pavements and when he reached the river began fairly to make progress. Into the silence he walked.

His face, washed yellow in the light of the street lamps, was set and severe.

" I cannot do with," quoted Richard ironically, " and I cannot do without."

They were the words of his friend, Signor Simi, the proprietor of Frascati's, the small Italian restaurant near Rush Street. He was reminded of his friend by an Italian who rose from space and floated with swarthy livid face past him under the yellow lamps. They had had great discussions on Green Chalybeate nights about drink and books and women. Once Signor Simi uttered solemnly in his broken English a hackneyed statement which stuck somehow in Richard's mind.

" I cannot do with," said Signor Simi, with his hands blandly apart, " and I cannot do without ! "

Yes, that was it. That was the trouble with them all. It was the trouble with him. He could not do with Shirley and he could not do without her. She must be sleeping now, with her hair spilt on the pillow and her lashes outlined like little black velvet fans on her cheeks, over her closed eyes. Sleeping ! Richard's lips turned in a slow inward smile. And she was his. Ah, but she was not his ! How could anyone be his if he himself were not his ?

" All my fault," muttered Richard. " All my fault."

He turned off Madison Street into one of the sombre avenues cutting the near west-side along the river into reticulations like a gridiron. They were cruel streets out this way. No trees shone in smaragd green, and little sun managed to penetrate the dark canyons frowning with house-tops. A little boy stood playing in a gutter, a dark little boy of one of the southern races, and Richard watched him seriously groping along the kerb for cigarette butts. Well, that little boy, too, had a problem. They all had problems. Only some were worse. Some were one's own fault.

He padded along the pavement through one grim avenue to a burst of light where workmen were gathered into a knot gesticulating. He slowed down and listened. He had been walking very fast. They were talking about bootleg whisky. Well, here were some people who agreed—just *agreed*—on something without questions or recriminations or explorations or subtleties. He rather envied them. It would be amusing to be able to define all life in the terms of bootleg whisky. Further along the street a woman hovered in a shawl against a doorstep, and Richard felt in a way she was no more an outcast than he.

"It isn't that Shirley is casting me out," he whispered. "I'm casting myself out. I've *got* to cast myself out."

It was necessary to make an emergence.

It was necessary to wipe things clean and start all over again and pull oneself up by the boot-straps a million miles.

It was necessary just to get away.

Richard didn't blame Shirley as these decisions came to his mind. But he knew now they couldn't continue to live together so far as he was concerned. The shadow of the past was too deep upon him. For his own salvation, if ever he could look himself in the eye again, he must emerge. He must see clearly this once or he could never hope to see clearly again. Always he would be bound, always hog-tied, always hamstrung, always the victim of mental malaises and rheums, spiritual distempers. And it was all so ridiculous! So tragically ridiculous! So futile. Who could trace the journey of his mind this last week over these precarious and tortured ways? All he knew was that a difference had come upon them, and not even their physical bond could span that difference. He loved Shirley—yes. But he owed something to himself. That was why he must . . . he could hardly say it to himself . . . must . . . go away.

"Go away," he repeated.

His eyes clouded and he didn't see the row of tawdry shops squatting along Archer Avenue. Ahead of him were lights as this diagonal street cut itself through the shambles behind the stockyards : far ahead, many miles, were rivers and green grass and prairie. But this about him was Chicago, the cruel part of Chicago, the ramshackle miles upon miles of crooked huts sweeping desolately to the bad lands. To the right, against the

o

red glow of the steel mills, he could see the lines of gas tanks, cylinders poised stolidly against the gloom. In the sky he saw flares and a red shudder vibrated across the shadowy heaven.

" Go away," said Richard.

The trouble was he and Shirley were essentially monogamists. He knew that was true of himself and he was sure it was also true of her. They belonged to one another. He knew very well that there could never be anyone else important for him. With others he must be spiritually impotent. And he knew pretty well there could never be anyone else in a creative important sense for Shirley. That was all wrong. It was insanely wrong. But it was so. Richard smiled again, bitterly. They belonged to one another, yes. Shirley herself admitted that. But they belonged to themselves first.

" Go away," repeated Richard.

Still down Archer Avenue till it crossed Halsted Street he walked, feeling the city silent and asleep about him, silent and asleep and . . . tense and . . . waiting. Waiting for another day. Always there was another day. He took a deep breath and decided that the fact of another day was the saving grace in the little mad futilities of life. Except, perhaps, in cases like his own. There another day did not matter much. His days didn't build, they didn't accumulate, because with Shirley somehow one began anew each twenty-four hours : what went before was only vague experience, it was not a pediment, a plinth ; always they began over again, over again. . . .

And it was so *useless*. Just because . . .

Why ?

Oh, he didn't know. He couldn't tell. All he knew was that he must go. If he went, if he ran away from her, then in a peculiar sense the accounts were straightened, the decks cleared, the pendulum in equilibrium. Then in their hearts they could each be easy. She ran away from him : he ran away from her : it was the same. It was the only solution. Since Shirley the other night had pointed out this bogey, this chimera, as the vital fact underlying their troubles and brooding over them, the fact that he could never be easy because she had once left him, ever since Shirley pointed out that fact, he had seen his own escape as the only solution for them both. Yes. And she must see it too. In fact, she hinted at it. Wise Shirley ! She would understand why he, too, must go. (But it was so *silly !*) She would understand. She went away : she came back ; he went away : he came . . .

But he thought that if he did go, he, he, would never come back, never, never. (He hoped so, at least. . . .)

Into the silence of the dark city Richard kept on walking.

ii

It wasn't easy, this business of seeing clearly.

First of all there were so many things to see clearly about.

There was so much that he wanted to know and had to know. Not merely about Shirley. Not merely about love and marriage. That was a large part, but it wasn't all. There was a great deal else. Richard pressed his lips together and began to think of all that rest. After all, he knew, so far as he himself was concerned, the best thing in life was the ceaseless pursuit and satisfaction of an intellectual curiosity. Elementally that was all that counted. To know. To *know* things.

(And afterwards, of course, to *do*, to *do* things.)

That was why he was so profoundly sorry he was not a surgeon, or an architect, or for that matter a master carpenter. They were people in their own spheres who

did know. They had to know. It was their business.
It was their business to take one small plot of knowledge
and cultivate it. Within limits that plot of knowledge
and what it accrued became theirs. They were masters
of something. And he, he was master of nothing, he
was sure of nothing, he knew nothing. That was why he
had turned to chemistry as a finite thing which could be
definitely studied, which stood on factual terms, which
had a bottom and sat on it. Well, if he dropped everything else and first assembled an education and then
worked eighteen hours a day for eighty years, why then,
perhaps at the end he *might* know something—about
chemistry. The science of chemistry itself wasn't
important. The point was to *know*.

Richard turned down a side street where the shambles
of decayed buildings were tumbled to ruin. He was
nearing the stockyards. He was nearing that amazing
city within a city where for miles on miles stretch the
pig-wallows, the cow-pens, the steaming valleys of
blood, the towering dens of killers. He could smell
pungently burnt hide and blood as little puffs of wind
flurried down the alleys. He was far from his own
ground now, far into the maze of the city away from the
river, where huts wallowed in mud for desolate acres,
where living was a stinking gasp from an *abattoir*, where
streets were naked promenades of human misery. It
was all mud and blood and filth and death. The aroma
of death was deeply impressed on these wretched hovels.
He looked at the dark houses brooding in shadow on
the unpaved streets, and wondered how many tragedies
the bare masked windows concealed.

But the point was to *know*.

To know a lot of things and see them clearly and then
assemble from them a satisfaction of the awful curiosities
of life.

(And all the time Shirley asleep on the pillow, her thick

hair dark on the pillow, her eyes shut and her breathing
soft like a child's . . .)

But where could one begin? How could one start?
There were so few verities. There were so few facts.
It was a fact that the square of the hypotenuse of a
right-angled triangle was equal to the sum of the
squares on the other two sides. It was a fact that the
Mauritius issue of 1875 was the rarest of known postage
stamps. It was a fact that $\frac{mm_1}{D^2} = F$. It was a fact that
bubonic plague was caused by the micro-organism,
bacillus pestis. It was a fact that the First Book of
Cæsar begins " Gallia est omnia divisa in partes tres." It
was a fact that the sun shone. It was a fact that the
Battle of Hastings was fought in A.D. 1066, and the Battle
of Mycale in 479 B.C. It was a fact that

$$Na_2CO_3 + Ca(OH)_2 \longrightarrow 2NaOH + CaCO_3.$$

Yes, these were all facts. But good *Lord!*

Even if they were facts they didn't count much.
Richard, however, was interested in them. It was all
part of that curiosity. If only he could get over wanting
to know the *why* and the *how* of things—why the sky
was blue and how para-typhoid differed from alpha-
typhoid, why certain herbivores had three toes and how
the gold points stabilize the sterling exchange, why
the law of conservation of matter acted the way it did
and how Sarouks differed from Kermanshahs and
Khorassans and Oushaks—and so on interminably.
Well, he could answer or begin to answer those
questions. Those were easy ones. But if he ever really
got started!

The trouble was he didn't *know* anything.

Well, no one knew anything.

Look at Jacques Loeb. He started sixty years ago
studying dogs. Year by year he began to study simpler

and simpler and yet simpler things, until at the end, as he died, he was studying colloids, which are not even living things, but finding them of such incalculably complex and mysterious nature that they were not even a beginning. That was a good thing to remember. Yes, look at Jacques Loeb. And look at Martin Arrowsmith.

Richard had progressed through the bad lands now and his footsteps echoed in moody silence. He met very few people. It was very late, and he had been walking a long while. This was a district where people slept at night, slept the sleep of exhaustion. Ate and slept and worked and bore filthy children. Ate and slept and worked and tangled themselves in greasy bestial embraces. Ate and slept and worked and rolled in their own dirty pinguid fat. It was a curious city, Chicago, surely the most cruel and strident of cities, but also in a way the most vivid and vital, the most brawling and dynamic. He was veering away from the yards now and the tang of blood vitiating the air was gone. But far to the left the sky still throbbed with fire from the mills. He looked in that direction almost longingly. It was his city. He loved it. He would always love it.

And now he was leaving it.

(Shirley asleep on the pillow, very quietly breathing, with her face to one side shyly and a red smile curving her lips.)

But about knowing things.

Well, there could always be a start. There must be a start unless his life was to be wasted. He must start soon and he must start alone. If he ever did intend penetrating to the core of things, searching out the realities of existence, there had better be soon a beginning. Reality. That demanded escape. Well, he had made up his mind to escape. He would escape. Queerly, none of this would have happened this way if Shirley hadn't come back. It was she who had jabbed him out of his rut. It was always Shirley.

But there must be a beginning. He must go.

Richard was a little tired now and he walked more slowly.

Oh, but it was all because he was young. It was all a symptomatic restlessness—the restlessness of these hurried changing post-war years, these troubled unstable years. Everyone was feeling it. Only it hit different people different ways. If you were lucky you just got drunk, if you were unlucky you started thinking and then left your wife. If you started thinking, really thinking, it was the end. There was no hope, he thought grimly, for any intelligent and sensitive young man, once he started *thinking*. One might just as well give up. And yet it was the only thing to do.

" Only stupid people are happy," he muttered. " Only dull people."

What was the meaning of it all ?

Just youth. Restlessness. *Weltschmerz.*

Crying aspiration and clouds of iron. Flight without wings and an awful inhibited futility of mind.

Well, the only cure for all that was to get out and get out quick, and get away and try to achieve perspective. That was a good idea, achieve perspective. Not an easy thing to do. Something like seeing clearly. Well, he would do it. Anyway, he would try. He might try in Europe.

Either a hut in the foothills somewhere near the Italian lakes (what was that place Shirley told him about, Cadenabbia near Bellagio ?—always Shirley), or else the British Museum with a million books staggering about you. (Shirley had told him about that too—always Shirley.) Alternate a year of each. Alternate a year of each for ten years or so, and then maybe you might begin. But it was a long grind. Just to get an educa-

tion. To know something about politics and biology
and women's furs and worm-gearing and endocrinology
and economics and Lazarus and the ornithorynchus
paradoxus and the Andromeda nebulæ and Duccio and
Wedgwood china and the Risorgimento and sculpture
(sculpture!) and the anatomy of negation and the
dynamo and The Perfumed Garden and how to get a
shave in Spain and what's the best cigarette in Zanzibar
and the divine right of kings. *Know* something.

Richard laughed a little, still bitterly.

But knowing wasn't all. That was just the beginning.
After you knew a little then perhaps you might begin
to *do* things. That was what counted, in the end. *Doing*
things. Not necessarily finite achievement, not necessarily power (though that would be sweet!), but at least
the consciousness of effort, real effort intelligently
conceived and capably carried out. There was much to
do in this world! Richard was absolutely convinced,
he had a sublime silly personal faith, that there was much
for him to do. Well, it was time to get started. It was
time for him to . . . go.

(And Shirley asleep quietly, perhaps reaching forward
a hand to touch him, perhaps wondering in her sleep
why he would go, why he had gone.)

He saw that he had escaped the lowering tunnel of
26th Street and had reached first Western and then
Kedzie Avenue far out beyond the smoke stacks and
chimneys. Here was a new Chicago. He stood at a
bridge rail and looked over the slow green gloss of the
river, still flowing insanely backwards. But he was many
miles from that other bridge. Here the river was spread
out, seeping over its banks, but on its banks still the
railroad tracks crucified the soil. Far away were visible
the towers of the skyscrapers with fire-escapes zigzagging
up the shiny walls, but here was only tired desolation,
only the smouldering backwash of industry. The very

dust here was weary, and it might easily become angry dust. The river was turgid beneath his feet, swaying its surface scum. There was no real current here, only a listlessness, no real water, only mud. But far away were towers piled in easy strength and far to the left the red glow pulsed from the steel mills. Richard thought of Carl Sandburg's lines, hog butcher of the world and stacker of wheat and player with railroads, and he thought the iron poet was right.

Chicago! Chicago! It was like a drone, a chant.

But it was a cruel city.

iii

"And then," Richard said to himself, "there is the business called love."

What was it, anyway?

He himself had seen it work so many ways. Usually in a restless sort of way.

All of them were restless. Paul and Marjorie were the quick restlessness of adolescent romance, Austin and Mary the restlessness of sophisticated ennui, Agatha the restlessness of suppression, Leon and Doris the restlessness of sex, Phil the restlessness of relentless activity, he and Shirley the restlessness of undisciplined and impotent intelligence and feeling. And all of them lovers. . . .

"Yes," muttered Richard. "Myself and Shirley. We're lovers. We're perfect lovers. We can't do with one another and we can't do without one another. Yes: perfect lovers. And now just because we're both asses and neither of us can see clearly . . . or perhaps we see too clearly . . . I've got to clear out.

"I've got to clear out just to satisfy myself I *can* clear out.

"If I don't clear out, I'll never be worth a damn again as long as I live.

" If I don't clear out, I'm lower than scum, and Shirley won't ever look at me again."

Richard was walking south now with his face still clenched and puzzled and soon he would be out of the city proper, soon he would reach the first suburbs. Already the houses were thinning out, and he was far beyond the bloody miles of hog-pens. There were trees again now, and he felt his last view of the real city had been from the bridge, with its squat gas tanks in the distance and the burnished towers of the skyscrapers. Now he was coming to green grass and the smell of wood smoke and the baying of dogs and prairie, the sweet flatness of prairie. He walked quickly and no longer felt tired.

" But about love," thought Richard.

The nature of reality was part of love, and also seeing clearly, and also facts.

Sometimes love started like the big Rachmaninoff Prelude with booming chords swelling from the strings, throbbing in passionate reverberation. He could remember the music and could see it in his mind : it started like a Coda ; it was a death-chant of love. And sometimes love was thin and piping like For Nobody Knows And Nobody Cares, thin and piping, weak-lunged, knock-kneed, pigeon-chested, bow-legged, emasculated, water-brained, hump-backed, spavined . . . yes, sometimes it was like that.

A green haze was over the open streets and as Richard walked almost in silence he came further out of the sprawling city into the suburbs, further into gardens and pastures and green fields.

" The trouble is," he thought, " I'm too damn decent. I can't take people when I want 'em. Always there is something which says No. That's the trouble with being born a monogamist."

He nodded. He was right there. He and Shirley

were decent people. They were monogamists. They had each other and that was all and that was enough. It was fine in a way.

"Yes, fine," thought Richard. "But . . ." Anyway, finer than playing around like Austin and Doris and the rest. That was so easily dirty. And there was only boredom after a while in dirty things. Finer than being unknowing children, like Paul and poor little Marjorie. Yet he supposed even they must know some whisper of the meaning of love. And finer perhaps than Mary with her fidelity to a shadow in the past . . . yet Mary was a real lover. . . .

"Fine, I suppose," he repeated defiantly. "But . . ."

And then, one always learned first the unimportant things about love. It became easy, after a while, to be "attractive to women" (silly phrase!). He laughed, a little stridently. It was a ludicrously easy thing to do. It was the most painfully, the most excruciatingly easy thing to do. It always worked. There were just three rules, and they were always the same and they always worked.

Chase her half a block and then run like hell for four miles.

Let her catch you and then be tender and masculine by turn, and if necessary chase her a little again and then run like hell for forty miles.

Always take her "No" for a "Yes," always, always.

That was all there was to it, and it was a silly shocking ritual for grown men to bother with. Every woman knew it, and it was time the men came to their senses and called the bluff. But somehow it was part of love. He walked on, shrugging. It irritated him a little. It was so easy. So ludicrous. He kept on shrugging.

But what was *love*?

"One-third glands, one-third nerves, one-third blood-pressure," said Richard first.

No, that was a little cruel.

" One-third myopia, one-third hallucination, one-third aphasia."

No, that was worse.

(And while he walked Shirley was asleep, with her hair spilled on the pillow and the slow curve of her arm gleaming in the soft light, asleep and yet wondering, wondering . . .)

But what *was* it ? Of what elements did it consist ? What was its essential nature ? What caused it and how and when ? What were its controls ? (As the bacteriologists said.) What impulse set it in motion and what stopped it again ? What were the *facts* about love ? What was its ætiology, its case-history, its preventives, its prophylaxis, its stimulants, its irregularities, its prognosis, its diagnosis, its therapeutics, its cure ? What was the *reality* of love ?

He shrugged again. He didn't know. No one knew.

Here was the most important single force in the world, and no one had ever explored it scientifically. No one had ever defined even its primary terms or studied its preliminary assumptions, no one had ever tried to calculate it, to reckon its origins and implications and ramifications, to weigh its sociology or discount its neurology. No one had ever decently *studied* it ! Incredible ! A crazy world ! No one knew anything about its ethics, its logic, its metaphysics, its epistemology, or even its psychology. Nothing *real*, that is. What were the professors doing anyway, with such a subject for a Ph.D. thesis ready and waiting ?

(But about Shirley, now . . .)

Richard thought of Austin's words. Syzygy. His lip curled sardonically.

Well, maybe love *was* just syzygy. The intimately united and apparently fused condition of certain low organisms during conjugation. " Certain low organisms." . . . Ugh ! What talent for words the scientist-fellows had ! . . .

But syzygy meant lots of other things. Coming from the Greek συξυγιά, it meant primarily "yoke." In astronomy it meant the point of an orbit, as of the moon, when in conjunction or opposition. In mathematics it meant a linear equation between fundamental co-variants of a quantic, or in some cases any linear function of a set of variables. In prosody it meant a group of two coupled feet, denoting a tonic coupled foot like the ionic. In zoology it was the immovable union and practical concrescence of two joints of an arm of a crinoid to form a single segment. . . .

Well, well. Syzygy. A yoke.

And life was like that, too, sometimes. Not only love, but life was a syzygy.

(The intimately united and apparently fused condition of certain low organisms . . .)

Oh, forget such nonsense.

But granted that love was comprised to some degree of glands and nerves and blood-pressure, there were other ingredients. Not less important were the ingredients omitted. There were so many things love didn't recognize. Very often it didn't recognize good looks or brains or success or money or beauty or even character. Often. Very often. Very often indeed.

There were few married people, few lovers, who could muster between them much of good looks or brains or success or money or beauty or even character. And yet they *had* become lovers. And yet they *had* married. The great illusion had been at work. The great illusion had worked. It was all so unaccountable, so unreasonable. What *did* make people fall in love ? *Why ?*

"What we need," said Richard, "is celestial ecto-genesis."

He laughed bitterly. That was a good idea. Test-tubes and retorts. Bunsen burners and Erlenmeyer flasks :

$$\text{Male } x + \text{Female } y \longrightarrow$$

He didn't finish the equation. He kept on walking.

(But Shirley, Shirley . . .)

Think of all the married people who always had been married, who were inevitably married. One could fancy no other husband in the world picking that particular wife, no other wife picking that particular husband. ("Why do I always keep running to the idea of marriage?" thought Richard.) Yet the mysteriously endowed two did find one another. They were endowed with faculties of attraction only they themselves could find. They met and they loved. It was like the marching of the stars. It was as ineluctable as the sunrise. It was ordained by God.

"Anyway," muttered Richard confidentially to himself, "any woman can marry any man, all things being equal, any woman can marry any man if she really sets out to do it. Man runs the race, but he runs it looking backward."

He scowled.

"But if the woman does marry the man under such considerations, she's likely to make them both damn miserably unhappy afterwards."

And why, wondered Richard, did brilliant husbands almost invariably marry dull wives, and brilliant wives marry dull husbands? What did they see in one another? Why did all the lovely girls he knew, girls intelligent and high-spirited and high-hearted, with a zest for life and a courage to meet it, have for a little while their little day, have for a while their little flurried triumphs . . . and then marry dullards, then marry sapheads? Dullards who weren't even physically attractive, sapheads who weren't even *sensitive*. Nice fellows and all that, but

. . .! Why did girls like . . . oh, he could think of a dozen . . . to marry men who came home every night and gobbled dinner and smacked their lips and read the paper and went to the bathroom and took off their coats and turned on the radio? But *why*?

Love.

" No," said Richard in horror. " Not love. Inertia."

Love.

" The funny thing is," he admitted, " it seems the lovely brilliant girls who can fall in love with dullards as well as with people with brains and looks."

(And Shirley, Shirley . . .)

He mused.

Love.

" Maybe they don't think they're dullards. Maybe only I see them as dullards."

Richard grinned, almost the first whole-hearted grin of that walk, and he walked on. There was no doubt he was tired. There was no doubt, too, that his brain was tiring. He wasn't thinking nearly as clearly as he had two hours before. Well, keep it up another mile or so, anyway. He was feeling happier in this country air. His shoulders were high, and he breathed deeply. The city showed behind him as a smudge of smoke. The fields were clear now like bracken. They were like pictures by those early impressionists who first began to break up light, Renoir and Sisley in 1885.

" Anyway," he thought, " there's only one recipe for a happy marriage. Don't marry anyone till she can make you tingle all over by moving a little finger four feet away."

Love.

He *was* tired: it was getting light now and he had been walking anyway four hours.

(And Shirley sleeping, sleeping as dawn came to the city, sleeping with her fist to her chin and her black hair splashed over the pillow, as dawn came to the city, breaking like some wild thing over the hills.)

Richard's lips moved together, but he still walked.

Shirley, Shirley . . .

Love.

iv

It was light now and Richard was weary. He had been walking since eleven o'clock, and the distance must be close to twenty miles. He was out of the near western suburbs, and by cutting through a field he reached an avenue of trees near a branch of the river. It was the Des Plaines River though, he had passed beyond his own river. He felt no temptation to sit down or rest, and still an implacable impulse kept him walking. Perhaps if he had walked long enough he might reach really open country. (Prairie!) Between the rows of trees the light was dim, and the stars low in the sky were patterned between crossing branches. The footing was insecure and several times he slipped, tripping into a gulley and muddying his shoes. Floundering out of the mud and regaining the path, he walked along the edge of a gulley between the trees. He listened to the rustle of wet leaves underfoot and saw an obscure aperture of light beckoning at the end of the valley.

Love.

And that wasn't all, either. That, too, was only a beginning. (Everything was only a beginning.) There was the business of life itself.

A crazy, crooked business. So much a searching without a finding, so much an unreasonable frustration. Like a boat on choppy seas without a rudder. Like a light for ever concealed behind clouds. Like Tantalus and the shining fruits beyond him.

Oh, but it was too easy, it didn't mean anything to mutter such black similes.

He might be Leon. Poor Leon! What was happening to Leon, anyway?

Forget these juvenile miasmas.

His face eased as he plodded through the dank leaves and felt the tree-trunks as he passed. Dawn had come now and the open fields would be lucent. But here under the trees it was somnolent and brooding. He slipped through the difficult footing and saw suddenly approaching him a man. The man looked like a tramp. He asked for a match in an unsteady voice, and Richard gave him one. Richard held the light and the tramp ignited a cheap cigarette. They hardly uttered a word, but when Richard impatiently started to walk on again, the man turned and, without speech, accompanied him. They walked side by side, floundering through the little valley of trees, Richard shrugging his shoulders slightly; he didn't want company. The tramp appeared to walk more unsteadily than the evil footing demanded, and Richard turned to observe him more closely and discovered he was drunk. The man staggered a little and lurched through the dead leaves, and as they walked still without speech Richard took his arm firmly to steady him.

Love. Life.

What was it, anyway, he did want to see clearly?

Everything.

That was the trouble. That made it hard.

And Shirley, Shirley . . .

Richard was in such a stupor of bodily fatigue that his mind was blurring. It seemed to him as he plodded through the leaves with the man on his arm that his brain had never been quite so muddled. He was lucid enough to recognize blackness in the muddle, but not to disentangle it from the blackness which was no part of his muddle, but with which he stupidly tried to enmesh it. It was all cloudy now, and his brain felt on fire, fruitlessly, as his feet swung slowly through the

P

dark slippery avenue of leaves. Life was a sort of
Augean stable, never cleansed, always choked with dead
leaves, slippery avenues of leaves.

The stranger beside him was still silent and had
thrown away his cigarette. Richard turned to offer him
another and discovered to his amazement that the man's
face was flooded with tears. His face was laved with
silent tears. Richard stopped: and then because
there seemed no real reason for stopping, he shrugged
slightly and went on walking, firmly guiding the man's
drunken footsteps. The stranger looked at him once
or twice, but his eyes were masked by the tears. Richard
was impatient and puzzled, but he maintained silence.
They were walking now through a veritable tunnel of
dusk, and the trees arched overhead to caress with their
branches. It seemed to grow darker and Richard felt
his mind grow dark also. His legs were weary, and he
was surprised to discover himself laughing. The man
with tears still pooling his eyes turned to him sharply.
He thought Richard was laughing at him. They walked
in constrained silence then, and when they finally emerged
from the little wood at the archway of light Richard
discovered that he too very slightly was crying. " Drunk? "
questioned the stranger dimly. " Yes," answered Richard,
" very drunk." The man turned then and released his
arm. He turned about and re-entered the slumbering
wood, and Richard looked over his shoulder to see him
disappear into the gloom.

Richard paused to look after him uncertainly. Then
he strode on.

What would Mr. Stern say when he left, when he said
he was going: doubtless Mr. Stern would mutter
something about the Shogunates of Ashihaga. What
would Agatha say? What would Phil and Leon and
Mary say? Well, it didn't matter. He couldn't help
what they would say. They didn't count.

Shirley would know.

She would know that he went because she once went : that he went because his insane predisposition to balance made him desire settling the accounts, washing the slate clean. She would know it was the only way. She would think he would come back. Also she would think somewhat of his pride . . .

Richard laughed harshly.

He discovered with the jangled laughter he was stupid with mental pressure and bodily fatigue. He turned across another field toward a road and reached the road. There was a ditch to surmount and he found himself almost incapable of surmounting it. He dragged himself across it wearily and climbed to the high-crowned road, falling to his knees once. " If I were the hero of an autobiographical novel," he said to himself, laughing bitterly, " doubtless having discovered life is a blank wall, having discovered I know myself but that is all, having penetrated this emotional cul-de-sac, I suppose I should re-enter that field now and roll like an animal in the dew." He laughed harshly again and turned resolutely but unsteadily along the road. The dawn was full now and market wagons were parading the road toward town. One offered him a lift, but he shook his head, declining it. He walked.

(Shirley awake, yawning with her white teeth showing, yawning widely and lifting the lashes like little black velvet fans, Shirley awake, Shirley looking for Richard, and wondering, wondering . . .)

" Oh *God !* " he cried passionately.

Why had she come back, anyway ? Damn her, *damn* her !

Stumbling a little and with his legs trembling, he found himself nearing a village. The quiet of the village was amazing. It was clean with manicured doorsteps and everyone was still asleep. The village breathed rhythmically like a person in its sleep. Richard walked to the railway station wearily and then decided instead to take a taxi and drive back to the city.

That stranger? Was he a hallucination? Was it all a hallucination? Had he really been walking these many miles? Was he really going to leave Shirley?

He twisted his head nervously and laughed a little again.

The stranger. A funny business. The stranger had felt community and he himself had felt it also. That business of community could be a funny thing.

Yes, they were both drunk, only Richard was drunk on a more dangerous intoxicant than alcohol.

Yes, it was a relief to be convinced of the essential meaninglessness of life, because then nothing mattered, nothing mattered at all.

Like Cronshaw's carpet. The Persian carpet. That was a good idea and a good book!

Richard re-entered the village street. Well, he could get a taxi at the garage here and drive back to the city. The village was on something of a hill, and he could see beneath him in the distance the smouldering wedge of smoke which was Chicago, sprawled along the lake front for thirty miles. The dawn was full, and a pallid sun was clear-cut in the pink horizon over the lake. The sun hung there like a brittle pearl set in the pink clouds. Richard watched it with lips tight and laughed once more. He must stop this silly laughing! The sky was ribboned with colour, and far to the east he could still see red puffs of flame from the steel mills throbbing and shuddering over the cold sky.

v

It was all clear now.
He must go.

In the taxi the revivifying wind awoke his brain and sharpened again his senses. As the machine slipped over the roads through the Sag Valley, through Beverly, through Palos Park, through Summit, through Argo, where the great corn-products plant stood behind barbed wire like a fortress, through Naperville and Cicero, as the machine wound past the first link of river and over the crest of Ashbourne and into the city again, Richard saw indeed that this strange night had not been in vain, that indeed he knew his will.

It was still very early and only a few knots of traffic impeded his car across the boulevards. He was in Chicago now ; he entered it like a cloud : he was deep in smoke and wind and dirt, deep in a typhoon-city always dimmed from external view, always swirling within itself, menacingly, mercilessly. The tang of the blood-pens near the yards came to him as he whisked through the decayed flat-lands. He passed the region of gas tanks and grain elevators and windowed factories, and came again to his own ground, the parks splayed in green and the tall tower-buildings near the lake. He sat back as he watched the car stretch out to rustle north along the boulevards. Chicago !

Shirley would understand.

Only he was *not* coming back. (That is . . .)

Love. Shirley. Shirley . . .

Across the shoulder of the city Richard progressed, and then cut over the haunch of Lincoln Park. He was near his own neighbourhood now. It was about seven o'clock and the city was stirring. In an hour it would discharge its floods, and the great daily redistribution of population would brusquely begin. Then the crowded trains and the shrieking cars. Then the noise and push and smoke ! And also in a way the impressive beauty of great strength in mighty and deliberate progression. In an hour now. The car turned off Sheridan

Road and bumped to a halt before the Bryn Mawr flat.

Richard got out and mechanically paid the chauffeur. He entered the apartment. He opened the door and climbed the stairs. He saw it was seven-fifteen, and he was very tired.

Chapter Fifteen

SHIRLEY ASLEEP

AND while Richard was walking through the westward streets to open country, Shirley indeed slept peacefully with her lips slightly apart and her breathing slow. But toward morning she stirred in bed and discovered Richard was not there. She awoke and first stroked her chin in the dim light, as her puzzled eyes concentrated to accept this absence. Then she sank back slowly and listened to her heart beat, listened to her heart increase its tempo till she could feel it like a pulse.

She pursed her lips. Upright then in bed, she switched on the light and blinked before the dazing glow. She sat there, her hand still to her chin in the old puzzled childlike gesture, and then smiled. She smiled, but still her heart beat disconcertingly. A quick survey showed her Richard had packed nothing. She sensed then what he was doing. A long walk perhaps in the darkness, a long fatiguing walk till his heart was washed clear of trouble.

Shirley slipped back to the pillow. She thought:

" It would be a strange thing if I should go out now and Richard found the flat empty in the morning."

Hmmmm.

" That would be a queer discovery for Richard, because it's about leaving *me* he's thinking."

Her smile paused. What a sensation it would be! It might shock him into clarity and their situation to resolution. Still, it was something she could never do. It was a trick. That was the sort of thing she must do genuinely or not at all. No, he must come home, must come home and find her quietly asleep. That was the best way. He mustn't even know she missed him, until first he should tell her of his walk.

" The pity of it," she thought, " is that he has to hurt himself so much to hurt me."

It was, she thought, a sort of spiritual masochism. It was necessary to lacerate himself because Shirley must be lacerated first. And it was all so silly. Could anyone trace the queer working of Richard's mind which prompted him to his choice ? He had chosen by this time, she was sure. She looked at the peeping green of the trees, bursting through the dawn just outside the window, and she knew he had chosen. And she thought she knew which way. It was too bad.

She shrugged.

He was a fool. She was a fool. They were both fools.

She shrugged again, and then smiled and murmured to herself :

" The funny thing is, Richard is really a *splendid* sort of person somehow."

(And at the time he was saying :

" The funny thing is, Shirley is such a *dear*—such a superior and *splendid* dear.")

Shirley turned off the light and made brave to discard the business from her mind. She was somehow above it. She couldn't help Richard : he had this fight for himself, and it was only a pity he had to be hurt making it. It was always a pity to hurt people. But somehow she felt she wasn't immediately or personally concerned : she would acquiesce however it came out. Elementally it didn't matter. Nothing mattered. It was all futile. Whatever happened, she was always Shirley, always herself.

And she, too, had work to do.

But it was a change to be alone in that big bed and rather lonely in heart. . . .

Hmmmm.

She dropped off to sleep soon enough, but it took a little longer than usual, because for so many moments her heart kept up that ridiculous thump-thump, so that she felt it alive and palpable within her, pulsing echoes throughout the dim and sleepy room.

Chapter Sixteen

RICHARD AND LEON

i

THE door-bell rang and Shirley paused over her egg. Richard, too, was eating. In a reaction from fatigue he had been talking excitedly the last half-hour, talking excitedly and laughing a good deal and pacing up and down the room. He was very sleepy. She made him eat breakfast and then hoped he would go to bed. She was worried a little at his face. She was worried because he was taut and a little strident, with his eyes queer. When the door-bell kept ringing she picked up her napkin impatiently.

"Postman," said Richard.

It was about eight-thirty, the time when the first mail usually came.

"I don't think so," said Shirley. "Different ring."

He felt that no one important could be ringing at that hour of the morning and he kept on eating; when she went to the door, opened it, and admitted Leon, he was considerably surprised.

"Sit down," said Shirley, "and I'll cook you an egg. Poached or fried?"

"Neither," said Leon. "Richard, I want to talk to you."

Now Leon, whatever his faults, which were mostly the faults of sensitive youth, was not often rude, and she turned to him a little concerned. His face was pale. His fingers were twitching, and he talked somewhat breathlessly, as if in stress of emotional fatigue.

"Of course," said Richard, after watching him; "just wait a moment and I'll be with you."

Shirley didn't like people to be rude to her, and she was a little nettled. But she looked at Leon again and said gently :

"Do have an egg or toast or something. Sit down. And you might, Leon, take off your hat. It's a dreadful hat, anyway. Here——" and she handed over some cereal.

Leon tried to eat, but it wasn't much of a go. He was bent over the plate and the table was silent. Shirley finished, lit a cigarette and retreated to her own room. Richard waited. He looked at Leon and saw his face very white over the plate. He wondered if any muddle in Leon's brain could match the muddle in his own.

Leon, too, was silent a long time.

"Let us," he pronounced finally, "go into your laboratory. There is somethink I must tell you and somethink you must do for me. Come."

Richard rose and walked with Leon out to the garage. He fitted the key to the door and reflected it had been a week at least since he had done any work within. Dust was sprayed over the tables and an old precipitate of aluminium hydroxide was gummed and yellow in a tube. He opened a window to dissipate the faint tang of acid, and turned to see Leon staring at him.

"Now," said Richard, "what is it ? "

ii

Leon told him.

"Well," said Richard, after something of a pause, "that's nothing to worry about."

Leon just looked at him.

"Of course it isn't," Richard went on. "Just what they call brantigam impotenz."

Leon continued, haggard, to look at him.

"It's just a symptom, Leon," proceeded Richard bravely. "Just a symptom, not a complaint."

There was a long pause again and Richard reflected uncomfortably he couldn't imagine a more painful thing to have to talk about.

"No," finally said Leon, "it is all very much deeper and more important than that. Don't lie to me, Richard. It is somethink very deep in me, and I suppose it must be broken down."

"Nons . . ." said Richard. "Yes."

"And . . ."

"What," broke in Richard, "do you want me to do ?"

"There is only one think for me you can do."

Then he looked away, and Richard saw his lips come together.

Poor Leon ! Richard found it difficult to focus his mind, but he saw it was just the sort of thing that would happen to Leon of all people in the world, to Leon more acutely and passionately than to anyone else. What a climax for his love-affair ! It was so ridiculously hard to be consoling or to give advice just because the situation itself was so ridiculous, if also pathetic. And what could he do ?

"There is only one thing," said Leon again.

Richard saw it was a shock to think concentratedly on one problem for ten hours, and then find a new one hurled at him. In a daze of fatigue he tried to force his mind to Leon. And such a problem ! Then he happened to think he might cure Leon's major trouble by giving him a minor one to worry about. That often worked. But it was risky. Still, the situation was dangerous, and merited dangerous remedies. He thought of Shirley's "You never forgive a person after you do him an injury," and hesitated : then he looked at Leon's grey face and said slowly :

" Did you know, Leon, that Doris has been seeing
Jack—Shirley's brother, Jack Bowdoin ?   I wondered
if you knew, and I wanted to tell you.   If it bothered
you it need bother you no longer.   Because I have seen
Jack and he won't see Doris any more."

Richard spoke very quietly and persuasively.

" I knew all about that," said Leon, " from the
beginnink."

That was a lie.   Richard looked at him sharply and
decided it was a lie.   In fact, since the night of Mary's
party Leon had never heard Doris refer again to her
anonymous cavalier.   Richard pursed his lips.   Pride.
It was a strange thing, the pride of young Jews who
suffer and pretend they're not suffering.

As for Leon, he felt little shock as Richard told him ;
it didn't matter, only larger things mattered now.

He saw still in the tubes some of the colours Richard
had made for him the other day.   Chrome, magenta,
puce, ivory, Afghan green, sage, bitter-sweet, scarlet
. . . But he was beyond all that now.   He was looking
at the KCN bottle and thinking of the odour of peach
kernels.

" You see," Leon said, " I have been trying to learn
how to suffer.   Think !   It was only ten days—only a
week—since we first talked about sufferink, you and I,
Richard.   And I fear I have learned much about sufferink
in those ten days."

" Yes," said Richard again, and felt an unsympathetic
pity.   Why was it the troubles of someone else were
somehow always a little unreal and grotesque ?   But
what to *do* with the boy ?

" The philosophy of sufferink," muttered Leon slowly,
" is something I fear I do not understand.   I thought
sufferink would be chastening.   But now I find it is not
that at all.   It is something deeper.   Yet what can I
do ?   Well, there is only one thing now I can do."

Richard was thinking : " I am an unsympathetic pig. My mind is not with Leon at all."

Leon had arisen and was walking to a shelf in the laboratory. Now Richard did turn sharply, and suddenly he saw what it was the boy wanted. He was amazed first and then shocked. Good Lord ! Of course ! Oh, but it was *pitiful !*

" And," Leon was saying, " I want you to help me."

" How ? " asked Richard.

He knew very well now what Leon wanted, and his mouth choked a little. He found it difficult to articulate the monosyllable.

" How ? " he repeated.

" I want you," said Leon, turning full and clear on him, with his eyes glittering, " I want you to give me poison. *Poison !* "

iii

" Nonsense," said Richard sharply.

But somehow he knew that it was not nonsense, not nonsense at all.

Leon's lips turned in a slow and painful smile.

" You are my friend," he said quietly. " You are my only friend, and yet I come to you with a think like this happened and you say ' Nonsense.' " He paused. " Well, well."

" Don't be an ass," Richard went on, his voice still sharp. " You're mad, Leon, mad to think of such a thing. Go home and get some sleep."

" It is true," said Leon meditatively, " that last night I had but little sleep."

" I didn't sleep at all. I walked all night. You're not the only one with troubles. Good Lord, *you* have nothing to worry about. I tell you nothing is wrong with you, it's nothing to get sick or excited over. Go home and sleep it off. Don't bother me with such

insane nonsense. Run home, I tell you ; run home and
forget it, forget it, sleep it off."

Richard was insistent and in his voice was a note of
unaccustomed clamour. He was talking insistently
because in the haze of his mind he hardly knew what he
was saying. How his eyelids wanted to droop ! He wasn't
thinking of Leon—confound Leon—he was thinking of
tragedy and himself and Shirley. Over and over again
in his heart rolled with savage vehemence his decision
to go.

" Don't be a fool," he said bitterly.

Leon was very silent and was sitting down again.
A pool of sunlight was silvering the floor. Leon drew
his shoe along the pattern in the linoleum and reflected
that sunlight was good for life. It was not good for
him. He had learned how to suffer, and suffering was
too much for him. He was going to die. He withdrew
his toe and then tapped it on the floor once or twice
hard. And then, of course, death was such a beautiful
thing.

" I want you," he repeated in a stony whisper, " to
give me poison."

" You're mad. Don't be a fool."

" Of course I'm mad. All of us are mad. What has
that to do with it ? I want to die, and I want you to
give me poison, because you are my only friend. I
want to *die*."

" You're mad."

Leon tossed the hair from his forehead.

" Really, Richard, now it is you who are being stupid.
You are tired and you are findink it hard to think. But
that is no excuse. Come. I have asked you a favour.
Answer it."

Richard reflected that he had never known Leon
before to be so positive, so assertive. It appeared that
the shadow of death strengthened and encouraged

him.   Then Richard was suddenly scared.   His mind
sharpened a little.   So tired his chin was falling on
his chest, he yet managed to see suddenly, it dawned
on him startlingly, that Leon meant it, that Leon
did mean to kill himself, that Leon *would* kill himself . . .

He leaned back shocked.   Then he began to talk, to
talk fast.

"Listen," he turned close to Leon and drummed on
Leon's bony knee with a finger.   "Listen."   He pushed
the finger upward till it wavered before Leon's nose.
"Listen.   I wish to tell you something.   You are
bluffing.   Do you understand ?   I look at you now and
say flatly that you are bluffing.   You are a coward !
You are afraid to die ! "

Richard talked burningly, and Leon withdrew in
dignity before the truculent finger.   Richard had
an idea now.   It was a risk and a slim chance, but
the only one.   Good Lord, he had to *save* this
boy !

"Nonsense," it was Leon's turn to say.

Richard brushed aside the remark.   Yes, his idea was
the only one.   He leaned forward :

"I repeat," he went on more slowly, thinking for
words, "I repeat that you are a bluffer and a coward
and afraid to die.   Listen.   I will give you poison.   I
will give you the bottle, you can take the bottle, the
whole damn bottle, and you will be afraid to eat a morsel ;
you will keep it in your pocket and be *afraid* to eat a
morsel—because you are a bluffer and a coward and
afraid to die ! "

Richard paused and discovered himself standing high
over Leon.   He was excited by his idea now ; it was
more than an idea, it was a salvation.   His voice was
tense but clear, as he realized more certainly he had
a life to save.   He hadn't realized that first.   But now

he was convinced that Leon did really mean to kill himself. And he must work fast. His brain was far ahead of his speech, and he must control himself and *convince* the boy.

" I do not," said Leon finally, " quite understand."

" Of course you don't," Richard rapped out carefully. " That is because you are not only a coward and a bluffer and afraid to die, but also in addition you are very stupid. You are stupid ! In short, Leon, you are a fool. But I will explain to you, because in addition to all these things, you are another thing—you are my friend. Listen. *Listen,* do you hear ? I will explain in words of one syllable. I will give you this KCN, this white crystalline potassium cyanide which looks so much like peppermint candy. I will give you the whole bottle. But you will *not* swallow it. You understand ! You will *not* swallow a bit of it. You will take it home with you and you will keep it in your pocket, and you will not *touch* it."

Leon looked at him in blank amazement.

" I put it squarely up to you," Richard went on, with slow clarity. " I do what you ask. I give you the poison."

Richard forgot his weariness. He shook his head violently as if to dash sleep from his eyes, because now of all times he must not be weary. This was a battle of wills pure and simple, and his will must be the stronger. It was becoming a fight.

(But Shirley, Shirley . . .)

" I put it squarely up to you," he proceeded slowly, taking breath in his tired excitement ; " I do this because of two things. First, because you are a coward. You will not swallow the poison, because if you do *it will prove you a coward :* and then you will die and never be able to prove to me, your friend, that you are not a coward." Richard paused. He was leaning over Leon's

Q

face with the finger still pointing. " I want you to see that very clearly. I say that you are a bluffer and a coward. Now it is up to you to deny that, to prove me wrong. Now, Leon, it is a poor thing to be a bluffer and a coward. And you have pride." He paused again : he was deeply moved now : he had posited an intellectual problem with a human life at stake. " All this is one reason why I will give you this poison. I give it to you because it is necessary for you to prove yourself. It is very necessary. This is a real crisis for you, Leon. You must forget all about your silly sufferings. It is time to cast all that behind you and be something of a man. You must learn to live and write and create, but live, *live* first of all. Therefore—*because* you must live—I give you this poison. I give it to you so that you will have a *real* struggle and so that you can win that struggle. You see, I am putting a high stake in the scales. You must win for that reason also. You must keep that poison in your pocket until you have beaten yourself and can return it untouched to me with easy mind. Until you can return it to me laughing. Then you will have won. You will not be a coward then and not a bluffer, and you will never again be afraid of death. You will have conquered death and conquered yourself and made yourself your own master." Richard was in a passion of excitement : he took the boy's shoulders and shook him, pleading with him. " It is your only chance and it is an uncertain chance. You must fight it out yourself. You must have the means of death at hand and you must *not* die."

Richard was done now and he sank back. " Do you see," he whispered, " do you *see* ? "

Leon watched him, impressed and amazed at his fervour.

" I want you to see it yourself," repeated Richard. " You must see it your*self*."

Leon nodded slowly. Richard leaned back and felt exhausted. Leon kept on nodding.

Then, thought Richard, he had won. But it was all a muddle. In reaction he thought : " Perhaps Leon ought to die." Why not ? Why not let a man die if he wanted to ?

But it was a problem and an exciting one. He was moulding Leon with his bare hands. He was putting forward a narrow path before him and inviting him to walk, while to either side the slightest misstep was death. " Do you *see* ? " he repeated in exhilaration, almost in wonder at himself.

" Perhaps," thought Leon quickly to himself, " it is Richard who is mad."

And Richard was thinking :

" All this is madness. Leon is mad and I am mad. This is all a dream, a nightmare. All last night was a dream. I never took that walk. All this week is a dream. Shirley has not returned. Leon is mad and Shirley is mad and I am mad most of all. We are all phantoms dreaming, and all this is a mad dream."

On the shelf the bottle of white cyanide was twinkling in the sun.

It was mad. He was *dreaming*.

But he tossed his head almost violently and found himself awake. And he felt he had taken the only way. If he had tried any other tack he would have failed. Remonstrance would have failed with Leon, and also savage rebuke and also pity. Also would have failed dismally any flat refusal. Leon would have simply walked to the nearest drug store and bought strychnine. He was saving a life, and he had chosen the only way. The only way was to take Leon's mind in his hand and mould it. By giving him an intellectual equation to ponder over, he had taken the matter from the realm of heart and soul and put it into mathematics ; he had interested him in the philosophical and metaphysical implications of his decision and so made him forget the decision itself.

" Do you *see?* " he asked Leon again : and Leon nodded. Yes, he had taken the only way. He had won . . . if Leon's mind would work that way. But it was a terrific chance to have taken. . . .

All this time Leon had been silent, and all this time, too, Richard kept staring at him like a hypnotist. Leon's lips trembled and sagged a little. Richard felt something of the exultation of an evangelist. He was doing more than save a soul, he was saving a life. By will power. He clenched his fists in a sort of ecstacy and struck Leon violently on the cheek. Leon whimpered. Richard leaned over and took him in his arms. He embraced him and then said :

" But I mentioned another reason. You will recall I mentioned another reason." Richard spoke very quietly and persuasively, the words barely dripping from his mouth, but he was still staring at Leon's drooping eyes like a mesmerist. " It is not a good reason, but I must voice it. It is that I am your friend. And if you killed yourself now, Leon, it is I who would be your murderer. That would not be a good thing. It would be a very awful thing. I would be your murderer. It is not a good thing to think of that."

Richard paused and took breath, and felt a tremendous exhaustion sap him. He rose, hardly steadily, and reached for the poison, thrust it into Leon's hand.

The only way . . .

(But Shirley, Shirley . . .)

" And must I take it with me ? " whispered Leon.

" Yes. Yes ! "

" And I must not swallow any ? "

Leon barely muttered the words, and his face was hanging.

"Yes," whispered Richard. "Yes!"

Richard was quivering with fatigue and relief and Leon seemed barely able to stand. He rose and put both Leon's hands on the bottle. Leon in dull mechanical acquiescence put the bottle into his pocket. Richard steadied him and they stumbled over the pool of sunlight toward the door.

"Go now!" said Richard.

"Yes," whispered Leon.

"Go now," repeated Richard, his voice rising. "And remember you're a bluffer and a coward and afraid to die! Remember all I have told you. Remember if you do take that poison then you *are* a bluffer and a coward and afraid to die, and you can never come to me laughing and say you have conquered and proved yourself. Remember that you must win this great fight and remain my friend and prove yourself by not dying unafraid of death."

"Yes," whispered Leon.

He walked limply off, and Richard saw him turn stumbling down the street.

Richard felt a mortal tiredness surge over him and he went back to the apartment with his mind washed clean and empty. But he felt a prophet. He was happy. He had won.

iv

Shirley was waiting for him, just a little anxiously.

"What did Leon want?" she asked.

"Nothing," said Richard abruptly.

He was too tired, too tired . . .

Shirley pursed her lips and was about to repeat quizzically "Nothing?" when she reflected Richard had better sleep. Whatever he had said to Leon, evidently it had exhausted him. Look at Richard! He was tottering.

"I think," he was saying, with a slow painful smile, "that it's almost time . . . I went to bed."

"Dear!"

He groped for her and kissed her with tears standing a little in his eyes.

"Yes," droned Richard, "I think, maybe, I ought to go to bed now."

His smile was faint and warped and Shirley felt an intolerable ache in her heart that she couldn't help him win this his own battle, that he must fight it and win it himself.

He stumbled toward bed, and as he mechanically undressed ("Oh, damn this shoe!") he thought of Leon again, and his heart chilled. What a fearful chance to have taken! But it was the only way. Otherwise he knew surely as fate Leon would have killed himself somehow. Perhaps shot himself. He had been Leon's last chance. The only way.

But . . .

Murderer.

The only way . . .

Murderer.

"Oh," said Richard aloud passionately. "*Oh!*"

Shirley was listening outside the room, and his cry turned her sick and weary.

"My dear," she called, "*do* sleep now. Forget all about it. *Do* sleep."

"All right."

He drew the shades and to hearten Shirley tried to chuckle, and the sound brought her hand to her breast. He slipped into bed and his eyelids sank weighted. He breathed once, deeply. She walked to the window fronting the street, and looked out a long time. She sighed. . . .

As Richard fell into dead limp slumber his brain kept whispering to him, teasing him horribly:

" I shall forget her. Please God I shall forget her."

Over the room rug the placid sun dripped pools of amber light.

Chapter Seventeen

DORIS

i

DORIS BARRON, too, had reached some sort of climax, some sort of full stop. In the room near the river she stood and surveyed a heap of bags and boxes. She was moving. She was leaving the little flat near the river. She was going home.

She had decided quite reasonedly to return to her father in his great empty house on the south side, on one of the little streets flanking the University campus. She had had a month of freedom now, and it was beginning to bore her. Her father would understand. He was a wise man. When she left him, saying she wanted to live by herself for a while, just by herself, in the same city, and still a student at school, still in touch with home but by herself, he had only smiled slightly, this absent-minded heavy-browed geologist, and told her to go her own way, to take care of herself and to go her way. Dr. Barron wasn't too deeply interested in his daughter. At that time he was engaged in research in crystallography, and was interested in the fact that microscopic air bubbles in artificial gems apparently were always cubical. His wife was dead. Doris had never known her mother.

And now she was going home . . .

" Bother ! " she said.

She wondered if she would have been a different sort of person if her name had been Dora, say, rather than Doris. Or Dorine, or Dorinda. Or even Dorothy. What a queer difference it made, just this difference in names ! Doris was a pretty hard name to live up to.

Still, how awful to be named Dora! But names were
funny. The Dorothys had an easier time of it. And
think of the difference between Elizabeth and Lizzie
and Betty and Bess. Between Lucy and Lucienne. Or
between Suzanne and Susan.

She looked bitterly over her piles of books and clothes
and papers and miscellaneous luggage.

It was all over now. Done.

She was going to be a nice little girl, now, a nice
little girl with sleek golden hair and innocent lips.

" Bother ! " she said again.

The trouble was she had tried it alone. No wonder
she had been eager for . . . company. If she had had
a girl for friend, now . . . a girl like . . . well, even
one like Shirley. Shirley was a pretty good sort, even if
her brother was such a vulgar little ass. Doris had no
regrets for Jack. Yes, someone like Shirley would have
been good. (Only Shirley didn't like her.) Or Mary . . .

Men were fools. Men were boasters.

She closed the yawning trunk and with effort buckled
a strap over it. It was nearly done now. She had better
ring for a taxi. All over, all over. Her father again :
the old silent man who looked at his daughter absently
once in a while and asked if she had had enough for
dinner. She wondered if she would like him if she knew
him better. Some people did. He was a famous man.
She wondered what he would say if he knew about
her recent adventures. Heavens !

What a bore life was !

" Bother ! " said Doris a third time.

ii

Her thoughts drifted to Leon. Her lips compressed,
and she tried to dismiss him from her mind.

It had been Leon who had caused the collapse of her

little scheme. It was because of him she was going home.
She would never see Leon again.

If Doris had been in love with him it might have been
very terrible for her. Probably she would have had no
recourse but to get a man, some man, any man. It would
have been a simple physical necessity. But because she
didn't love Leon she didn't feel that necessity. In fact,
with Leon had come an immense revulsion toward all
that sort of thing. Doris bit her lip and scowled. It was
a revulsion. No doubt of that. How long would it
last?

"I hope," she murmured, "not long. That's not a
good thing to have inside of you."

It had been bad enough as it was. The fumbling, the
hooded excitement, the humiliation. Most of all it was
that last. Of course Leon would feel the humiliation
deeper than she. But however he might feel at heart,
he had a clear way out. He could never look her in the
eye again. Well, it served him right. But as for
her . . .

She remembered how first she wanted to call up any
man : Jack, Austin, anybody.

But Jack was a little itching boy, and she didn't *like*
Austin, Austin was horrid . . .

In the end, after only a day, Doris sank back into a
sort of emotional fatigue which helped to dissolve the
hurt. She could shrug Leon away and with him the
scene. The humiliation sank like a shadow and became only a resentment. But now she would always
resent him. She wondered if he had learned anything
about suffering. Probably not. He was too much of a
fool.

Anyway, she was going home. She had learned something during her little month, if only the fact that no
man is good-looking in his B.V.D.'s. She had quenched
that curiosity, and felt her independence, and lived

alone. She had made her first real contacts with life
and her first experiments. And she had had a lesson.
Also Austin would probably give her a good mark in
French.

And now she was leaving it all. She reached vaguely
around the room for final odds and ends. She wondered
what would her father say. Probably no more than
what he said when she left. Probably he would be thinking about the cleavage in isotropic crystals, smoking his
big black pipe and writing in his fine hand over innumerable scrawled papers. Yes, she was all ready now. She
reached for the 'phone and called Calumet 6000 for a
taxi.

iii

While her taxi was coming she glanced through the
papers. Only the morning papers had been delivered.
She was surprised to find on the society page the official
notification of Paul and Marjorie's engagement. She
had thought that announcement printed long ago. Still,
this was May 22nd and Mary's party had been only a
little over a week before. It seemed months. What a
strange week it had been for her! One week and three
men. Rather, one week and two and a half men. She
smiled rather bitterly to herself.

In another part of the paper she read a long story
under Philip Hubbard's signature. Phil was a nice
person. She must get to know him better. It would
be amusing to try to make him out. Too bad he chased
around so much with Jean Tilford trying to make that
lovely girl fall in love with him ; too bad he saw so much
of a sybarite like Millan. She must see Phil some day.
She must try to be friends with him.

" I wonder," said Doris seriously to herself, " if I ever
can be friends with a man. Any man, I wonder ? I
doubt it."

She paused.

"I think I'd like to try."

Her face was still a little bitter, and when she tried to smile it didn't quite come off. She looked at herself in the mirror and remembered the day she had kissed herself, just after Leon . . . Leon had made love to her. That seemed a very long time before. But it was only six or seven days. She had been growing. All of them were growing. They were flung into a situation and one week took hold of them and pulled them onward through the years. Why, she would be twenty soon ! *Twenty !*

Doris sighed. She picked up the paper again. Phil's story was about a hanging and was very dull. She noticed next to it a story about a girl named Cade. Agatha Cade. Wasn't that the name of the girl in Richard's office ? Well, maybe not. Anyway, the Cade girl had disappeared from her home. Her employers were a bond firm in La Salle Street (" Yes," thought Doris) and reported no word from her. She had been gone for twenty-four hours now and her parents appealed to the police. There was some hint of dragging the river.

" My Lord ! " thought Doris.

Well, it wasn't Richard's fault.

Leon, Leon . . .

No, it wasn't his fault either.

Doris sighed again and put Leon out of her mind. She rose : she slipped on a fur and powdered her nose in the mirror. The taxi had come. . . . She could see it before the window. . . . And she must hurry. She was beautiful. Yes, she was very beautiful. . . . Well, that was something. That was a certainty.

The taximan was ringing.

" Bother ! " breathed Doris once more.

Her little body was brave somehow as she walked into the sunlight, brave and upright and perhaps puzzled, but unafraid, cool and direct and unafraid in the slim tailored jacket and abrupt skirt : and as she met the sunlight Doris had no regrets.

Chapter Eighteen

THE RED PAVILION

i

LATE that afternoon Shirley heard the telephone bell ring sharply.

"May I speak to Richard?" said Phil's voice.

"He's asleep, Philip," she answered.

"But it's important, very important. I must speak to him."

He was urgent and she said, uncertainly:

"Can I take the message?"

"No. Hardly think so. It's rather bad news, Shirley; let me talk to Richard, *please*."

"Just a moment," she concluded. "I'll call him."

Shirley found him still sound asleep, and he didn't waken fully for several moments. Then he stumbled sleepily to the 'phone.

"What?" she heard him say.

Then:

"Oh God! *What!*"

"What's the matter, Richard?" she whispered, next to the 'phone.

"Ssh! Wait till I hear Phil." Richard was wide awake now. "Yes, Phil? What . . . what was that you said? I didn't . . . hear."

Then Shirley squeezed up to the receiver and, together with Richard, she heard Phil's intense, hurried voice. He said:

"Leon is dead."

"Oh!" she breathed.

"Dead!" exclaimed Richard. "Oh, I knew, I *knew*."

His voice fell and he whispered away from Shirley, with his cheek against the mouthpiece: "Murderer . . . murderer . . ."

"What was that?" called Phil.

"Murderer . . . murderer," Richard's voice sagged.

Shirley brushed him aside and picked up the receiver. Her voice flamed up. "Tell me, Phil, Leon is *dead*? How . . . when did it happen? Tell me. How . . ."

"We've just had word from the city press office," said Phil rapidly. "He was identified by cards in his pocket. He was walking toward his flat about eleven o'clock this morning, and two witnesses have said . . ."

"Listen, Richard," broke in Shirley.

"And two witnesses said he was stumbling as if he were drunk, and they noticed his unsteady step as he passed. But the doctors say he wasn't drunk. Evidently he was excited about something or just preoccupied: you know how Leon is . . . was. Well, he was crossing Sheridan Road and Irving Park, in this vague kind of stupor, and a motor bus ran him down."

"*What?*" exclaimed Richard.

"Yes. The poor kid evidently never knew what hit him. The driver said he didn't have a chance. Just walked in a sort of trance under the wheels. The doctors say he died almost instantly. They rushed him to the Columbus, but he was dead already. Not much resistance, I guess. Did you know the poor kid was only nineteen? The police found a bottle in his pocket containing some sort of white stuff, but it was smashed to bits. Dope, maybe."

"Only nineteen," muttered Richard.

"Oh . . . *oh!*" exclaimed Shirley.

Richard's face was contorted in a spasm of pain that was also relief, and Shirley puckered her lips to keep from laughing hysterically. She did half-laugh and found herself choking with a sob. Richard was still clutching the 'phone mouthpiece as if it were a stanchion, and swaying a little.

" I'll go over to the hospital and fix things up," finished Phil. " Please don't either of you bother. I'll call later about the funeral and so on. Do you know if he had any people in Chicago ? I don't think so. Fearful shame, isn't it ? The poor unlucky kid. Still, no one's fault but his own. Don't worry about anything and let me take charge. That's all. Good-bye."

Richard sat down haggard. Shirley looked at him.

ii

Later Shirley knew that Richard wanted to be alone, and she left the flat, ostensibly to shop for dinner. She was cheery when she kissed him good-bye, but her heart was clouded by the pain in his face. She was one of those people who belong to the closed-eyes-when-kissing school, and ordinarily he did also. But this time, when she looked up to him after the kiss, she saw his eyes were drawn and open. They had been open. They didn't seem to see her.

But Shirley left the apartment clear-eyed and determined to be sensible : she went into the garage and very prosaically drove out the car.* It would be good to drive : to feel cool wind comb through her hair and the subtle energy of the accelerator throb under her foot. She swung it capably into the boulevard, turning the big wheel, and felt it stretch out southward like an eager plaything. There was a long line of cars waiting at Wilson Avenue and for blocks the automobiles paraded in single file, nuzzling one another.

" Now," thought Shirley, " it is nonsense to let this

* I fear I have neglected all along to describe Richard's car. It was one of the new four-seater Jordan playboys, a lithe and powerful affair, painted deep blue with stream lines of lighter blue defining its grace, and a stork stolen from a Hispano-Suiza flying from the radiator-cap.—J. G.

agony continue. The devil with it all! Either I'm
going or he's going. If I go, I suppose it will kill him.
If he goes, it may kill him too. But that's the safest.
Let him go. I'll not stand this chaffing any longer."

Her lips were resolute.

At the corner of Irving Park she thought naturally
enough of Leon. There was some broken glass shovelled
into the curb and some dark stuff on the pavement.
She looked away. Poor Leon. She felt genuine pity.
Again it was something which seemed meaningless.
Wonder why Richard was so extraordinarily upset?
Not like him to lose control like that. Well, he was
sleepy. But did he know why Leon was so dazed? She
pursed her lips, then drew in breath. Hmmmm. So
that was it! Well!

Oh, the *poor* kid!

For a mile or so Shirley drove with brows very taut,
and if her lips were resolute they were grim also.

She was nearing the Loop and the buildings grimaced
welcome as her car shot down the chasm of the Avenue.
Where was she going? She didn't know. Anyway, it
was good just to drive. She forgot the shopping subter-
fuge. Why hadn't Richard taken the car instead of all
that walking? Because poor dear Richard was a fool.
Absurdly, as she stopped before the Blackstone and heard
the thin whine of music within, she wanted to dance.
She felt free now and happy. She was away. The
flat had been getting intolerable. She hadn't realized
how intolerable it was till she got out. She hadn't danced
for ages. Well, this had been rather a full week! One
didn't have time to dance on such days. She remembered
a remark Richard had made to her years and years before.
He had said:

"Dancing with you is like swimming with no clothes
on."

The dear idiot! And now he was going. Yes. There

R

was no doubt that he was going. He would probably be gone when she returned. She realized now, and for some curious reason it made her smile, that she had left the apartment because it would make it easier for him to go. Shirley almost bumped into the car crowding the boulevard ahead of her at this realization. That was an astonishing thing! And quite true. She didn't know it then. What an *astonishing* thing! So *that* was why she had kissed him quickly when his eyes were taut and funny and had run out. Stupid of her to take the car. (But she hadn't known it then!) He might want the car. Well, it was too late now. *Well!*

Shirley tipped her hair in the wind and drove on, and her driving was somewhat reckless. She would be near the campus soon. She thought of Marjorie and her chubby child's lips. And of Mary and Austin also. She liked them all so much, so very much. She could hear Mary say to her, " Isn't it too appallingly appalling? " in her best helpless manner. She could see Austin, pensive, icy, brilliant, muttering acidities. And she wondered suddenly why it is it takes a man, even a grown man, so long . . . so very long . . . to realize that to a woman sexual pleasure might be as important or unimportant as you wish merely for its own sake, that to women it was as legitimate and ingrown and innate as to men. It was just that men didn't see that until it was blasted into them. A queer thing. But there were so many queer things. Why was it every man deep in his heart held a peculiar intense conviction that he among all other men was the most effectively ardent? And so many other things. The fidelity of women, for instance, the *ludicrous* fidelity of women. And the more ludicrous caprice of men.

But her thoughts in Jackson Park near the Wooded Island drew her back toward Richard.

For a few moments she had driven them away from

Richard, but she saw that was procrastinating cowardice. Always face it, face it right away. That was best. *Then* run away, if necessary. Well, then, face it. She had left the apartment so that Richard, without lacerating himself, freed from the stigmata of lacerating her, could the more easily go. She didn't know that then, it had been purely intuitive and instinctive and unconscious : but she knew it now. Well : *why had she done that?* Of course, she could bluff herself and say that it was because she loved and pitied him, because they were both splendid and high-hearted fools, because unselfishly she wanted to ease his burden and his path. Well, now, if she said that, *was* it bluffing, wasn't part of it true? Ye-es. In facing it she didn't want to topple backwards in mock modesty. Ye-es, then, part of all that was true ("Very worthy of me," she muttered, "damn!"), but that wasn't all. No, not all of it.

"Not by a long shot," she said aloud. "It was *I*."

Her lips were still firm and her chin high. She moved one hand from the steering wheel and brought it to her lips. She made the only reasonable deduction the fact afforded : it was a deduction which she didn't want to make and which overwhelmed her, it was such a bountiful relief. The deduction was merely that she wanted him to go. Yes, that was it. Fundamentally, deep down, she wanted him to go. She *wanted* him to go.

"Not just for his sake," she shook her head quickly, "not just for his sake. For *mine!*"

Yes, for hers.

Shirley was amazed at the relief she felt. It was like a load removed from her head. She made herself say it aloud, "I *want* him to go," and felt even further relief. It was a ridiculous thing. But it was true. It was necessary not only to their happiness, but to their salvation. They each had work in the world. They each must be free. Neither must suffer from such succubi as had tortured them this last week. No more of such haggard chaffing. No, he must go. She was glad he must go. Not only for his sake, for hers. She was glad.

She breathed. She was still driving recklessly. She shot dizzily past a cordon of cars and swung out toward the lake, toward the beaches blurred with people, swarming with colour, the heads like apples in a tub. Pas à pas on va bien loin, she thought.

Then she drove a long time and drove fast, without daring to think at all.

There was glee upon her and she giggled and laughed till she felt moisture on her cheeks. But perhaps that was only the wind. She felt glee first and then her teeth clenched and she wanted to bite something. She wanted to bite something hard, and her teeth gritted. She kept on driving, grinning like a maniac. She drove a long while.

" Must give him time," she thought.

Afterwards she was calm again, and her emotion retrogressed. She still felt an overwhelming relief. She neared Mary's house and turned down 56th Street to pass it. There were a few lights within and shadows floated like wraiths against the curtains of the big room. Shirley wondered whose shadows they were. She knew one of them. It had died eight years before. On the way back she was shiftless and drove carelessly. But passing the old bridge again she awoke with a new consciousness that for moments past Richard had been quite out of her mind. That shocked her a little, but it was a good thing, and she laughed. What had been in her mind was always there, always the deep irradiation, always the lava bubbling under a crust ready to surge over. She was thinking about work. Ah, it was good to work !

There was so much to do ! She would start in earnest now. She would start in earnest to-morrow morning. (Maybe to-night !) She would get something done if she died for it. She was brought up sharply by the thought that work would be impossible to-night or to-morrow morning unless Richard had indeed gone. She felt guilty then, she saw she wanted him to go so much. She wanted him to go because it was all clear in her mind now. She had made up her mind, it was all settled, she couldn't stand a new shift in values. And she wanted to work. That consciousness again brought her mind to its feet, and she saw there was no use denying to herself the hope that Richard would be gone. He must be gone now. He *must !* It would be too savage an anti-climax, too absurd a commentary, if now he was still staying. Well, if he was staying she would go. Shirley's lips were grim. *She* would go. This nonsense had lasted a week and it was wrecking them both. Let it stop.

The funny thing was she *loved* Richard. She nodded. She did. *Dear* Richahd ! But . . .

In sculpture, unlike painting, planes were more important than curves. That was because you could walk round a statue. From the *Maya* sculptures down to Epstein and Mestrovic the greatest people were those who went after planes and got life into 'em. That was an awfully hard thing to do, to get life into planes. Well, it depended on how you went about it. Now the next thing she tried . . . she wondered vaguely of the great days in the future when she could superintend her own piece-moulding and hire a scarpellino or two perhaps . . . perhaps work herself in marble, hack and hammer and carve at marble. *Marble !* She was excited. But marble or no marble she mustn't forget to buy some new stearin to-morrow . . .

Shirley was so determinedly hopeful that Richard

must be gone, she decided to give him more time. She swung across Lincoln Park at Diversey and turned south again. Give him a little longer. Give him half an hour. Oh!

For half an hour longer then she drove, in and around Lincoln Park, cutting through it a dozen times, and though her route was aimless, now her driving was neither reckless nor inattentive, but cool and direct and capable. Finally she turned north once more and took the drive up to Bryn Mawr. She looked over her shoulder once or twice to see the shadow of the city and the smoke-blurred towers.

Richahd, Richahd. . . . But he must go.

Yes, to-morrow morning, she began it. Maybe to-night. Still, the light was pretty bad, even for sketching. But she was like a really good writer, she could work anywhere, she could work in a boiler factory. Hmmmm. It *was* going to be a good statue! It *had* to be. But maybe she couldn't do it now: maybe she didn't know enough. Anyway she must start soon. Now.

"No," said Shirley aloud suddenly. "I won't call it *La Désenchantée* after all. I'll call it *The Bereft One.*"

iii

Richard awoke as from a dream to find Shirley gone, and he groped for the telephone and rang up Phil.

"Listen, Phil."

"Yes."

"*Listen*, will you?"

"I'm listening."

"That bottle."

"What bottle?"

"You know, the bottle they found smashed . . ."

"Oh, yes. On Leon."

"Yes. Listen, Phil." Richard paused earnestly.

" That bottle contained poison. Phil. It contained potassium cyanide."

" Yes. Well ? "

" Listen, Phil. I gave that bottle to Leon. He wanted to kill himself, and I *gave* him that bottle. I can't explain, but . . ."

" Forget it ! " cut in Phil sharply.

" But . . ."

" Forget it, I tell you ! " Phil's voice was hearty. " Forget it, old boy, and go to sleep. I'll tend to everything. Just *forget* it. Don't tell anyone else and *forget* it."

" But . . ." began Richard, and then listened blankly into the receiver.

Phil had cut off.

Richard sank and pondered in the deep chair covered with chintz like strawberries in cream. His head ached. He was having a hard time to think straight. He cupped his chin on a fist and struggled with himself. Now in that pool of light toward the door Shirley would come in. She would be in soon. She had gone a long time before, three years before, but she would be in soon. The taste of that last kiss was like dust on his lips, but she would be in soon.

" Like dust," repeated Richard solemnly.

Yes, in that oval pool of light Shirley would enter, and he would catch a first glimpse of her in the tall mirror, her lips a little parted and her face shining. Ha ! She would pull off her hat with the old gesture and push her hand through her hair. She knew exactly the gesture. He knew exactly how she would come in. He had seen her so many times. And he must never see her again.

" Never again," said Richard.

He stood up abruptly. He discovered himself catching hold of the table and knocking over a book. It was

The Philosophy of " As If," by Henry Vaihinger. He was very tired. He must walk very straight and watch his steps closely. He must not fall. It would be terrible if he should fall. He must walk past that pool of light (that was where Shirley was), he must pass through Shirley, he must then grope his way to his room somehow. Then he must be going.

" Be going," repeated Richard.

Shirley was standing in the pool of light, her sweet oval face gleaming. He must not look at her, but must pass straight through her. Ha-ha! That was a funny thing, pass right through her. She was standing there, poised and watching, with her face floating in the mirror opposite, and he must pass her. He swayed unsteadily and began a cautious approach. He must pass her, and that wasn't an easy job at all.

" Pass her," he muttered to himself.

Richard did pass her, and in his room he sank on the bed and felt himself limp. He must go now. Right away. (" Right away," he repeated.) It would never do for her to find him when she returned. That was why she had gone, of course, she had gone so that he might the more easily go. Dear Shirley! He knew that, even if she didn't. He laughed, a little sharply. His laugh was off-tune and jangled. (" Jangled," said Richard.) Mustn't laugh like that again. Must control laughter, control it, yes. Yes, she had gone out, kissing him that way, had gone out three years ago, so that he could go. He must go now. She had been away a long time. Three years was a long time. He must go. He had no choice. He had something now to expiate and that was Leon. Murderer. He must go away, far, far away, and forget all about Shirley and Leon. He had killed Leon. Ha-ha! (" Stop that damn silly laugh!") He could forget them easily enough. Yes, he must go far away and achieve perspective and begin

again to think things out for himself and see clearly
and know reality and grasp life. ("And forget Leon.")
This had been a terrible week, and it wasn't fair just
because he was a silly ass to give Shirley any more terrible
weeks. Dear Shirley! ("I shall forget her," muttered
Richard.) Yes, he must go . . . right away . . . pack
a few things and go . . . get out . . . get *out*.

His face he saw swimming in the mirror, and he fumbled absently for toothbrush and pyjamas and things
and tossed them into a bag vacantly.

He had to pass that pool of light again and Shirley
was there waiting for him, poised in that pool of light.
He laughed a little bitterly and thought it was unfair of
her always to be near him. That was the trouble, she
was always near him, he never got away. When she was
away in Europe she was nearest of all. And she had
been away in Europe all of this horrible week. Well,
he must kill that nearness. Kill it. No, kill Leon.
But he had already killed Leon. No use killing him
again. Ha-ha! What would Leon say, being killed twice?
That was hardly fair, and he was very proud of always
being fair.

"Being fair," he said to himself.

He reached a small dabble of wax Shirley had left on
her table and dropped it into his bag. A little sketch
in clay for a model was on the table also, and he
looked at it with his eyes ill-focussed. Then he toppled
it over. It crashed into many pieces and he giggled.
He walked to the bureau top and pulled off the cloth
cover, so that the combs and brushes and bottles of
perfume and things also crashed to the floor. He surveyed the ruin and tossed a few of his books into the
ruin. He laughed hysterically. Also he felt very tired.

"Very tired," he repeated.

But he must be going. He left his valise on the bed
and forgot to lock it. He drifted into the corridor and

supported himself by pushing both his hands out straight from the shoulders against the wall. That was a funny way to walk. Ha-ha! Yes, it would be a shame to kill Leon a second time. Before him now, but from a different direction, was that damn pool of light again, and Shirley was still there. She had come back from Europe, then. She was hung in the pool of light and shone there. That was unfair of her when he was trying so hard to be fair. She had no business being so beautiful and making him love her.

"Love her," he said.

He sprang on the pool of light, drawing himself for the leap like a tiger. He crashed through it and then cautiously looked back over his shoulder. He was surprised to find himself on the floor. And Shirley was still there! Richard clenched his fists and raised them over his head and rose and then smashed them down on her cool smiling face. But he didn't touch her. That was a funny thing! He could see her as clearly and yet she wasn't there when he hit her. Oh, but, of course, she was still in Europe. Ha-ha! He walked to the 'phone and decided to call Leon and tell him he was going to kill him again. He gave the operator the number quite steadily, but she spoke sharply into the 'phone because he said after he gave the number: "I am going to kill him again." But she rang the number anyway, and for a long time it kept ringing. Leon must surely answer soon. But the number kept blankly ringing. "No answer," said the operator. Richard let the receiver slide down and laughed a little. That was a funny thing. No answer! And from Leon!

But why go to bed now? It was only six o'clock. Six o'clock. That meant Shirley would be home soon again. ("I shall forget her," said Richard.) But he must go before she came. It was only fair. He looked about him vacantly and then straightened his shoulders.

He looked at the pool of light and saw to his relief she was no longer there. He had killed her, then. He took a deep breath and walked to the door. Well, that was finished in that case. He had killed her. Good Lord, he had killed two people! Ha-ha!

He felt better now and he must remember clear back through the years to the words Shirley had used, so long before, almost at this time of day, on this same kind of day, in this same apartment. He remembered them, and he rolled them on his tongue. Well, he would say the same thing, only putting in her name, of course, not his. The figure in the pool indeed had disappeared, and he felt no longer unsteady. He turned to the empty room and said aloud, clearly and openly, " I think I'm going, Richahd." Well, there, he had said good-bye to her. He listened for an answer, but there was no answer, and he braced his shoulders again. The room was dusky with twilight, and he moved almost cautiously toward the door, moving his feet in whispers. He opened the door without looking back. He shut it gently. He went out.

iv

Shirley returned later. She opened the door and peered in the dimness just as she had done ten days before : but this time there was no doubt in her mind. She knew Richard had gone.

She dashed the room full of light, and when she saw the havoc in the bedroom and his unclosed bag her lips trembled a little. She bit her upper lip and found herself trembling. She was trembling all over. Then she stooped down and quite calmly and methodically picked up the mess. She picked up the fragments of her smashed model and tidied the floor. It took about ten minutes. When she rose, much blood had flown to her head and her face was flushed.

She looked at herself and laughed a little and reflected she had brought no dinner, and she was hungry. She went into the kitchen and made herself a tomato sandwich, eating it as she sat on the sink with her legs dangling. She decided after all not to try to work to-night.

She walked to the front room and murmured just once, "Dear Richahd." She saw that the chintz chair was mussed, with the coverlet pulled out of place and crumpled, and felt it was still warm. She patted it smooth with her lips strangely twisted, and then sat down on the warmth and cried a little.

She sat for a long time till dusk submerged the room completely, and the shadows trooped toward the corners in long waves. To one side she saw a couple of gutted candles, and she remembered their silent dinner. She remembered many things and somehow they did seem poignant now.

She thought with bitterness that she and Richard had fumbled their lines in this week's play. It was unreasonable that the curtain was down, that this indeed was the end. It was a pity there could not be just one more rehearsal. Then she knew somehow it was not over. She knew she could not be glad if deep in her heart she should reach the ultimate realization that the end had verily come.

She knew Richard must have that cognizance too, otherwise he never could have gone. They had both bungled so badly they felt it due one another to pretend they could not have another chance. They had pretended very well and the pretence had been helped by that strange insurgence which both confused with youth. But she knew they must come together again.

Shirley sighed deeply and moved to the window. She pushed aside and grasped the curtains and looked into the street brooding in the twilit dusk. The street was empty and only far away could she see tiny figures flooding into the city, plodding slowly with their heads weary and hearts bowed. . . .

She watched them and hung poised by the window a second, her arms upraised slightly and her hands hidden in the fabric of the curtains. She withdrew her hands and the window fell dark. She turned to the room and she felt she could see in it some final resolution of their trouble, some memory of the past so deep it could find its outlet only in the future, some further passion into the shadows.

THE END

PORQUEROLLES, FRANCE,
    APRIL—JUNE, 1925.